Sybil

Sybil

BY LOUIS AUCHINCLOSS

GREENWOOD PRESS, PUBLISHERS
WESTPORT, CONNECTICUT

*The characters and events in this novel are
fictitious; any resemblance to actual persons and places
is wholly accidental and unintentional*

Copyright, 1951, by Louis Auchincloss

All rights reserved

Originally published in 1951
by the Houghton Mifflin Company, Boston

Reprinted with the permission
of the Houghton Mifflin Company

Reprinted from an original copy in the collections
of the University of Illinois Library

First Greenwood Reprinting 1971

Library of Congress Catalogue Card Number 75-108840

ISBN 0-8371-3728-4

Printed in the United States of America

Part One

Chapter

One

SYBIL met Philip Hilliard on the night of her twenty-first birthday and at a dance, too, just as Aunt Jo had always told her that those things happened. It was a subscription dance, the last of a series of semiannual parties that had begun when she was fifteen. She and her mother had attended them regularly, one as a member, one as patroness, through the long years to emerge where they had started.

"It was a compromise that Mother and I made at an early date," she was to tell Philip much later. "I didn't want to go to any parties in New York, and she insisted that I would regret it. Not the parties but never having been to them. We finally agreed on two a year. It was a 'package deal,' the minimum course from crushes to matrimony. And the silly thing was that she hated being a patroness as much as I hated going. We used to stare gloomily at each other across crowds of people who, we both assumed, must have been having a good time. But that was the way Mother was. She believed in suffering."

"But wasn't she right in the end?" he asked. "You met your man, didn't you?"

"Oh, but that was never *her* idea," she said promptly. "That was Aunt Jo's. Mother believed in suffering for suffering's sake. An ulterior purpose would have been vulgar."

Sybil's power to examine her parents dispassionately had been acquired at an early age. It seemed as though there had never been a time when her mother had impressed her, as mothers of other children impressed them. It was not because she did not love her mother, for she did, in her own careful, undemonstrative way. But she sensed the egotism behind the perennial worry in her mother's eyes; she divined that what preoccupied and absorbed Esther was the proper fulfillment of her own functions as a parent rather than the happiness and welfare of her children. There was strength, of course, in this kind of worrying; it pervaded the narrow brownstone house and its atmosphere of varnish and bronze figures; it affected Sybil and her brother, making them responsible for any untoward maternal alarm. They were acolytes in what seemed the never ending ceremonial of Esther's dreary task of doing right. But in her heart Sybil dissented; she had always dissented. Did she exist only to be a daughter to her parents, a niece to her aunt, a task for them to perform, a joy that they were meant to enjoy? She couldn't remember a time when she had not been asking herself this question. It was even visible in the portrait that Aunt Jo had had painted of her and Teddy as children, that large, sentimental canvas, gilt-framed, that hung in the dining room of Aunt Jo's house at Easton Bay. It showed them on a marble bench in the garden, her brother with his curly hair and radiant smile, so different from the small dark creature at his side, in her white dress and wide blue sash, holding a Pekingese tightly in her arms and staring out of the picture with eyes that already expressed her sense of the unfitness of things.

The dance that fell on her birthday, in the late fall of 1940, began as the other dances had begun. Aunt Jo gave a dinner before it, made up entirely of Teddy's friends, and Sybil sat at the end of the table while the men on either side of her, classmates of his at law school, talked across her about people whom she didn't know. When they arrived at the hotel where the dance was held, she sat by herself in the hallway and waited while the other girls went to the powder room. At the head of the big circular stairway her mother and the patronesses would be standing, with corsages and long white gloves, to guard the oval ballroom. She stared at the young people going up the stairway and laughing.

"Sybil! Hey, Sybil! Come over here."

It was her father, looking greyer and ruddier than usual in a tail coat that had not been altered for an expanding figure, standing near the men's coat room and talking to Millie Dessart's father. Her parents had dined, she knew, with the Dessarts; by now her father would have had his fourth whiskey and would have told Mr. Dessart, in confidence, that he doubted Uncle Stafford's ability, "wonderful though he was," to continue much longer as chairman of the Cummings Bank.

She went over to them, stiffening as he put his arm around her shoulder.

"I'll bet you hardly know our Sybil, Tom," he said in his loud voice. "She's as quiet as Teddy is gay. She's the literary member of the family. I bet you can't mention a date in European history that she doesn't know. But she overdoes it; that's the trouble. The past is good to know about, but it's the present we have to live in. Isn't that so, Tom? Tell her that's so."

Mr. Dessart nodded, and Sybil, who had felt her heart go cold during her father's little speech, was grateful for his boredom. None of these men had to listen to her father; she knew that. It was only when he cornered them at a bar, when he held them physically as now, at the bottom of a stairway, that they had, momentarily, to hear his jealous doubts about Uncle Stafford. What would it profit him, she thought grimly, if Uncle Stafford *should* retire? Wouldn't he simply lose his own job?

"Do you go to college, Miss Rodman?" Mr. Dessart was asking her. "Is that where you learn about history?"

She shook her head. People were always asking her that.

"No, Sybil wouldn't go," her father answered for her, giving her shoulders a little shake. "Would you, Sib? She's always been on the shy side. Likes to stick around home. No real harm in it, I suppose. Most people nowadays seem to overdo things. Sib's probably being sensible."

"I'm sure she is." Mr. Dessart smiled at her. "I wish my Millie would borrow a leaf from her notebook and stay home occasionally."

Sybil didn't answer. She suddenly knew that there was no point in trying, because there were no words to come. Then she remembered that she was twenty-one. She disengaged herself from her father's arm and turned away.

"Sybil," she heard his voice. It was a surprised, hurt voice. "Sybil, come back here."

She turned and looked at him evenly.

"Come back and say good night to Mr. Dessart. You know better than to walk off like that. Without saying a word. Or don't you?"

He was smiling now, to cover his fear that she wouldn't obey him. There was a plea in his eyes behind the habitual bluff of his masculinity.

"Good night, Mr. Dessart," she murmured. "Good night, Daddy."

She turned away, wondering if it was wicked to feel as she felt. It seemed wrong to be always picking him apart in her mind, the clear mind of an adult child at home, to be always examining him, piece by piece, and seeing in every piece and part the origin of some remembered resentment of her childhood. But was she bound, on the other hand, to fester forever in the illusion that they were a happy, loving family? It was an illusion that her mother had always fostered, dangling before her the hope that when she grew up, *really* grew up, she would see that it was not, after all, an illusion, or at least that she would understand the necessity of maintaining it. Now she had grown up, and the hope had not been realized, as she had known it never would be.

She went up to the ladies' room; she sat on the couch and smoked a cigarette. The girls who had been at Aunt Jo's dinner were still there, sitting before mirrors, the girls whom she had known and feared at school, but who seemed to have put that period behind them. They had incorporated into their settled personalities the mannerisms which she had once regarded as only temporary. This was what they were and would be; this was maturity. They nodded to her and smiled, gushingly, like adults, as if they had no memory of the small spiteful things which they used to say and do. Millie Dessart came over to speak to her, Millie, the worst of them all, with her small foolish features and her smirking air, Millie, the "perfect girl," as her friends described her, as feminine as a wedding present in a small gift shop.

"Are you going to sit here all night, Sib?" she asked, smiling. She was almost engaged to Teddy; it made her feel responsible for his sister.

"I might."

"Oh, come."

"Why not? I hate dances, Millie. You know that."

Millie laughed her affected laugh, the one that was worse than her loud one. She simply opened her mouth and tilted her head back without emitting a sound.

"I guess somebody will come along one day who'll change your mind about *that*," she said.

"Is that the reason you like parties?" Sybil asked. "Because someone's come along?"

Millie leaned closer to her.

"Don't give us away, dear," she whispered. And then she laughed again. Appallingly.

"But suppose I don't want to meet anybody?" Sybil demanded. "Suppose I want to stay the way I am?"

She saw the impatience flicker in Millie's eyes.

"You don't want to be an old maid all your life, do you, Sybil?"

"Why not?"

Millie shrugged her shoulders.

"I thought, of course, you wanted a home of your own," she said. "Like my family's. And yours."

There was a pause.

"I don't think I'd want to marry a man like Daddy," Sybil said in flat voice. "And I certainly wouldn't want to have a child like me."

Millie's eyes widened slightly, and she stood up. She was like a poodle, clipped and curled, that has put its paw up and been rebuffed.

"I think we should join the others," she said.

As Sybil went up the circular stairway ahead of her, for Millie had fallen back to look for Teddy, she watched her reflection in the mirror panels along the wall, surprised at the unaccustomed neatness of her straight black hair and red dress. It was true, she reflected, that she was different; it was not all in her imagination. Other girls did not have the brooding look of her dark eyes or the startled pallor of her complexion. She could not, however, make out even a hint of the tenderness, the gentle appeal that she could sometimes imagine in poses before her own mirror. She was hard looking, she thought, unattractively hard, as only the timid can be.

She stopped at the end of the line of people waiting to shake hands with the patronesses and watched her mother smiling and nodding in agitated fashion at friends of Teddy's whom she should have recognized but didn't. She was older than the other mothers; it was obvious that she felt out of place despite all her years of officiating at just such parties. Sybil could see in her nervous, darting hands, in the drawn, taut corners of her lips, in the tensity of her frame under the unlovely brown velvet, the attitude of unshakable integrity, of unneeded courage, of superfluous spirit that had always provoked and touched her. She could still want to rush over to her mother and throw her arms around her and bury her head in the brown velvet, even knowing, as she did, how stiffly she would have been rejected, how horrified Esther would have been by a demonstration so public. But why then did Esther have to stand there so bravely, her long thin nose elevated, her pale lips set, fighting for nothing against nobody? Can she never let me be, Sybil asked herself fiercely, as she clenched her fists, with all her misty kindness and ineffectuality?

She was opposite her mother now. Esther gave her one look and took her aside, away from the line.

"Darling, are you alone? Where are the others?"

"They'll be along."

"You came with them?"

"Yes."

Esther looked at her anxiously.

"Was it a nice dinner party?"

"I guess."

"Don't be cross, dear."

"Oh, Mother. *Please.*"

Esther continued to hold her by the arm as if she were afraid that she would break away and do something unseemly on the dance floor.

"I'll get Teddy. He'll start you off," she said.

"Oh, leave poor Teddy alone."

"Darling, he won't mind. There he is now. Teddy!" She beckoned to him, and he came over. "Teddy, will you start Sybil off?"

"Of course," he said. "I was just coming over. Don't worry about us, Mummie. We're going to have a tremendous time. You watch."

Sybil was irritated by the affected generosity of his "us." It was kind of him, of course, but he was always being kind.

"Of course, she's desperately worried about *you*," she said to him sullenly. "Nobody wants to dance with Teddy, do they, Mother?"

Esther did not answer. She never answered sarcasm.

"Let me have just a word with Teddy, dear," she said and took him out of earshot.

Sybil watched them, wondering at the contrast between them. It was underlined at a party. For Teddy seemed as much of the world as their mother seemed out of it. There may have been a touch of the cherub in his round face and curly brown hair, and a shade too much red in his lips, but his smile was brilliant; it made up for the rest. She knew only too well what they were discussing. Her mother would be reminding him that as a member of the committee she could introduce boys to Sybil and that he mustn't spend the whole evening fussing over her. He would be protesting, sincere in his protestations. She noticed the way her mother was swallowing, as she did when she was nervous, and how she plucked a piece of down off his coat. She wanted to keep him there, talking to her; that was the real reason for their conference. And she knew it, too; Esther knew everything about herself and was embarrassed by her knowledge.

"All briefed?" Sybil asked, when Teddy came back to her.

"All briefed," he answered, and they went into the ball-room together.

"I don't want any fussing tonight," she said as they started to dance, "I don't want to be introduced to people. If they don't want to dance with me I can sit with Mother."

"You cannot."

"Then I can go home."

"Now, Sib," he protested, "we brought you here to have a good time."

"I won't have you ruining your evening and hovering about the stag line looking for victims. It's indecent. After all, it isn't as if I were a débutante. I'm twenty-one."

"Then I won't," he said soothingly. "But there's one person you've got to meet. Phil Hilliard."

"Teddy, I don't know anything about horses and foxes ——"

"Philip is different," he interrupted. "Philip's not like that."

"Well, anyway, you can go and dance with Millie now. I see Howard coming over. Howard will always do right by me."

Howard Plimpton, like all the men at Sybil's dinner, had originally been a friend of Teddy's. He and Philip Hilliard and Teddy had been in the same class at Chelton School and later at Harvard. Howard, however, had not gone to the University of Virginia Law School with the group inspired by Philip, who loved horses and hunting country; he had been obliged by his father's death to leave college before graduating and to take a job in New York. He worked for a brokerage house, and he looked, with his brown crew cut and square shoulders, his small, firm, regular features, exactly as a Harvard man in a brokerage house should look. He was not, however, what he looked. One could feel, or at least Sybil thought she could feel, in the very expressionlessness of his blue eyes, in the stubbornness of his square jaw, in the jerkiness of his dancing, that something within him was being held there only by the tightest control. He and Sybil sensed in each other the same dissatisfactions. He sometimes took her out to dinner to discuss Mabel Henleigh, a foolish but attractive friend of Millie's with whom he was rather inarticulately in love. It was not flattering, perhaps, but Sybil had never been one to care about flattery.

"Is Mabel here?" she asked him, after he had cut in.

He jerked his head for answer in the direction of a very blond girl in a hoop dress who had both hands on her partner's shoulders and was teaching him, as they both stared down at their feet, a curious new step.

"Oh. Have you danced with her?"

"No."

"Won't she be mad at your dancing with me first?"

"I wish to hell she would."

Sybil considered this.

"I asked her to Aunt Jo's dinner, you know," she explained. "She said she couldn't come."

"She's always got another engagement."

They danced for a few moments in silence, a rather pleasant silence.

"Did you enjoy the dinner at all?" she asked.

"It wasn't bad."

She sighed. Over his shoulder she could see Teddy talking to a friend in the stag line. He was still keeping an eye on her, covertly.

"You say that so casually," she told him. "I envy your indifference. To me it was ghastly."

"You shouldn't care so, Sib. You should take it or leave it."

"I know. But the girls get me down. They all care so."

He nodded, without answering.

"You sat next to Millie, didn't you?" she continued.

"Yes. Which wasn't very nice of you."

"I wanted to know what you thought of her," she explained. "What did you think of her?"

He shrugged his shoulders as though to express the unimportance of what he or anyone cared to think about Millie.

"Do you think Teddy will marry her?" she persisted.

"I suppose. Isn't she what he wants? Doesn't she look like the kind of girl whom the budding lawyer of good family is supposed to marry?"

"Oh, Howard." She looked up at him reproachfully. Teddy, for all the difference in their lives, was the person she most loved. "Do you think Teddy's like that? I'm not like that."

"You're not like anything, Sib," he said. "But you'll come out all right."

"That's what the family keep saying," she said gloomily. "You make me sound like a game of solitaire."

As they danced again in silence she watched Teddy in the stag line talking to a young man who must have been Philip Hilliard. He was a tall and muscular young man, arrogant, she decided, and self-assured, the kind who would never dance except with the prettiest girl in the room. He was handsome, she conceded; he had the looks that went with youth and strength. But she wondered if she couldn't make out a bald future in that thinning blond hair and eventual puffiness in those round, hard cheeks. It was like her to notice such things. It was her tendency, she knew, to resent Teddy's friends of the big world, the ones whom he visited and whom he never seemed to ask to visit him. And then, as she looked, they broke away from the stag line together and came across the floor to her. She turned her face away, almost in panic.

"Sybil, do you remember Philip?" Teddy was saying. Howard had bowed to her and gone already to look for Mabel. They were standing in front of her. She nodded.

"I think we met at Chelton. Years ago."

"Did we?" he asked, and they started to dance. "I hadn't realized that. When was that?"

His voice was higher than she would have expected. She was suddenly sure that he was the sort of person who would never, even for the sake of being polite, pretend to remember something that he didn't.

"I guess we didn't actually meet," she confessed. "I saw you and Teddy on the platform on Prize Day. I watched you."

He laughed. It was a high, cheerful laugh, pleasantly vain. "Why?"

"I like to watch people."

"More than you like to meet them?"

"Perhaps."

"Would you rather watch me?" he asked.

She managed a smile.

"No."

And the conversation died. She tried to think of something to say. When it came, it was awful.

"Are you enjoying the dance?"

"Are you?"

He was bored. Bored already. When she looked up she saw that his grey eyes, smaller than she had thought, were roaming the floor. There was a patch on his cleft, oval chin that had escaped the razor; she noticed that the stubs were darker than the very blond hair on his head.

"It's conversation," she said. "I don't know how it's made. And as a matter of fact," she added in sudden perversity, "I don't care."

He was about to answer when Teddy brought up someone else to dance with her. This time she resented it, feeling suddenly that Teddy was not thinking of her. He was thinking of Philip; he was always thinking of Philip. Obviously it would be too hard on Philip, popular Philip, to dance for more than two minutes with anyone's sister. She turned abruptly away from them both and danced off with her new partner. They hardly exchanged a word. She looked gloomily around the big oval room and the throng of white-tied young men watching the girls dancing. She could see her mother, finished with the receiving line, standing in a doorway with another patroness and darting glances in her direction. The room had suddenly become a crib, and she was looking out through bars with moveable red and yellow balls.

"I think, if you'll excuse me — " she was starting, when the miracle occurred.

Philip cut in.

"You know this is most unwise of you," she warned him earnestly. "You may be terribly stuck."

"Well, you see, I'm a gambler."

"Teddy will always bail you out once," she continued. "But the second time you're on your own. That's our rule."

He looked down at her and smiled.

"You're a funny girl," he said. "Do you really dislike people?"

"Oh, no!"

"Who do you like?"

She thought.

"I like Teddy," she said after a few moments. "And I have an aunt whom I like. And I think I like Nicholas."

"Who is Nicholas?"

"He's my cousin. Or rather he's not really my cousin. He's my aunt's stepson."

He nodded vaguely.

"All family, you mean?" he asked.

"Yes. I guess so."

"Families go just so far, don't you think? Not far enough?"

She never knew what people meant when they said things like that.

"I'm at law school with Teddy, you know," he said.

"Yes, I know."

He smiled self-consciously.

"Do you like *me?*" he asked.

Her tone, when she answered, was serious.

"I think so," she said, and he smiled again.

She was wrong about Teddy. He did bail Philip out and

far sooner than was necessary. It was only too evident that he regarded any attention to her in the light of a favor to himself which simply increased his obligation to rescue. Obviously, now, Philip would not cut in again. Even if he should want to dance with her later in the evening, it would then be so evident that she was "sticky" that he would not take the chance. And then she realized, very clearly and suddenly, that she did not want Philip to see her stuck, to see her circling the room with an uninteresting and uncomfortable partner, passing and repassing the empty gilt chairs along the wall as if she were back at dancing class, with her mother's concerned eye roving after her and Teddy being, from time to time, such an angel. She saw her cousin, Nicholas, coming across the floor in his slow, deliberate gait, sent, no doubt, by her mother, or worse still, coming at his own instance, smug in the assurance of well performing his cousinly duty. No, she couldn't bear it; she would be stuck with Nicholas, and he wouldn't mind; it would be worse than someone else minding.

"Thank you," she said suddenly to her astonished partner. "I have to go now. I have to see my mother."

She had left the floor before he could protest; she slipped through one of the doorways, watching her mother's back, and hurried down the circular stairway past the table where grey-haired ladies at card tables were checking the cards of the new arrivals. She got her coat and went into the main hallway of the hotel. Opposite the ballroom there was a dark little bar with leather seats and empty tables. She went in and sat in a corner and ordered a brandy. She had to order something.

.   .   .

Philip, however, did come back, and for the third time. He had a taste for the unusual; he liked to collect and classify. He did so in an exact rather than an imaginative manner; his was not a reaching curiosity, but it was, none-theless, a curiosity.

"Where's your sister?" he asked Teddy. "You didn't give me a chance to dance more than two steps with her."

Teddy, surprised and gratified, looked around for Sybil. "I don't see her. She may have gone home. Or she may be in the ladies' room. Or in the bar. You never can tell what Sybil will do."

But this only intensified Philip's curiosity.

"Really?" he said. "I think I'll have a look around for her."

The more he looked, the more his interest developed. He covered the ballroom and the dining room, and he hovered for several long, self-conscious minutes outside the ladies' room. He even asked the doorman if he had seen a young lady with long dark hair leave the building alone. When he finally discovered her in the back of the little bar he stood in the doorway for a moment, watching her. She had not seen him. Then he asked the waiter to bring a bourbon and water to her table and walked over to join her.

"Are you waiting for someone?" he asked, with a slight note of sarcasm. "Or may I sit down?"

She looked up, very startled. Then her face seemed to settle into expressionlessness.

"Oh, no," she said. "I'm not expecting anyone."

He sat down beside her.

"You know," he told her, "that a girl's not meant to leave a party and go to a bar alone."

"It's all right," she explained. "Mother's on the com-mittee."

"Even so. It's considered odd."

She shrugged her shoulders.

"Why do you do it?" he persisted.

There was a considerable pause. She appeared to be thinking over her answer.

"I suppose," she said, "there isn't anything I really want

that I'd get for doing the things I ought to do."

His drink arrived, and he stirred it with the mixer.

"What is it then," he asked, "that you do want?"

Sybil looked across the room at all the bottles piled in front of the mirror behind the bar. She was feeling reckless. It was beyond her comprehension why he had followed her.

"I suppose what I really want," she said slowly, "is to have something terrific happen. Not necessarily to me. Or to anyone. But something to prove to everyone that I've always been right and they've been wrong."

He looked baffled.

"About what?"

Again she shrugged her shoulders.

"About everything."

But Philip did not have a speculative mind. He was first and foremost a collector, and a collector of facts that fitted into little drawers and cubbyholes in the mental chest that he had built for them.

"Like sitting in a bar alone during a party?" he asked.

She paused.

"All right," she said. "Like that."

"I don't see why that's so important."

She looked away from him. She knew that it was oddly important to her that he shouldn't be bored, but she had no idea how to choose a topic. Howard had been interested in what she had to say or else had done the talking himself. Her decision, however, was a wise one. She asked him a question about himself.

"It isn't important," she said. "We needn't worry about it. What do you want? To be a great lawyer?"

He expanded.

"Oh, no," he said. "I only go to law school for the training. It's a wonderful mind trainer, you know."

"I see." Her father was always saying that to Teddy. She had a picture of little runways and trap doors such as people used to test mice. "And, then, it's a good jumping-off point to other careers, isn't it?" This, she had learned, was the other thing one said about law.

"Exactly," he agreed, and she was relieved. "But I wouldn't care to be a lawyer," he added.

"Oh? Good."

He looked up in surprise.

"Why do you say that?"

"I don't know." She was confused again. "It doesn't seem like you. It's dry, isn't it?" She thought for a moment. "My cousin, Nicholas, is a lawyer."

He laughed.

"I guess that fixes Nicholas," he said. "Or does it fix the law?"

"It's not that I don't like my cousin," she explained hurriedly. "He's very good to me. In fact, he came here tonight just to dance with me. But you seem — well — more lifelike than Nicholas." She looked down at the table in embarrassment.

"Thanks," he said easily. "If it's meant to be a compliment. Tell me, Sybil. Did you come out here to get away from your cousin? Is that it?"

She flushed.

"Partly."

"You poor kid. Do your family never let you alone? I saw how Teddy was. Hovering around you like an old nurse."

She shook her head protestingly. She had no wish to throw the blame on Teddy, but what could she say? How could she possibly make someone like him understand?

"If you're not going to be a lawyer," she said, returning to the safer topic, "what do you think you will be?"

"I'd like to go into politics," he said. "I think that's what people like us ought to do. Don't you?"

She stared; she couldn't imagine what common denominator might exist between them.

"Like us?" she repeated.

"You know," he explained, a touch impatiently. "People with money and all that."

"But I don't have any money."

"Your family, I mean."

"But their money isn't mine. Anyway, I don't think they have any. It's all Uncle Stafford's."

He looked at her, perplexed.

"Anyway," he said, "it's what I want to do. Of course, I don't think the way most people here think."

"Oh?" Her eyes were wide. "How do you think?"

"Well, I guess I call myself a liberal," he said, with a touch of modesty. "Daddy, of course, thinks I'm a radical." Then, as she continued to look blank, he explained. "I've always been a staunch New Dealer," he said firmly.

She looked at him with admiration.

"Well, that's fine," she said. "So have I!"

It was the first time that she had ever really considered the matter. Everyone in her family was of a conservative turn of mind. Now, on the spot, she adopted a different creed.

"I thought you might be," he said approvingly. "You're independent. I like a girl who knows her own mind."

She smiled.

"Even if she sits alone in bars?"

"This girl's not alone in a bar," he said, smiling back at her.

And so they talked, very pleasantly, for an hour, and then he suggested that they go on to a night club. Sybil, however, to her own surprise, felt a sudden sharp reluctance to do so. All that was in her that could hold back, and this was a great deal, rose to swell it.

"I think, if you don't mind, I won't," she said, getting up. "I'm tired. It's the party, I guess. Let's go up and find Teddy, and he'll take me home."

Before he could protest she had taken her coat and was out of the bar.

.   .   .

Back at the dance, where the receiving line had disbanded, Esther Rodman stood in the doorway to the ballroom, watching the couples and fingering her small seed pearls. Occasionally she dabbed at her nose with a fussy little handkerchief that she kept stuffing back into her faded evening bag. Mrs. Dessart, Millie's mother, years younger than Esther and, like her daughter, delicately and self-consciously pretty, was standing beside her.

"Millie was telling me how sorry she was that the Anderton girl wasn't asked this year," she was saying. "She says the other girls all like her so much. Apparently they can't understand what happened."

Esther stiffened at the challenge in her tone. She was not sympathetic with those who bowed to the young.

"I understand that she had too much to drink at the party last year," she said. "I even heard that she had to be taken home."

"Oh, but Mrs. Rodman," Mrs. Dessart protested, "surely it was obvious what happened there. The poor child never had anything to drink before. That was inexperience, pure and simple."

"It's the kind of inexperience that rules one out of these dances, I'm afraid," Esther said gravely. "It may be accepted in many places. I don't doubt that it is. But not here. Not yet, anyway." She shook her head. "People are always saying how stuffy we are," she continued, rather loftily. "I can't imagine why they care so to belong."

She moved away to look for her husband. She had stayed late enough, and Teddy could bring Sybil home. It was the last of the dances with which she as patroness would have to be concerned. Perhaps they had not proved much, but at least Sybil could never complain that she had not had the chance to go. As she went down the steps she was not complacent, for she was never that, but she felt at least that she had tried. Esther had a feeling that any social formula, once established, should be maintained. Or at least maintained by her. On other shoulders than hers had been placed the burden of changing the scheme of things.

"I think it was a nice party," she said to her husband when she found him, coming out of the bar. "I'm glad that we won't have to go to any more."

"Did Sybil enjoy it, do you think?" he asked, as he followed her down the steps to the street, taking care not to lurch. "She was rather snappish with me when I spoke to her."

"Sybil's snappish with everybody."

"More so with me," he said sulkily, as they waited for a cab. "Much more. She's always looking down her nose at me."

But Esther was more interested in looking for a taxi.

"You've never been subtle with her, George," she said. "You were always tossing her in the air and catching her when she was little."

"Subtle!" He looked at the doorman, as if for sympathy. "Does a father have to be subtle? Is there no such thing as simple, ordinary family affection?"

"Don't be silly, George. Oh, there's a cab!"

He reflected sourly, as they drove home in silence, that he understood his wife no better than when he had married her. She had a habit of assuming that she and Sybil, and even Teddy at times, were beyond the jurisdiction of any general rule, an assumption which, leaving him out as it did, made him clamorously assert his own identification with a basic Americanism that he suspected her of despising. Yet even in such moments he wondered if he was not sounding shrill. Did she ever listen to him, after all? Did any of them? And yet when he, a minister's son from upstate, had married into what he had then regarded, however admiringly, as the decaying house of Delafield, had he not assumed that they would welcome his ungenealogical vigor?

"Well, evidently I'm too simple a soul to understand these things," he said as the taxi drew up at their door. "I'm sure that you and Jo, when you have your next meeting, will develop the topic more fully. You'll probably decide that Sybil was dropped by her nurse or frightened by a pink elephant. It will never occur to either of you that she may be just spoiled. Spoiled by her mother and spoiled by her precious aunt."

But Esther said nothing. She rarely answered, or even listened to him, when he spoke this way. She knew that it was important for his pride to say these things, and she ignored them as she would have ignored an habitual cough or twitch. She had not married George for his brains or his ambition. She had never really believed in the success that he had loved to talk about. She had been thirty when she had met him and living with her sister; she had wanted a family of her own. Even more, she had felt it her duty to have one. He had given her this; it was all as it should be. That he had not succeeded, that he had ultimately been grateful for a job in Jo's husband's bank, was not important. Jo had supported her before her marriage; it did not seem strange to be helped by her now. Had George been rich and Stafford poor, she would have done as much for Jo. Only men worried about such things.

Chapter
Two

WHEN SYBIL woke up the next morning she stared at the wallpaper with the faded shepherdesses that she had known from childhood and wondered what she had done the night before. Then, with a sudden contraction of heart, she remembered him. But if there had been a void, even for a moment, she thought desperately, sitting up abruptly in bed, might it not be recaptured? Alas, no. She lay back. There were more traps in life, it appeared, than those set by one's family. She thought of the young man from the bank whom Uncle Stafford had brought for the weekend to Easton Bay and how he had failed even to recognize her when they had met in the street three weeks later. It was perfectly natural; they had only exchanged two sentences. But why, she asked herself fiercely, why did this sort of thing have to keep happening to her? When she only wanted to be left alone? Why did she have to think of love as a cold in the head, as something one woke up with, something to get over? She sat up and pushed her hair back and looked at her dark brown eyes in the mirror over the bureau, put her hands to the hollow of her pale cheeks. Oh, Sybil! She turned in disgust from the deluded creature in the glass and jumped out of bed to close the window, reaccepting the room as her

own, as the room that had always been her room, with its
cream-colored bureau and bed, its wallpaper and its two
big brown lithographs of the sheep leaving and the sheep
returning.

There was a knock at the door.

"Is that you, Ellen?" she asked, getting back into bed.

"Are you awake? Did I hear you moving?"

"Yes. Come in."

Ellen came in. She was a large Irish woman with an
asthmatic wheeze, and hair, inadequately dyed red and
thinning, that showed wide patches of scalp. She clasped
her hands together and looked at Sybil out of dry little eyes
that simulated dismay.

"Did I wake you, child? Your mother says you're to sleep."

"Is it late?"

Ellen had been Sybil's nurse and still worked for the
Rodmans, having changed herself, as the years went by,
into a reluctant general housemaid. She preferred to regard
herself as a housekeeper, but this was sheer illusion, as the
other servant, a cook, paid no attention to her, leaving only
the family for Ellen to supervise. It was she who had succeeded in getting Sybil to the party the night before, at the
last moment. She had gone to her room where she was in
bed, pretending a headache, and had bathed her in such a
sea of Irish consolation, praising her so unreasoningly as
she laid out her dress and slippers, that Sybil had been
hypnotized into getting up. She came over now and sat on
the bed, patting Sybil's knee under the covers.

"Tell me. Were you the belle of the ball?"

"I was not."

"All the men were after you. Don't tell me they weren't."

"Ellen, you're an old silly. I was so stuck I had to run off
to the bar. All by myself, too."

"Sybil Rodman, you didn't dare!"

"I certainly did."

"And did your mother see you? Oh, good lord!" Ellen put both hands to her face and raised her eyes to the ceiling. "And what would your Aunt Jo have said?"

"I don't see that it matters what they thought," Sybil said with dignity. "I'm twenty-one. I can do what I like, can't I?"

"Will you listen to her?" Ellen protested, appealing as she always appealed, to the absent figures of Mrs. Rodman and Mrs. Cummings.

"Furthermore I ordered brandy. And drank it."

"All by yourself? Mother of God!"

It was the game that they always played after Sybil had been out. It never had anything to do with the realities of a situation; it was designed, in fact, to keep away from them.

"All alone. At first. Then a man followed me."

"A strange man! Off the street!"

"Strange to me, anyway. Yes. And to get into the building, I suppose he had to come off the street."

"And had he the cheek to address you? Oh, the dirty creature!" Ellen made as if to strike him.

"Of course, he addressed me. We had a very pleasant conversation." Sybil became almost demure. "I hope I shall see him again. The city, however, is large. It seems hardly likely."

"Will you get up and dress, Sybil Rodman," Ellen cried, leaping to her feet. "And not be telling me any such tales!"

Sybil got out of bed and gave her a hug, the hug of affection, of habit. She drank the coffee that Ellen had brought her and then dressed and went down the three flights to the front hall. She ran her hand along the varnished bannister as she descended the narrow, carpeted stairway, past the cramped little rooms, past the glassed-in bookcases surmounted by bronze deer and warriors, the portraits of long dead Delafield children, uncles and great-uncles of her mother, in round gold frames, into the black hall with the gaunt Italian chairs and the smell of cooking. Taking a deep breath outside on the top of the stoop she looked around and saw that it was a beautiful day.

To go to Aunt Jo's she had only to cross the street. In fact, the Rodmans' house belonged to Uncle Stafford who had bought it to protect his property and allowed his wife's sister to occupy it. His own house, however, unlike theirs, was impressive. It was the kind of house that Sybil as a child had believed that rich people had to live in. How else could one have told they were rich? Its façade of grey limestone was three times the width of their drab, brown front; it was covered with the half-columns and cornices and pediments that clustered the large city houses of its period. Yet big as it was it was still not big enough for the scale on which it had been conceived; inside, a marble stairway filled the front hall like a coiled snake, and the green plants in the conservatory were as crowded as in a jungle. The living room, where Sybil, who was her aunt's secretary, worked in the mornings was so cluttered with red, upholstered furniture as to seem of modest, almost cozy dimensions.

Aunt Jo was sitting on the sofa when she came in, reading a circular and flicking ashes from her cigarette into an enormous jardinière. Ten years older than Esther, she was everything the latter was not, cheerful and hospitable, worldly and self-confident. She had no looks, it was true, being stout now and heavy-featured, with elegant white hair tinted with too much blue, but unlike her sister she had once been handsome, as one could still make out in the sparkle of her large blue eyes, the contour of her smooth, puffy cheeks and the firm, straight line of her nose. Aunt Jo had converted the pretty girl of her past into the busy hostess of sixty-five, but one could still sense an almost epicurean laziness lurking beneath the smooth, hard surface of her activity. She had the kind of common sense that could uncover the ridiculous even in what she did herself, but at the same time a discipline, born of the same background that had endowed Esther with her conscientiousness, that carried her forward to the completion of each undertaken task. First and foremost Jo Cummings was a manager, and she liked in particular to manage her own family. She had even forgiven George Rodman his failure as a businessman for the opportunity that it had given her, childless herself, of controlling his domestic affairs. She might pay the piper, but she was most certainly going to call the tune.

"Well, did you have a good time?" she asked as Sybil came in.

"As a matter of fact, I did."

"That's good news. Who did you dance with?"

"Oh, several different boys," Sybil said, sitting down. "Mostly the ones who were at your dinner. It was nice of you to give that dinner, Aunt Jo," she added dutifully.

"Pish. I wish you'd let me give you a ball."

"It's a pity you should have only one niece and that she should be such a poke," Sybil said, picking up a pile of correspondence. "Millie Dessart would have been perfect for you."

"Millie?" Aunt Jo laughed comfortably. "She's a dear, but she hasn't your spark, child. Oh, I'm not really worried about you."

"Mummie is."

"Well, of course, your mother worries about everything," Aunt Jo said briskly. "That's the way she is."

Sybil's duties as a secretary were not onerous. She took care of her aunt's corespondence, helped her to fill her opera box and drove with her in the afternoons. She had not wanted to go to college, but, as her mother had put it, she couldn't just "sit home and read all day." Aunt Jo had suggested this compromise, not because she needed a secretary, but because she wanted to take Sybil under her direct supervision. Oddly enough Sybil, although aware of this, did not resent it. There was a self-confidence in Aunt Jo that her sister entirely lacked. Esther conveyed in her very solicitude for Sybil an uneasy sense that her daughter might, after all, have some hidden argument of possible validity behind her social intransigency. Aunt Jo, on the other hand, scoffed at the mere suggestion that anyone who did not openly admire her way of life could be anything but frustrated and envious.

"Here's Lucy Hilliard after me again. Another benefit," she said. "Did she subscribe to my tuberculosis thing?"

Sybil checked the list that lay on the sofa by the mail.

"I don't see her name."

Aunt Jo frowned.

"She's really outrageous, that Lucy. When you think of the money she has, too."

"Shall I throw away her appeal?"

"No." Aunt Jo shook her head, almost regretfully. "Put me down for four seats. I'll give her another chance. Lucy's one of those women who always gets one more chance. But that's life, my dear."

"Because she has money, Aunt Jo?"

Aunt Jo looked at her niece severely. She did not like to have it carelessly assumed that favors accorded to the rich were never disinterested.

"Not at all because she has money," she said. "Lucy Hilliard has that rare gift of making people do things for her. And of making them like it, too. Of course, she's outrageous." Aunt Jo smiled tolerantly. "She says the most awful things about people and does the most terrible things. And between ourselves I think she hits the bottle. But she has spirit. Great spirit. She cares about life, and people care about her." Here she paused to give her words full effect. "Nobody likes a cynic, child. Remember that."

"Philip isn't cynical. He must be like her."

Aunt Jo looked up.

"I didn't know you knew Philip."

"He's a friend of Teddy's."

"I know that. But when did *you* meet him?"

There was a pause; it gave her away.

"Last night."

"Last night?" Aunt Jo's sharp eyes were really on her now. "He wasn't at my dinner. Did he dance with you?"

"Yes. Is that so incredible?"

"I suppose Teddy introduced him."

"He did."

"Did he dance with you more than once?"

"Three times, to be exact."

But Aunt Jo was too interested to take notice of her sarcasm.

"Three times!" She nodded in satisfaction. "That shows that you made an impression. A definite one, too. And he's such a nice young man. So polite. And so handsome."

"And so rich."

"And what's the harm in that?" Aunt Jo positively glared at her. "Is that *his* fault? I wonder he danced with you at all if you talked that way."

"Oh, I didn't have to talk at all," Sybil explained. "I simply listened."

"You're going to have to watch that tongue of yours," Aunt Jo grumbled as she reached for another letter. She was thinking how unreasonable it was that the only thing that Esther had managed to hammer into the stubborn head of her daughter was a part of her own refusal to assess the world. What did they think they were going to live on, these feckless people, with the money bound in trust for Nicholas, when she and Stafford were gone?

"It's all very well for you to be so independent," she continued. "But somebody has to be practical in this family."

"You're the practical one, Aunt Jo."

"Well, I can't do everything," she retorted. "And I can tell you one thing, young lady. It worries me very much to see you go to one dance in a whole winter and be so casual about a young man like Philip Hilliard." At this she gave final vent to her sense of the unfitness of it. "A young man who'd make you a better husband than anyone I can think of!"

Sybil was terrified at the suddenness with which her aunt could sweep away the barriers that stood between her and what Aunt Jo regarded as the normal and fulfilled life. The majority, of whom Aunt Jo had always been firmly but not unpleasantly the symbol, "other people," those who set the standards and fitted easily within them, were always willing to welcome the recalcitrant at the first hint of a change of heart. As she sat looking down at the correspondence in front of her and visualized herself as married to Philip she gasped at her own presumption.

"Oh, Aunt Jo, how you jump at things," she protested in a voice moderated to conceal the sharpness of her own alarm. "It's perfectly absurd. A boy cuts in on me at a party and talks to me for a few minutes because I'm different from his usual crowd. What does it matter?"

Aunt Jo shrugged her shoulders.

"Well, as long as you don't care," she said, "I suppose we may as well drop it."

But Sybil was very far from not caring. The idea of Philip was with her in the following days and weeks as much as Aunt Jo could possibly have wished. That she barely knew him and might well not see him again she took entirely for granted. She had never been in love with anyone who had been in love with her or with anyone, for that matter, who had even been aware of her feeling. Hers had been shadowy affairs subsisting on memory and imagination, kept alive by her own half-reluctant promptings, as she sat by Aunt Jo on her afternoon drive and listened to the hum of the wheels as they passed through the darkening park on their way back from Riverside Drive or later, in the opera box, intent and still, hearing the strange wildness of Salome or Electra, or the clear nostalgic notes of Isolde. At such times she would learn some of the force and some of the penalties of love and even, in her own way, some of its joys. For Sybil, under her sullen exterior, was far from being, as Aunt Jo had implied, a cynic. In her solitary love life, in her solitary and endless reading of fiction and history, she was a deep romantic. The very sharpness of her reaction against her mother's concept of domesticity, her disgust at her father's jokes and pretenses, was evidence of a faith, not fully formulated, that life did not have to be that way, that life itself could be tremendous. She did not know if anything tremendous would ever happen to her; she rather doubted if it would, but she could assure herself that she would never, like her mother, make a compromise with life. She was sure that if she married it would be because she had found a person who would let her love him. She usually imagined that this would not happen. It was more real, somehow, to conceive of herself as disappointed.

There was certainly nothing in her life that seemed likely to produce a less unilateral romance. Nicholas Cummings, Uncle Stafford's son and more than fifteen years her senior, obviously but politely acting at his stepmother's suggestion, took her out for dinner once a week, on Thursday evenings. It was not very gay, but then she was not used to gaiety, and at least he never made her feel uncomfortable. He was a tall, slight, spare man with thin wrists and ankles; his long, thick hair was brushed back closely from the high forehead that surmounted his prominent nose and faintly questioning eyes. Nicholas seemed to pause on the threshold of life and to wave one past him — if one cared to pass. What he did, he did well; he was a member of the law firm that represented his father's bank; he collected early English law reports, and he played excellent bridge. His particular hobby, however, was the construction in his own fancy of a perfectly organized capitalist economy. He had so long given up hope for the survival of traditional capitalism in what he regarded as a now frankly socialist society that he did not even bother to be indignant, as did his friends and relatives, at the continuing nefariousness of the New Deal. He would simply shrug his shoulders and ask: "What do you expect?" with a mildness that gave people little hint of the disgust that lay beneath it, a disgust, indeed, that embraced in the same chilly grip each and every aspect of life in twentieth-century America. He and Sybil would dine, expensively but soberly, in old and familiar hotel restaurants and discuss the complex benefits of his new republic.

"What would you do with people like me?" she asked one night. "I'm an utter parasite. Would your system allow of parasites?"

"Oh, we've got to have a leisure class," he said decisively. "How else would beautiful things be appreciated?"

"I'm not sure that I appreciate beautiful things. Do you?"

He gave her a little smile.

"I'm a lawyer," he said. "Lawyers don't have to."

She sighed.

"You don't think I ought to *do* anything, then?" she asked doubtfully. "You think I can just sit?"

"But you do a great deal," he said politely. "You give a lot of time to my stepmother, and she certainly leads an active and useful life. We can't all be leaders to begin with, you know. Some of us must help."

Sybil was not versed in what people did or failed to do in the way of being useful, but she distrusted his assumption, sincere and consoling though it might be, that Aunt Jo's civic activity was the ultimate in good works. She doubted, for example, that Howard Plimpton would accept it.

"You don't think I could help more if I worked in a hospital?" she persisted. "Or for a community service?"

"I do not," he said, very definitely. "Social workers used

to be goodhearted old maids who distributed turkeys to the poor on Thanksgiving and read aloud to them in hospital wards. Now they're girls who have majored in psychology at New York University and intrude on the privacy of their neighbors to find . . . well, I'd rather not even guess what they find. No thank you. Not for me."

Sybil looked down at the tablecloth. It embarrassed her when Nicholas spoke this way. Whenever he referred to something modern, and therefore absurd, there was an edge of harshness in his tone.

"Nicholas," she protested, "Aunt Jo thinks that I'm cynical. But you're the cynic in the family. The real one."

"Me? Don't be foolish, Sybil. I'm a realist. There's a difference."

"And what am I?"

"You're a very attractive and a very intelligent young lady," he said, still in perfect seriousness. "And that is a perfectly good thing to be."

"You think I'm all right the way I am?" she persisted.

"Of course, you are."

Well, it was reassuring to think that someone thought so; it gave a lift to her spirits, but the reassurance was qualified by the fact that Nicholas was equally sure that he, too, was all right the way *he* was, and of this she was far from certain.

The only person outside the family whom she was seeing at this time was Howard Plimpton. He also took her out to dinner, but not to discuss economics. Their principal topic was Howard and Howard's life. He never apologized for this, simply stating that it was a relief to be able to talk to a girl who wasn't full of the "eyewash" that most girls were full of. Sybil gathered that his adored Mabel's own share of the general allotment of eyewash was a generous one. Howard, who in company was quiet and almost painfully polite, could be violent when alone. She felt, when he moved his hands in abrupt, quick gestures and frowned at her, that whatever he was repressing might make him explode at any moment into tiny pieces all over the restaurant.

"Your cousin Nicholas, if I may say so, Sybil, is a consummate ass," he said one night, when she had been quoting him. "He doesn't even live in the past. He lives in what he would like to think the past is."

Sybil stared. Nobody, except her father, had ever referred to Nicholas as an ass.

"He's very clever, you know," she protested. "Uncle Stafford says they take his advice at the bank on all sorts of things. He's written articles for the Wall Street Journal, and —— "

"Which has nothing whatever to do with his being an ass," Howard interrupted. "Oh, I don't say that he hasn't got some sort of an adding-machine mind. He's welcome to it. What I mean is that he doesn't have the faintest idea what life's all about. He's frozen tight. Do you think Nicholas has ever been in love, for example? Do you think he's even capable of it?"

She didn't like his saying this. It was the kind of thing that other people were apt to say about Nicholas, sneeringly. It was as if there were some duty to live fully, to enjoy oneself, a duty that she and Nicholas were secret allies in refusing to recognize.

"Everybody doesn't have to fall in love."

"Well, I feel sorry for the poor saps who don't."

"I've never been in love," she said defiantly, wondering, as she said it, if it wasn't perhaps true.

He looked at her for a moment.

"Don't worry, Sib. You will."

"I'm not so sure," she retorted. "And why, after all, should I want to? You're always going on about Mabel, and you admit she's a featherbrain. What's so wonderful about that?"

He looked pained.

"Can't you be a little more subtle?" he asked. "It's all

right for me to say things about Mabel. Not you."

"I don't see that at all," she said indignantly. "You call my cousin Nicholas an ass. Nicholas who's always been good and kind to me. I've met your Mabel. I don't think Nicholas is nearly so much of an ass as she is."

He winced.

"Look, Sib, that's different. You're not in love with Nicholas."

"I'm not at all sure I'm not!" she said heatedly. "It may be just what's wrong with me, and I've never known it! After all, he's the only person who really takes any trouble about me ―― "

But Howard was holding up his hands. He was laughing now.

"Okay, Sib," he said. "You win. There'll be no more talk of love tonight. I'm sorry."

When she let herself into the house that night she found that the lights in the living room were still on, and she assumed that her parents were up. She was tiptoeing up the darkened stairway when she heard her brother's voice.

"Sybil?"

She stopped in surprise.

"Teddy? But why aren't you in Virginia?"

She hurried to the door of the living room only to find him sitting there with Millie. They were not, however, alone. Philip was with them. They were all drinking beer. She simply stared.

"Phil and I flew up to New Haven for the hockey game," Teddy explained. "We decided at the last minute. How are you?"

"Have you been sitting alone at some bar?" Philip asked. "Oh, she has, Teddy. You can tell by that guilty look."

She felt a sudden disappointment that he did not look as she had pictured him. He was lanky, but he was thinner than she had remembered, and his voice was too hearty, and his eyes, well, his eyes were like other people's eyes.

"I have to do some work for Aunt Jo," she blurted out.
"If you'll excuse me."

"But, Sib, it's Saturday night — " Teddy was protesting.
She had turned and was already on the stairway.

"Sybil!" he called, but she hurried on. In the library she
turned on the lights and went over to the desk to get out
the minutes of Aunt Jo's hospital board meeting to type.
She did this automatically, because she had told them she
was going to. She sat down at the typewriter, still dazed,
and stared at the keys. Then she heard quick steps on the
stairway, and turned around as Philip came in.

"You're not going to leave me down there with Millie and
Teddy, are you?" he asked. "You've heard about three
being a crowd?"

His presence there, so suddenly juxtaposed against a background where every smallest object had a family affiliation,
was overwhelming. As she stared at him, however, her vision
readjusted, and he was again handsome. As handsome as
she had remembered.

"I thought you might have had things to discuss."

"They do," he said, sitting down beside her on the sofa.

"I don't. I'd rather be up here if you don't mind."

"Oh, I don't mind," she said quickly.

"Thanks." He smiled. "What have you been up to tonight? Were you really at a bar?"

"Oh, no." She shook her head. "I was having supper with
Howard. Howard Plimpton."

It was his turn to stare.

"The two of you?"

"You think we should have been chaperoned?"

He ignored this.

"I was thinking of Mabel," he said and gave a low whistle.
"Are you trying to cut her out? You're quite a girl, aren't
you? I'd never have suspected it."

"Oh, it's not that at all," she protested in dismay. "Howard and I are just friends. As a matter of fact, he takes me out to talk about Mabel."

"That must be fun for you."

"Oh, I don't mind."

"Why don't you go out with me some night? I promise I won't talk about Mabel."

There was a pause.

"Will you ask me?" she said gravely.

At this moment Esther came into the room, in a faded pink wrapper, tied loosely over her billowing nightgown. Her bedroom was on the library floor, and she had come down the corridor to get a book. Startled, and rather haggard, she stared at the couple on the sofa. Then she hurried across the room towards her book on the table as if crossing an open field under fire.

"Excuse me, Mr. Hilliard. Excuse me, Sybil," she murmured. "I didn't know you were here. I'll be right out."

Philip had stood up.

"Good evening, Mrs. Rodman. Can I help you find anything?"

"No, no. No, thanks."

She was making away with her clutched book when her husband, dressed only in his pajama bottoms, followed her into the library.

"Esther, why in hell does Ellen always make a point of hiding my —— Oh. Oh, I beg your pardon."

And pushed by his wife he disappeared with her into the corridor. Philip looked embarrassed.

"I shouldn't have come up," he said, sitting down again. "I should have stayed in the living room. I'm afraid we're disturbing your parents."

She shook her head.

"It doesn't matter."

But it did. It was as if her mother had done it on purpose,

stumbling in that way and clutching her wrapper about her, so pathetic, so exasperatingly pathetic, so unlike people of Mrs. Hilliard's kind who surely did not appear in wrappers, probably never needed them. It was as if she wanted to remind Sybil who Sybil was. Who did she think she was, anyway, sitting up there at night with a man like Philip, keeping him from the kind of girl that he must have really wanted?

"Maybe you're right," she said suddenly and got up. "Maybe you'd better go. But I would like to go out with you," she continued with a desperate boldness. "I'm much better away from home. Really. Do ask me sometime."

He looked at her closely, held by the plea in her eyes.

"Why sure," he said, with some embarrassment. "I come up lots of weekends. I'll call you."

She nodded and held out her hand. When he had gone she went back to her typewriter and stared at the keys. She could not even bring herself to think of what had happened.

Chapter
Three

TEDDY RODMAN was as different from his sister as a brother could possibly be. Where she was reserved, he was outgiving; where she was abrupt he was full of easy charm. Like Aunt Jo he enjoyed the world, or at least he seemed to; he loved riding and poetry and sport coats and long conversations about life late at night. He seemed at home with everyone, whether sprawled on the sand at the beach club at Easton Bay, where Aunt Jo went in the summer, giving advice to lovelorn subdébutantes, or sitting at an umbrella table on the club terrace, inhaling an absurdly big cigar and listening to the worries of his adoring mother and aunt. The only concern that his family had ever entertained was that the eclecticism of his tastes might foreshadow too novel a choice of career or girl friends. On these scores, however, as on others, he had satisfied them completely. The girl in whom he showed the greatest interest, Millie Dessart, was a conservative choice by any standard, and he had announced, promptly upon his graduation from Harvard, his intention to train for law. But it was as a son that he was most perfect of all, intimate, sympathetic and yet resourceful, as if at birth he had sensed his father's inadequacies and his mother's alarms and determined to protect them from themselves as well as from the world. George and Esther had never quite been able to take in the fact that they had produced so charming a boy; they were still inclined, from time to time, to rub their eyes and wonder what good fairy had deposited this welcome, if alien, bundle in any cradle of theirs.

If Teddy had always been the favorite of his parents and of Aunt Jo, it can be imagined that he was no less loved in the heart of his younger sister. She had worshipped him, however critically, since childhood. And Teddy, with the same sensitivity that had made him aware of his mother's and father's innate vulnerability, had understood his own importance to Sybil. He had never sent her off when his friends had come over to play, as most older brothers would have done, nor had he ever pulled her hair or cheated her on exchanges of toys. But their relationship was less one-sided than it may have seemed. Teddy's anxiety to please the world was the gauge of his need for affection, and in reckoning up his total of hearts won over he counted as the equivalent of several the unlimited if rather sticky devotion of his younger sister.

It was a relationship that had always been easier for him than for her. He had other friends and other interests, but to Sybil he was everything, and she was perennially jealous. She loved, during the long summers that they used to spend with Aunt Jo in Easton Bay, to sit beside him on the sofa in Uncle Stafford's dark library and look at the pictures in the illustrated histories, leather-bound and gold-topped, that filled the shelves. History to them was a dazzling succession, seen through royal genealogies, of stiff, brocaded, irresponsible persons, with pearls in their hair and pearls in their clothes, who postured in lithographs, always before crowds. Teddy would choose for his hero a Don John of Austria or a Tamburlaine, but to Sybil power was appealing when it fell into unlikely hands, as into the clutch of some discarded or neglected poor relation, who would in the end emerge, crowned and glittering, before a remorseful court.

She would be a Catherine de Medici or a Madame de Maintenon; her success would be the sweeter for earlier humiliation. And when the door would open and their mother, seeing her own childhood before her, would send them brusquely outside to play, hoping that by doing to them what her mother had done to her she would make them different from herself, as though only the innate perverseness locked within Esther Rodman could have failed to respond to such standard treatment, Sybil would think grimly of oubliettes and how she would have used them.

It would never have occurred to Esther not to send her son to Chelton School, in New Hampshire, in his fourteenth year. She regarded the New England church schools as among the absolutely unavoidable, if arbitrary, hurdles which every boy of her world had to take. It didn't particularly matter how he managed to get over the hurdle, but get over it he must. Otherwise, as the old argument ran, he would feel "queer" for the rest of his life. In this, if for somewhat different reasons, her husband was on her side. George did not come from a background where schools like Chelton were taken for granted; it was important to him that his son, if born a Rodman, should be educated as a Delafield. He might make fun of his brother-in-law; he might inwardly preen himself on coming from new and vigorous stock, but in this there could be no variance, and Teddy went off to a green campus surrounded by red brick, to football games in the fresh autumnal New England air, to narrow cubicles and cold showers, to strange new standards and the alarming universality of a single point of view. For several months he was unhappy; he had never before met hostility, but he was careful not to show it. He wrote his mother enthusiastic letters, not because he thought that she believed them or even because he wanted her to, but because he believed with her in the strange, arbitrary hurdles that marked the path of life which had to be overcome simply because they were there. Esther had conveyed to him some of her fatalism, however differently he may have expressed it, and he knew, if he wrote her that he was unhappy, that she would take him out of the school, and he knew, too, if she did this, that his father would be disgusted and that his life, in all probability, would be ruined. Chelton, above all things, taught its boys to believe in their own futures, in their great responsibilities. To Sybil alone could he unburden himself without fear of catastrophe.

"Our life here is very regular," he wrote her, after the first month, "which I suppose is good. I have not made many friends, but maybe I will have better luck when the football season is over. I play it rottenly. The boys who play it best have the most friends. Some of them, like Philip Hilliard, seem to have it in for me, but maybe it's because I don't know them well. There's a wonderful library, but I can only go there for a half-hour after lunch. I am reading Dumas and will finish 'The Diamond Necklace' by Christmas. Please read it too, so we can talk about it."

Sybil burned all his letters for fear that her mother might ask her for them. Esther had a way of doing this, because, being full of secrets herself, she imagined that secrets were wicked. It hurt Sybil to burn them, but, after all, they were engraved on her heart. She had to be strong, because she was the underground in a war against parental occupation. If Teddy was always weakening, it was not entirely his fault; he was under great pressure from Esther who was always calling up her reserves in the form of games or schools or odious, undesired playmates. Chelton to Sybil was nothing but a confession of weakness on her parents' part; they dared not leave Teddy with her at home. They dared not face the competition of the library and the quiet life. They were afraid, she reflected bitterly, that he might actually enjoy himself, and the surest remedy was to pack him off to a school that had decades of experience in the art of making life unpleasant. But it had to be borne. The time would come — some day — when they would stand forth on their own and confound the older generation. In the meanwhile they could only bide their time.

The time, of course, had never come. By Christmas Teddy had made friends with Chelton, and a new world had opened to him in which there was no place for her. And through the years it had continued this way. There had been Christmas vacations and dances to which he now seemed to want to go and summers in Europe, given by Aunt Jo, with other boys, and then Harvard and the bewildering world of clubs and people who took Teddy for granted, and finally law school and its odd, superior jargon and Millie with her air of proprietorship. Sybil had watched it all, at first with bitterness, later with resignation, but always in silence. She had not been one to make scenes. And Teddy, for his part, had always been aware of her basic disapproval. He sometimes wondered if there might not be, in her silent aloofness from the patter of his life, a grim but somehow commendable loyalty to the high integrity of their shared childhood. If there had been a betrayal, surely it had not been hers.

"I didn't know he would scare her so," he said to Millie that Saturday night after Philip had left, having stuck his head in the doorway to tell them he'd been "booted." "I thought she seemed to like him at the dance. Before he cut in on her the second time I knew he was going to. It was instinct. Nothing like that had ever happened before. Oh, I don't mean cousins and friends of the family. But to have a guy introduced and have him want to cut right back — well, that's something, Millie! For Sybil, anyway. She's changing!"

Millie, however, was very far from detecting the smallest change in Sybil's conduct.

"I'm probably scared myself by more things than Sybil is," she pointed out rather sharply. "As a matter of fact, she doesn't seem scared to me at all. People who are supposed to be shy get away with murder. Why can't she come in here and sit down and be civil for a minute? Why does she have to make me feel the way she makes me feel?"

"Like what?"

"Oh, like — like a doll."

She clenched her fists in emphasis, and when Teddy, still smiling, took one of her hands in his and pried her fingers apart, he wondered at the strength of people like Millie who had no strength outside their own trembling faith in the one way and the only way to be. It was her sense of the majority behind, of public affirmation, that buoyed Millie up, her belief that women everywhere cared about the things she cared about. And what was it but cowardice in him, the desire to be like others, that drew him to her pretty face and neat hair, her white round shoulders, her flat trim figure and the grey dress with the spot that she had not noticed yet, that would appall her when she did notice it, that she would think of for weeks, wondering how long it had been there?

"She's jealous of you, Millie. All intelligent girls are jealous of you."

"Oh, Teddy. You're never serious. It isn't right never to be serious."

When he had taken her home, later that night, and kissed her on the stoop and reminded her that she could still marry him if she wanted, which, as they both knew, she still did, but only after he had graduated and had a job, after he had earned all the things that Aunt Jo could give him anyway, he came back and stared at himself in his mirror. Was the day over? Could he go to bed now? There was a knock at the door.

"Teddy, I want to talk to you a minute. Just a minute, dear."

He turned.

"Yes, Mummie."

She came in and sat down on a corner of his bed, puffing at a cigarette. She looked tired, and he hated to see the ashes on her wrapper. He went over to his bureau and took the cuff links out of his shirt, arranging them side by side on the white cover.

"I've been meaning to say this to you for some time," she went on. "You worry too much over Sybil, dear. You oughtn't to. People have to make their own way."

"If they can."

"But you can't make it for them, dear," she protested. "I saw you at that dance and how you looked after her. And again tonight. Is it fair to Millie, Teddy? Wouldn't she rather be at a night club?"

He smiled a bit sourly at his reflection over the red bow tie in the glass. It was so like Esther, who had never felt or really believed in the tug of romantic desire, to conceive of it as a sort of prelude to marriage, a necessary but rather tricky exercise in which younger members of her own sex, like Millie, strangely but somehow justifiably demanding, required things of her own children which they, like herself, would find it hard to simulate but which they, again like herself, would have to learn to accomplish. He thought he could see the exhaustion behind the glitter in his own eyes as he stared. For was she perhaps right? Were they all alike?

"Sybil's got to have her chance, Mummie," he said.

He waited, but Esther showed no disposition to leave. She continued to puff at her cigarette.

"I suppose the psychiatrists would say I've rejected her," she said gloomily. "God knows I never meant to. But they say you can't fool children. Even when you're being sincere. Or think you're being sincere. It seems to me I've cared for her very much." She sighed. "But you can't beat the subconscious, I suppose. I know I've always been more congenial with you. But you were always nice to me, Teddy."

"Oh, I'm wonderful all right," he said, pulling his tie off. "Go to bed, Ma. You look done in."

"What does she expect, anyway?" Esther continued, almost peevishly. "I didn't make her go to college. I didn't make her come out. It seems to me I've let her have her own way in everything."

"Of course you have."

"Parents get blamed for everything now," she went on. "When I was a child, if I was naughty, it was my fault. Now, if Sybil's naughty, it's still my fault. When does it stop?"

He shrugged his shoulders.

"Teddy," she said, getting up, "you're not up to one of your schemes, are you? You didn't lure Philip here so he'd see her, did you?"

He raised his hands in mock dismay.

"Really, Mummie!"

"It wouldn't be — well, seemly, you know."

"No, Ma. Now go to bed."

"You're sure?"

"Of course, I'm sure. Good night."

He came over and kissed her on the cheek, gently, but drew away as she was about to put her arms around his neck. He loved her very much, but he hated her embraces, those smothering embraces in which she, ordinarily undemonstrative, still tried to enfold him, before going to bed, before going away, on birthdays, on Christmas, embraces that expressed so violently her passionate need to feel that she was being a good mother. It was a bit hard, he reflected, as he turned back, after closing the door behind her, to the contemplation of his own image in the big mirror, to have to do all his family's jobs for them. In life, they appeared to believe, things simply happened; it was vulgar to interfere. It was he who had to act out their romance, he who had to be the serpent as well as the flower. He looked into his own shining eyes and stuck his tongue out. To hell with them, he said out loud. Oh, Teddy, Teddy, how could you? And he laughed, rather recklessly, to himself.

Chapter

Four

NO TWO FAMILIES could have been more different than
the Hilliards and the Rodmans. Sybil's mother and her
aunt, Jo Cummings, had a strong and oppressive sense of
the responsibilities incurred by having been born who they
were ("whoever that was," as George Rodman used to
retort). Their point of view was congenial to the Long Island
summer colony at Easton Bay of which Aunt Jo was so con-
spicuous a member, a point of view that perhaps too often
found its expression in large hats and soft voices, in big,
dark shingle houses and small, cautious beach clubs, in a
great deal of housework and a triumphant domesticity.
"When Easton Bay girls are pregnant," Philip's mother used
to say, "they even show it in their hats." The Hilliard girls,
her daughters, though mothers themselves, never seemed
to show it at all. But that, of course, was just the difference.
They spent their summers in Glenville, only a few miles
from Easton Bay, but Glenville was all brick and no shingle,
all sweeping, well-cut lawns and grilled iron fences. Glenville was aloof from the world; it was a land of gateposts,
large gateposts of stone surmounted by lions or eagles, or
deceptively small ones of red brick, through all of which,
however, one had the same glimpse of a long winding tape
of blue gravel disappearing into the trees.

The Hilliards, to begin with, were rich, much richer even than Uncle Stafford. They had the impregnability that comes of being born with money, of having married money, of scarcely being able, as far as they could peer through the branches of their family tree, to spot a twig unendowed with its independent competency, so that the entire great oak, trunk and foliage, gave forth an air of having stood for a multiplicity of individual and profitable things back to the dawn of American history. Philip's parents had large red-brick, Georgian houses both in New York and in Glenville, furnished comfortably and rather splendidly in eighteenth-century English. They had an old beach house on the dunes of the south shore of Long Island, full of wicker furniture and stained sporting prints, where they went in August to relax. Their taste was sufficiently good when they cared, but they cared very rarely. They entertained constantly, and almost always the same people, except for a small, changing element drawn from the world of arts and letters. They served excellent food to which they paid little attention and excellent liquor to which they paid considerably more. They never, of course, went to church, for they believed in nothing except, very casually, the few principles of social formality which they had not yet discarded. They liked animals and people who liked animals and prided themselves on a tweedy, rustic toughness of mind and manner. They liked to think that they were down to earth and hard to take in. Noone, however, had ever tried.

To describe them more individually, Seymour Hilliard, Philip's father, was a silent, rather disagreeable man of forbidding manner who spent most of his time on his place in Glenville, even when his wife and children were in town. He talked at considerable length in a harsh, emphatic, self-assured voice on subjects that he knew something about, such as dogs and horses and hunting. He had a large farm on his country place which he ran with great efficiency, and he took an active interest in local politics, mostly because he hoped to arrest the steady march of low-priced housing developments that kept ominously moving out towards Glenville from the city. He was dogmatic, narrow and able; one could see in his conservative dress and in the unimaginative exactitude with which he inventoried every tree and shrub on his place his essential kinship with the counting house world in which, however, he rarely appeared. It was his wife who supplied the glitter which dazzled people. Lucy Hilliard, large and handsome and somehow detached from her dyed blond hair and her big gold jewelry, would fix one with a look that seemed to say: I can take anything from you except the insincerity of what you call your real beliefs. Drop them and we can talk. She said whatever was on her mind as it came to mind; there was no person living for whom she would make the smallest adjustment. She and her husband were mutually indifferent; it was understood between them that neither would ever ask a favor of the other. Lucy kept open house in New York both when he was there and when he wasn't. She was entirely casual about her dinners; she simply liked to have the house full. Her oldest daughters, Lila and Felicia, who were always with her when she entertained, had married men who were not, in Lucy's opinion, "stuffy." In other words, they were never so busy as to be unavailable when she needed them. Fun to Lucy was her only god, and she liked to worship it in the company of her offspring.

Philip, as the only son, occupied a special position. More was expected of him than of his brothers-in-law; he, after all, was a Hilliard, and Hilliards did things well if they did them at all. There was nothing to be despised about success; Lucy would have been delighted to see her son an ambassador or an explorer. But, most importantly, he could never be allowed to become "stuffy." And Philip had recently been showing signs of this. His politics, for example.

There was danger already of his becoming a bore. It was for this reason that Lucy currently had her son under a close observation, even keeping track of the girls he saw.

While she was still in Glenville the following Monday morning, after a weekend in the country, Felicia telephoned. Apparently Philip had lunched with her on Sunday and had talked for an hour about a girl called Sybil Rodman.

"Thank you, dear," her mother said. "You can never catch these things too early. It's like stepping on matches. Any girl he picks at this stage will be grim."

When Lila, her other married daughter, who was visiting her, came in to say good morning she found her mother propped up in bed with the Social Register on her lap. The big sunny room was filled with the Monday morning atmosphere of Lucy's imminent return to the city; bags and hatboxes, open and half-packed, were scattered over the floor. At the bureau Lucy's maid was taking things out of a drawer, and Arlina, the youngest, was trying on her mother's lipstick at the dressing table.

"This Rodman girl," Lucy said, as Lila came over to her. "She's a sister of Teddy's, I see. I didn't even know he had a sister. There must be something wrong with her or we'd have heard of her before now."

Lila, who was tall and bony like her mother, with large eyes wide apart and a detached air, sat on the edge of Lucy's bed.

"Oh, yes," she said. "Certainly. I know about her. Teddy's told me. She's difficult. Shy and hates people. Couldn't stay at schools. You know the type."

Lucy snorted.

"Just what Philip *would* fall for," she exclaimed. "The most dangerous of all!"

"You can't think him such an ass, Ma."

"Men make asses of themselves over neurotics," Lucy retorted. "Every time. Look at this girl's mother. Esther. I remember her at school, and I can assure you there was never a greater frump. Yet even she got a man. A vulgar one, I grant you, but still a man. And she did it just by looking gloomy. Arlina, put down that lipstick!"

"But Philip's always gone in for the sleeky type," Lila pointed out. "Or the brash and noisy. Like Julia Anderton. He wouldn't fall for a shy girl."

"Wouldn't he? A little girl who 'understood' him? And whom only he 'understood'?"

Lila shrugged her shoulders.

"What can you do?"

"Nothing, of course," her mother answered. "Now. Wait and see. And then have her around for dinner. If it keeps up."

"Won't she frighten him off?" Lila suggested. "Won't she expect a marriage proposal after one kiss?"

"No, you're wrong there, Lila," Lucy said, shaking her head. "Those girls will do anything. And they always get in trouble. That's why they're dangerous. I tell you, my child, you don't know them!"

. . .

Lucy was right in not underestimating the appeal of the unsophisticated. Philip had in fact been fascinated by Sybil; she had given him, as his mother had divined, a sense of being the first explorer in a field of untapped possibilities. The girl was different, and it was obvious to him that he had made an impression. Not that he was unused to making impressions, but it was pleasant, in this case, to think that his had been the first.

When he called her up two weeks later from Virginia to ask her if she was free the following Saturday night, she could hardly believe it. She admitted, of course, that she was. Then she called Teddy. He, too, was coming up that weekend, and she remembered that she had agreed to dine with him and Millie. When she told him about Philip, he only laughed.

"Of course, silly. You needn't make excuses to me. I'm only a substitute until another guy comes along. And when that guy's Philip, grab him!"

"Why, Teddy?"

"Because he's . . . well, because he's a catch. Anyway, do as I say, sweet. When has old Teddy ever let you down?"

All this was very alarming to Sybil who was quite alarmed enough, in the first place. She could see that to Philip she was something unusual and amusing, something out of the ordinary run of girl that he knew, and she felt sure that she would not be able to live up to his illusion of her individuality. The more, therefore, that she saw him, the sooner would his disillusionment come. But what could she do?

Her picture of him was not clouded by her involvement. She was quite aware, for example, that his conversation on the night of their first meeting had been less interesting than Howard's. Or even than Nicholas'. There had been moments when he had actually been boring. Philip's mind was like a street lamp at night; it lit up everything in the sector that it illuminated, but if one ventured the least bit beyond that, all was black. Yet when she had sat beside him that night in the bar, her only desire had been to keep within the lighted arc. It had not been hard. If Philip was sound, he was also predictable. She had some of her mother's feeling that this, in any event, was the way men were.

She was waiting in the little sitting room off the front hall when he called for her that Saturday night. No one had ever told her that it was not the thing to do, but this was just as well, for Philip, highly punctual himself, regarded it as a virtue. He took her to a night club, very dark and crowded, with an entertainment that nobody listened to.

"What have you been up to all week?" he asked when they were seated at their table. "Going out every night, I suppose? Gay as hell?"

"Oh, no." She shook her head, missing the humor in his tone. "I haven't been going out at all. I go out very rarely. I went out Thursday night with Nicholas —— "

"Have you been thinking about me?" he interrupted.

"I guess so," she said.

"Nice things?"

"Oh, yes."

He nodded and then looked up at the waiter to order cocktails.

"I was telling Ma about you this afternoon," he said. "She knows Teddy, of course. But I told her you're not like Teddy."

"Oh, no, I'm not like Teddy," she agreed hastily, as if afraid of being caught in a fraud. "Teddy's different. Everyone likes Teddy."

He shrugged his shoulders.

"Sure," he said. "Teddy's fine. He's always at the right place at the right time. But being popular isn't everything. You'd be popular, Sybil, if you'd give people a chance to know you."

She glanced for a second into his friendly grey eyes. They seemed to radiate normalcy, and she turned away in pain at the thought of what different things he would be thinking if he really knew her. She wanted to reassure him, to console him, to give him whatever it was that he wanted. But she couldn't talk about herself this way. Even for him.

"I'll try," she said. "To let people know me, that is."

"That's the girl. Come out of your shell. Show yourself off. Ma said she wants to meet you. Let me take you there for dinner some night."

Sybil looked up in alarm. She had heard a great deal about Mrs. Hilliard from Teddy who, with his usual hyperbole, had described her as "terrific."

"What's wrong?" he asked, laughing. "You look as if I'd asked you to dine at the morgue."

"Oh, no, Philip," she said. "I'd love to meet your mother. Teddy tells me she's wonderful. Only I don't think I'd fit into her atmosphere."

"Why not?"

"Oh. You know." She stirred uncomfortably. "I'm sure everybody there's so quick and gay."

"Oh, that." He brushed it off with a gesture. "Ma and the girls overdo that sort of thing, I grant you. But deep down they're okay. You'll like them. Really. When you get to know them."

Sybil reflected on the improbability that she would ever get to know "Ma and the girls."

"You should never let people like that worry you," he went on reassuringly. "They're all living in the past, anyway. Ma and Dad and Felicia and Lila. And the aunts. Only you don't know about the aunts. Daddy's old maid sisters. They're really something. Of course, Ma's the best," he said, more reflectively. "She's at least not always bitching about the government. Even if she is fundamentally conservative. If you ever tie her down. But the thing about Ma is that she doesn't give a damn."

"And should she?" she asked.

But to Philip life was a parlor game where people had to choose sides. He could not comprehend the femininity of seeing facts without issues.

"Of course, she should!" he exclaimed. "How can people do any good in the world if they don't believe in anything?"

Sybil looked at him wonderingly. Once again she was outside the lighted circle.

"Maybe she doesn't want to do any good," she suggested.

"I don't think my mother does any good."

"Oh, they all do a lot of charity work, don't they?"

Sybil's silence indicated the amount of good that she thought was accomplished by that.

"You're a cynical little creature, aren't you?" he said, laughing.

"Oh, no, Philip."

"You sit there quietly while I blab along, and you're probably thinking what a dope I am."

She shook her head in protest.

"What do you want to do?" he continued. "With your life, I mean?"

"Oh, nothing in particular." But this sounded too empty, even to her, and she added, after a moment: "I like to read."

He stared.

"But you can't just read."

"I can't?"

He raised his hands in dismay.

"Don't you want to get married?" he asked.

So there it was again, the inevitable question.

"I don't know," she said miserably. "I really don't."

"But all girls do."

"You take people for granted, Philip," she said, almost sharply. "You don't admit of exceptions."

"All right," he agreed easily, seeing that she minded. "So you want to read. What do you read mostly?"

"History."

"You feel it gives you a better understanding of what's going on today?"

"No."

"Then what do you read it for?" he asked.

"Escape." When she saw that she had shocked him she became abject. "It's pretty obvious, isn't it?" she asked. "But then I'm obvious. Just recently," she continued desperately, as he still said nothing, "I've been reading all the books I could find on Isabella. Isabella of Castile."

She could see that he was afraid that she would tell him about Isabella. He need not have worried. Already she wanted to go home. She wanted to be alone so that she could think about him. He would find her out, eventually, as everyone found her out, but she wanted first to build an image of him that would survive his disappearance. For she knew, even if only in a confused and troubled way, that something important was happening to her, something more than the passive dreams of her past romances, something more even than the simple and consoling experience of standing before the warm fire of his unassailable opinions and listening to his high laugh or watching his small eyes move back and forth, those grey eyes that seemed not quite to fit with the Americanism of his blond hair and the pugnacity of his jaw. She decided that he was the handsomest man that she had ever seen, knowing perfectly well that he wasn't.

When he took her home that night he tried to kiss her in the taxi. She did not like the way he did it, but she was not prepared to hold anything against him. He put his arm around her and pulled her over towards him. He did it easily, as if it were entirely to be expected that she wouldn't mind.

"You may say you're an escapist, Sybil," he said. "But here's something you're not going to escape."

She put both hands on his shoulders to hold him off.

"No, Philip, please!" she cried in a voice so tense that he drew back.

"What the heck?"

"I'm sorry," she said. She was trembling all over. "I'm terribly sorry."

He shrugged his shoulders and settled back in his corner of the seat.

"Have it your way," he said sulkily. "I'm not begging."

She had a sudden and disturbing sense of the crudity behind his disappointment, the quick, almost brutal repudiation of herself.

"You mustn't hold it against me, Philip," she said, shrinking back into her corner. "I like you a lot. Really, I do. It's
just that — well, you'll have to give me time. Oh, what am
I saying?" Her mouth was open with dismay. "Of course,
you won't give me time. Why on earth should you? It's
just that I'm — all wound up."

He looked at her in surprise for a moment and finally
smiled.

"Take it easy, Sib," he said, and they parted, after all, on
good terms.

Chapter
Five

TEDDY AND PHILIP went back to the university together the following night, and Sybil once again was left to contemplate the extraordinary event of this new friendship in her life. She was not, however, allowed to contemplate it alone. Esther had been briefed by Teddy; she had been told about Philip and warned not to interfere, but she could not resist, by constant indirect references, the temptation to glean further information as to how things were progressing. She would peer at Sybil cautiously across the dining-room table and ask if the Hilliards still had the house they used to have in Glenville or if Lucy Hilliard was as handsome as she once was. Sybil, of course, told her nothing, but she hated the questions and finally went down to Easton Bay to be by herself and think how best to cope with these new complications in her quiet life. Everything there was soaked in the melancholy dampness of a premature spring, and as she walked up and down Aunt Jo's terrace, listening to the plop of raindrops on the broad leaves of the rhododendrons, she thought with agony of the clumsiness of her conduct in the cab and how much better she might have handled herself. Then, one morning, Philip called her from Charlottesville.

"Hi!" he said. "How's Queen Isabella?"

"Where we left her, I guess."

"You shouldn't just read that stuff," he continued. "I was talking about it with Teddy. You ought to write something."

She wondered if he had called her up to tell her this.

"Oh, no," she said.

"Sybil," he said, with his usual definiteness. "I'm coming up the end of this week. Ma's giving a party on Friday night. Will you come?"

She felt her heart stop.

"Oh, Philip. She doesn't want me, does she?"

"Sure she does. As a matter of fact, she suggested it. Eight o'clock and dress. Okay?"

She supposed that she must have accepted for he rang off and left her to her desolate thoughts. She could hardly do a thing all the next day but walk about the grounds debating whether or not she should call him and pretend to be sick. Yet it was always possible, wasn't it, that Mrs. Hilliard who, according to Teddy, really cared for Philip under the parade of her apparent indifference, might see in her something of more durable value than the brassy emptiness of girls like Julia Anderton? Stranger things had happened, hadn't they? As she looked in her mirror that night and pulled a comb through her long, straight hair she saw herself for a moment, modestly but clearly, confirming a point that Mr. Hilliard had made with a reference to the fall of the Byzantine empire. Not, of course, with even a hint of pedantry. Simply as if the illustration had been torn from her by its relevance to the general discussion.

"Ah, but, Philip, it's not true what they say," his mother would exclaim; "there *are* girls who are educated!" She threw the comb down. What a fool she was.

She came into town that Friday afternoon and walked with Ellen in the park. Ellen started their old game of picturing the success that Sybil was going to have that night. Sybil, however, for the first time, did not like it. It was too much on the level of the desperate hope that she had entertained in the country, and she wanted this hope to be more than a game.

"No, Ellen," she said abruptly. "We won't talk about me. Not today."

That evening she dressed early and came down to the dining room to sit with her parents while they had dinner. She was too nervous to be alone.

"Where are you going, dear?" her mother asked.

"To the Hilliards."

Esther looked at her with a gloomy speculativeness.

"To Lucy's?" she said. "How *is* Lucy?"

"I don't know. I've never met her."

"I've always thought that deep down Lucy Hilliard was probably a nice woman," Esther went on in the rather condescending tone that she adopted towards people whom she had known as a child. Having once seen their vulnerability she could never again be impressed. "If I were you, though, I wouldn't have anything to drink there. I imagine their drinks are very strong."

"Now, Esther, leave her alone," George interrupted. "She's going to a snappy dinner, and she looks ready to conquer. Go to it, my girl," he said with an approving smile. "Knock 'em silly!"

Sybil, however, was very conscious of not looking ready to knock anyone at all silly when, a half-hour later, she entered the big oblong drawing room at the Hilliards' with its eighteenth-century English canvases of ladies in wide hats against leafy backgrounds, its varnished Chippendale and its noisy, well-dressed occupants. Philip, seeming too much at ease, came across the room to greet her.

"How's the girl?" he asked.

"Oh, Philip, I'm scared to death," she said, looking around.

"What on earth of?"

"Of everything."

Lucy Hilliard, her blond hair curled into tiny ringlets

tight against her scalp, her long freckled brown arms folded, stood in a corner of the room talking to Lila, unmindful of all her guests but one. Two large grey poodles, elaborately clipped, stood at her side looking up at her.

"There she is now," she said nodding towards the door. "You're certainly right about her being a mouse, Lila. I can almost hear her squeak from here."

"But she's pretty, Ma. You'll have to give her that."

Lucy put her head back as she took Sybil in.

"In a way," she conceded. "If you like that tubercular type. I remember your father used to like it. My God, Lila, what asses men are! I almost lost him to a consumptive about the time you were born."

"Here she comes, Ma."

Sybil came up with Philip and shook her hostess' hand with a quick, awkward movement.

"It's so nice of you to have me tonight, Mrs. Hilliard."

"Not at all, my dear," Lucy said heartily. "I used to know your mother. I can still remember the day at Miss Heely's School when she went up on the roof and sat out all morning in the rain. Of course, she got the most frightful cold, and Miss Heely asked why on earth she'd done it. She said she wanted to be naughty. Apparently, she'd never been naughty before. Has she been naughty since, my dear?"

The others laughed, and Sybil felt, under Mrs. Hilliard's bold stare, as though she and her mother were allies for the first time.

"Which is more, Ma," Philip pointed out, "than could have been said of you."

"Listen to him," Lucy said turning to some others who had come up. "Everyone knows I was little Eva. You had to be good in those days to marry a Hilliard. Now I'm not sure. They're going cheaper." She turned abruptly back to Sybil and pointed to the drinks on the table. "What's your poison, dear?"

Sybil stared at her.

"My what?"

"Gin or whiskey? Get her a drink, Philip. Be a little help, child. And there's Viola," she said going over to meet a large, smiling lady whose little features were almost lost in her broad, powdered face. "Viola, my dear!" And she spent the rest of the period before dinner having a talk in a corner with Viola Paton which nothing could interrupt.

At dinner Sybil found herself on Mr. Hilliard's left, with the entire length of the table between her and his terrifying wife. He seemed a more restrained and dignified individual than the others of his family, and she looked at him hopefully, wondering if together they might not find a topic. These hopes were soon shattered. Mr. Hilliard asked her some perfunctory questions about where she lived and what she did and then, not immediately finding the spark that he required, he dropped her completely and turned an attentive and occasionally smiling face to the conversation on his other side. Mr. Hilliard never made the smallest contribution to the talk at his wife's dinner table, but this did not keep him from being easily bored by anyone who failed to come up to his own high standards of repartee. He felt that his right to be amused was absolute and that it was the privilege of Lucy's friends, on his rare visits to town, to perform this function. Sybil could not conceive why the conversation that was going on should amuse a man of his gravity of demeanor, but it obviously did, for he occasionally laughed, the way Philip did, with an unexpected loudness. The group at dinner was obviously homogeneous, although there was a wide discrepancy in ages. Lucy's friends, evidently, made as little of age as Esther's made much of it. They talked and laughed very boisterously, and the main topic of their conversation was the oddities and vagaries of the very rich, a group which they all seemed to know but from the absurdities of which they were apparently emancipated.

She kept glancing covertly at her hostess down the table, watching her gold jewelry gleam in the candlelight as she moved her long arms. At her end of the table they were talking now of less personal topics. Sybil could hear an argument of Scottish habits as opposed to English; she caught a reference to Scottish history and the name of Mary, Queen of Scots. Then she no longer even pretended to be listening to Mr. Hilliard's conversation with Viola; she stared down at her unfinished lobster in terror that Philip might ask her to arbitrate a point. It was the foolish terror, she reasoned desperately, of the self-conscious; surely he could not be so unfeeling. But fear was never to be controlled by reason, and, worse still, it could attract the very catastrophe that it anticipated. She glanced once more down the table to reassure herself only to find that Mrs. Hilliard was looking at her.

"Why ask Philip," she heard her say in a suddenly public voice, "when I understand we have a Macaulay in our midst? Sybil Rodman," she called down the table, "you know everything. At least, Philip tells me so. When were England and Scotland united?"

The table blurred as Sybil felt thirteen pairs of eyes upon her.

"In 1603, I think," she heard her voice, thin and trembling. "When Elizabeth died. Except the parliaments didn't unite until Queen Anne. Which was much later, of course." She could hear the pedantry in her tone; she could feel how little it fitted the atmosphere. She fastened her eyes on Mrs. Hilliard's, in a kind of fascination; she saw their faintly curious amusement.

"Philip, my child," Lucy said, turning to her son, "for once in your lifetime you seem to be right. The girl's extraordinary! You certainly couldn't have met her in the company you usually keep. Let me ask you something, Miss Rodman. What do you possibly see in him? Tell a despairing mother."

There was laughter around the table, a terrible laughter.

Sybil sat in frozen silence while Mrs. Hilliard continued to smile at her.

"I think Miss Rodman must be one of Philip's political friends," Lila broke into the silence from the middle of the table. "Aren't all bright girls liberal? Are you liberal, Miss Rodman?"

"Oh, shut up, Lila," Philip retorted.

The conversation promptly broke up, as it always did at the Hilliards', at the first note of anger. Sybil turned in relief to Mr. Hilliard who was now speaking to her. He had taken in Lila's remark, and he lectured her in dry tones on what he thought of young people who, like his son, enjoyed without gratitude the accumulations of their worthier progenitors. Sybil did not listen to his words, but she felt their chipped hardness against her eardrums. It was the hardness, however, of indifference, not of antagonism. He and his guests might look at her without affection, but it was also without interest. The small family world that she had stood out against was at least a world of some love; it was this that made her egotism possible. Tonight she was facing not a world, but *the* world. In whatever different guises it might show itself, whether at the Hilliards' or at Aunt Jo's, it would always wear the bright clear look of an indifference to Sybil Rodman. She glanced down the table at Philip and saw how oddly at ease he was in this world.

"I have accepted a great many things from my parents," she told Mr. Hilliard with sudden courage. "And I have never felt gratitude. Why should I? I should never expect gratitude from children of mine."

Mr. Hilliard stared at the tone in her voice, but he did not hear her words. Like her he had not been listening.

"That's what I mean," he said inconsequentially.

Sybil's courage, however, deserted her again after dinner in the living room when Lucy Hilliard beckoned her over to sit on the sofa beside her.

"You must give your mother my love," she said in a more friendly tone, "and ask why I never see her."

"Mummie goes out very little," Sybil explained.

"I've never known anyone who admits to going out a lot," Lucy said dryly. "Except myself. I go out all the time, my dear. I like people. Unless they're dreary."

Old Viola readjusted her shawl and snapped her black eyes, the only features that seemed to move in her broad face.

"We're not going to be dreary tonight, I trust," she said. "Will we have a word game, Lucy? I've now learned the nine muses. I shall be the star."

"Oh, of course, we'll play," Lucy rejoined. "But you won't be the star, Viola. We have Miss Rodman tonight. You heard her on Scotland. We'll make her 'it.' "

Sybil thought she had experienced every panic in the dining room. It was obvious now that she had not. What lay ahead made dinner itself seem a mild cross-examination before the rack.

"Oh, Mrs. Hilliard, please," she protested. "I can't play games. Really. Let me watch."

"Nonsense. You'll be marvelous." And Lucy proceeded in her brisk manner to outline the rules of a guessing game where the person who was "it" had to be a character beginning with a certain letter and all questions had to be connected with the same letter. Sybil listened and nodded dumbly, realizing in her misery that she wasn't taking in a word of it.

"Do you get it?" Lucy asked. "If you do, let's get the men in."

Sybil's eyes beseeched her.

"Oh, Mrs. Hilliard, I *really* don't think I can."

Lila, at least, was not totally without sensitivity.

"Leave her alone, Ma," she said. "If she doesn't want to, she doesn't have to."

But to Lucy the battle of the parlor game was not one in which quarter was allowed. She had never in her life felt a fear like Sybil's, and she literally did not realize what it could be. Besides, she had a feeling that such fears, if they really existed, should be suppressed.

"Nonsense," she said loudly. "Of course she has to. Just once. She'll put us all to shame."

When Lucy got up Sybil was already feeling the relief that comes with desperate resolution. She got up suddenly and left the room. Going upstairs she walked down the wide hall passageway until she came to a doorway where a maid was standing. Entering, she found herself in a large bedroom with white couches and tables and English landscapes that was obviously Mrs. Hilliard's. She sat down in a chair by the fireplace and lit a cigarette. Here she was, she reflected grimly, and here she would stay. It was the end of a chapter, but when had she not known that it would end? She rested her head against the back of the chair and thought bleakly of her future. She could be in love with Philip, if love was the dark tide that had been tugging her away from her only moorings, stiff and stubborn moorings, too; yes, she could love him with a love that made his mother seem as remotely ineffectual as her own, that made her world even more absurd than it had been and her imagination the only reality, but it was a love, as she had known from the beginning, that would have to subsist on very little. It would have to fill, too, the library at home and the long meals with her parents and their monotonous preoccupations, but it could and must, and she would be able now to turn herself, almost with calm, to the sharp task of terminating the actuality. When she heard Mrs. Hilliard's voice in the corridor she did not move. She did not even sit up when Lucy came into the room and stopped in surprise to see her.

"What's wrong, my dear?" she asked in a voice that was almost solicitous. "Are you ill?"

Sybil looked at her for a moment. Her heart was beating again, but she was not afraid. There had been an impulse, if only for a second, to tell her that she didn't care to be made a fool of. But what would have been the use? Lucy was the universe. She had to be accepted.

"I don't want to play games," she said flatly. "I thought I'd sit up here. I'm sorry."

Lucy contemplated the dark rebellious figure before her. She was almost touched. As Esther had said, she was not a bad woman. But her interest, even when aroused, was flickering. In another minute Sybil would be in her past, and Sybil knew this.

"But, my child, you can't just sit here," she protested. "Of course, you don't have to play if you don't want to. But at least come downstairs and watch."

Sybil shook her head.

"I don't want to feel a fool," she said. "I want to go home."

It was Lucy's turn to be concerned. The thing was becoming an incident, and incidents at her house were only created by her. Besides, there was the danger, if the girl left, that Philip would be angry. Really angry.

"I never heard of such a thing," she said brusquely. "We won't play games if you don't want. But, for goodness' sakes, cheer up and come on down."

Again Sybil shook her head.

"It's my fault, Mrs. Hilliard," she said sincerely. "I don't know how to behave. Please let me go."

Lucy stared at her, nonplussed. Never in a lifetime of giving parties had she been made to feel like a jailer.

"Well, of course," she said after a pause. "I'll tell Philip to take you home." And again an instinct of pity overtook her. "I'll tell him you have a headache. Good night, my dear. Come again. When you're all over this. Whatever it is."

Sybil followed Mrs. Hilliard downstairs and waited in the hall while the latter went in to get Philip. She would have rather gone home alone, slipping out the front door unnoticed, but that was not to be. Philip appeared almost immediately in the doorway, his eyes filled with the inquiring, specific solicitude that he always showed towards her.

"What is it, Sib?" he asked. "A headache? What rotten luck."

"I'm sorry, Philip," she murmured. "I can get myself home. Please go back to the others."

"Don't be silly." He put on a coat and helped her into hers. "Are you sure it's just a headache?" he asked as they went out into the street. "And not the party?" He laughed uneasily.

"Maybe a little of each," she said. "I'm not used to all this. That's all. Really."

There was mostly silence in the cab during the short drive to the Rodmans' house. Sybil could feel the new distance between them and counted the blocks as they passed. In a few more minutes, however interminable, she would be in her own room, with the door closed and locked, living in a world that could be corrected and alleviated by imagination. It would be better that way.

.   .   .

Back in the Hilliards' living room Lucy was describing the episode to the others with her customary vividness.

"She was simply hiding, the poor creature," she said. "Absolutely scared to death. When I spoke to her she snapped at me the way trapped animals do. I assure you, it was something!"

Her audience, however, was touched.

"You scared her, Lucy," Viola said. "You should remember that everybody's not as tough as this crowd. We're old crabs that have had time to grow our shells."

"And our claws!"

This last was one of Mr. Hilliard's rare contributions to general conversation, and it was received with an outburst of congratulation. They never quite despaired of making him a true member of the group.

Lucy did not like opposition, but she was quick to recognize it and to change the subject.

"Don't mention this to Philip when he comes in," she warned them. "After all, the poor boy's rather gone on her."

Philip found them busily engaged in a word game when he returned. He was furious with his mother and sulked on the sofa with a magazine, refusing to join them. He waited, however, until everybody had gone, except Lila and her husband, who always lingered to discuss a party, and then turned on his mother.

"I think you were very mean to Sybil tonight, Ma," he said, staring closely at the cigar in his hand. "I think I told you that she was shy."

Lucy was standing before the fireplace looking down at him.

"Darling, I couldn't be sorrier," she said. "The whole thing, I admit, was grim. But how was I to know that she crumpled if you touched her? You didn't tell me that. You didn't have 'Handle With Care' stamped on her."

"Oh, Ma, you exaggerate so!" he said impatiently. "You know it's terrifying for a young girl to come to one of your parties. And then, if on top of that, she's made fun of —— "

"I didn't make fun of her! I just spoofed her a bit."

"How was she supposed to tell the difference?"

"Well, I didn't realize, Phil," Lucy retorted with a shrug of her shoulders, "that my poor friends were such dragons. We'll all be in cages the next time she comes."

"If she ever does."

Mr. Hilliard and Lila watched them with the satisfaction that other members of a family watch a rift between the two closest. The intimacy between Lucy and Philip, inevitably, had excluded them.

"Now, Philip," Lucy said in a more coaxing tone, "don't be that way. She'll come again, and we'll all be lambs. You watch." She sat on the arm of his chair and put her hand on his head. "She's a dear little thing, but she wants spirit. We'll feed her on spinach."

He shook her hand off impatiently.

"Darling," she said with a mocking inflection, "how can you treat me this way?"

Philip went off to his room, still furious, but realizing nonetheless that she had won. However small an opinion he may have had of his mother's dinner parties, he did not like a friend of his to appear ridiculous at them. And Sybil had certainly cut a sorry figure that night. He thought this out angrily but clearly as he stood by his window and looked down at the street. All in Sybil that had caught his imagination, her sullen quality of not belonging, of not even wanting to belong, her honesty and the sense that she conveyed of emotion, strongly repressed, had put her at a hopeless disadvantage before his mother. Not that he was ignorant of Lucy's game. He knew his mother and most of her tricks. But even when he could see the game, he could see that it put Sybil in a different light. He realized that he must have been harboring the illusion that Sybil, placed suddenly in company, would somehow shine. He had wanted her to be unique and unique because she had been discovered by him. But could she ever fit into his world? He had to shake his head. Reluctantly, because there was a helplessness behind the girl's deliberate nature, like the sense of ill-health in her pale skin and large dark eyes, that appealed, almost maddeningly, to what he liked to think of as his protective nature. But then he shrugged his shoulders and opened his diary and turned to the back where he kept a list of girls' names in alphabetical order. Beside "Rodman, Sybil" he noted: "Mentally alert. Physically attractive. To me, anyway. Likes me. Probably too much. Sexually shy and inexperienced. Bad in company, but a good talker when alone with me." He then put a "3" beside her name which had a code meaning of third-class marriage possibility.

Chapter

Six

TEDDY AND PHILIP were both at home on vacation during the following week. The day after Lucy's unfortunate dinner party they played squash at Philip's club. Philip, as usual, was the victor, although Teddy, who cared terribly, played as hard as he could. Afterwards, as they were dressing in the locker room, Philip told him about the party and how Sybil had walked out. He was rather self-conscious in the telling of it; it was obvious to Teddy that he was trying to protect himself in advance against whatever Sybil's version might be.

"But Sybil doesn't get headaches," her brother pointed out.

Philip shrugged his shoulders.

"Maybe it was just an excuse."

"An excuse for what?"

Philip laughed a bit nervously.

"Oh, for getting out of a dull dinner," he said.

Teddy did not press the point, but he knew about Lucy Hilliard's dinner parties and could picture what Sybil's discomfort must have been. It occurred to him that he might not have been doing Sybil the favor that he had thought he was doing in introducing Philip. People might, after all, want to work out their own lives.

It was not that he did not think well of Philip. Philip had been, since their early days together at Chelton, Teddy's idea of everything a man should be. Where Teddy was undecided and hesitant, Philip was direct; where Teddy was complicated, Philip was uncluttered. Philip went after his objectives in the shortest, straightest manner; Teddy, despite all his apparent ease and enthusiasm, was not even sure what his objectives were. Teddy knew all about Philip's diaries and lists of girls and admired their simplicity even when he smiled at them. He was always touched when Philip consulted him on any of his problems, and he was always surprised at their easy solubility and at the extreme, rather naïve candor with which Philip outlined them. He, on the other hand, would never have dreamed of bothering Philip with any but the least consequential of his own. But that was their relationship. That, as a matter of fact, was Teddy's relationship with most of his friends. It was his understanding of Philip that made him see why he would be attracted by a girl like Sybil. Oh, we're subtle, we Rodmans, he reflected, and laughed to himself at how much condescension there really was in his own admiration of Philip.

He went home, put a red flower in his buttonhole and came downstairs to find his mother and Sybil in the living room. Esther was reading the newspaper. Sybil was looking at the floor.

"Come, Sib," he said. "I'm taking you out to lunch."

She looked up.

"Why?"

"Because. Come on."

"Teddy, lunch is ordered here," his mother protested. "It's all ready, dear."

He waved the idea aside.

"Sorry, Mum. I have reasons."

Sybil found herself sitting, a few minutes later, in Teddy's favorite French restaurant while he fussed with the waiter over the details of a meal in which she could not take the least interest.

"You shouldn't waste your money on me," she reproached him. "Or is this on Aunt Jo?"

"It's on Aunt Jo, of course," he lied. "And I know all about last night," he said, turning at last from the waiter. "So you won't have to tell me a thing."

Her eyes widened.

"Did Philip tell you?"

"Certainly he told me," he retorted. "All about how you ran down the stairs and out of the house. Like Cinderella. Except it was way before midnight."

"I know." She shook her head glumly. "It was awful. Perfectly awful."

"I can imagine."

"Oh, Teddy, you can't!" she protested. "You see, you love that sort of party."

"Of course. I'm desperately popular. There's no question about that." He dismissed himself with a gesture. "But tell me about Phil. Was he nice about it?"

She nodded.

"Do you like Phil?"

She hesitated.

"Oh, I like him, yes," she said.

"I mean, *really* like him?"

There was another pause.

"Teddy, you must never breathe a word of this to him," she said desperately. "You really mustn't."

He looked into her worried face and laughed.

"Now don't get into a stew, Sib," he said. "These things can be worked out. Tell me," he said curiously, "are you really in love?"

"I suppose so."

"You don't seem very happy about it."

"Is it anything to be happy about?" she demanded. "What about you? Are you in love?"

"But all the time," he answered with an uneasy cheerfulness. "Ever since I fell in love with the wife of the math teacher at Chelton. It was all very beautiful and all rather silly."

She considered this.

"Are you in love with Millie?"

He flicked the ashes from his cigarette with an elaborate gesture, as though dismissing the subject.

"I won't tell you," he said firmly. "Because you don't like her."

"Millie's not good enough for you," she said flatly.

"Neither is Philip," he retorted. "For you."

She stared at him in astonishment.

"Oh, Teddy," she protested, "how can you say such a thing?"

For the rest of the meal they discussed matters of the heart in more general terms. He described his abortive romance with the teacher's wife and laughed at himself and at his friends, but in his mind he was turning over the question of what he could do for her. He had only to look into her eyes and see the capacity for suffering that was there.

"Do you know something, Sib?" he asked her. "You've never been down to visit me in Charlottesville? And here it is, my last spring there."

She looked at him doubtfully.

"Why do you want me to come to Charlottesville?" she asked. "Do you want to throw me at Philip's head?"

But he only laughed at her.

"Anything in that line, young lady," he said, waving to the waiter to bring him his check, "you will have to accomplish for yourself."

Chapter
Seven

WHEN TEDDY WENT back to law school he left Sybil
with a general invitation to visit him any weekend that she
wished to select. He was careful not to press her or to tie
her down. At the time she had no idea of taking him up on
his offer. She could conceive of nothing more terrible than
giving Philip the notion that she was chasing him. After
only a week had passed, however, a week without communication of any sort from Philip, life became dreary as she had
never known it. She even lost enthusiasm for Easton Bay
and stayed in town to mope in the library or take long walks
around the reservoir in Central Park with Ellen and her
mother's ancient Airedale. Even her reading stopped; her
mental life consisted now in conjuring up romantic situations where Philip, fallen from his present altitude, was de-
pendent on her for his very bread. It was not agreeable for
a person of her self-awareness to consider rationally the day
dreams to which she was more and more turning. She lived
the prisoner of her own contempt.

What made her finally decide to go to Virginia was the
realization that she was again forgetting what Philip looked
like. Her preoccupation had been so intense as to corrode
the mental image, which gave her the distressing sense of
being moved by a strong emotion without an object. It was

true that when her mind was suddenly distracted, his image would return, clear and triumphant, as if to wipe out the temporary disloyalty, but then, in the very intensity of her joy at recapturing him, it would again fade and blur. Yes, she would go to Virginia. She really had no alternative.

She took the train one night, two weeks later, and Teddy met her in Charlottesville the following morning. It turned out that she had selected the worst possible weekend. There was a dance on Saturday night, and Millie was coming down, and what was even worse, Philip had invited Julia Anderton. Teddy, however, presented all this to her in its most favorable light. Millie was not coming until later in the day and was staying with friends; Sybil could occupy the bedroom in his apartment while he slept in the study. If she wanted to go to the dance, he would get a friend to take her. It would all work out.

"But I won't be in your way at all, Teddy," she promised him. "I'll go for a walk this morning. And the movies tonight. Don't give me a thought. I've come to see the university, anyway."

Teddy's apartment was within walking distance of the law school and while he was in classes that morning she strolled on the lawn below the rotunda and took in the proportions of Mr. Jefferson's architecture. It was early spring, the time of year when the university looked its best; she walked round and round the lawn, under the arcades and out, enjoying the white columns and red brick and feeling, as she watched the students go by with their books, an odd nostalgia for a campus atmosphere that she had never known. When she found herself in front of the law school she realized that she had come to it without knowing where it was, and as she stood on the steps to the terrace, reading the inscription over the doors, they opened, and a group of students came out to smoke by the balustrade. She was turning to make her escape when she heard her name called.

And, as she had known it would be, it was Philip, coming towards her, smiling, with his stiff stride.

"Hey, Sybil! I thought it was you. I saw you from the window. Teddy didn't tell me you were down!"

"I just arrived," she murmured.

"Going to the party tonight?"

"Oh, no, I don't think so," she said hurriedly.

"Of course. You don't like parties, do you?" But his laugh was pleasant. "This one's different, though. No older people butting in. I've got a girl coming down for it. Julia Anderton. Do you know her? And Teddy's going with Millie. We'll fix you up with a date."

"Oh, no. Philip. Please."

"Sure. You've got to come. I want to show you that a party can be fun. Do you like Charlottesville? Have you been here before?"

She told him where she had been, and he told her what else to see, and so they chatted until he had to go back to class. She said good-bye and turned abruptly to go back to Teddy's apartment. It was all that she could do to keep from running. She was almost too excited to walk.

When Teddy came in at lunch time he knew that she had seen Philip.

"You don't waste any time, do you?" he said with a little laugh. "We've got to fix you up with a date for this party now. It's a pity Philip had to ask Julia down. Except she's just another on his list. Don't give her a thought."

She thought of Julia, so big and brusque and sophisticated. She wondered if Philip could really be interested in her.

"Where's Millie?" she asked.

"Millie gets here this afternoon." He looked slightly self-conscious. "We're going to meet for cocktails, the three of us. You don't mind, do you?"

"Mind? Of course not. Why should I mind?"

.   .   .

Sybil did rather mind, but she was in no position to object. It was angelic of Teddy, as she well knew, to take the trouble about her. They all met for cocktails in Teddy's apartment that evening, Millie, Sybil, Teddy, and a young, freckled, talkative Southern Boy who had been the only unattached male whom Teddy could get for Sybil at such short notice. She developed an aversion to him almost immediately, and he, finding her uncommunicative, directed his charm towards Millie. Sybil observed the latter carefully. Millie was even more possessive about Teddy than usual. It was obvious that their relationship had passed into a more definite stage and one that precluded the necessity of her being simply pleasing. She had an air of efficiency, of "no nonsense about me," that was implicit in the neat waves of chestnut hair on either side of her straight part and the brisk way in which she puffed at her cigarette. She was very much the proprietress in Teddy's apartment, and Sybil bristled to see it.

"It was such a good idea, your coming down, Sybil," she said. "I hope Teddy makes you comfortable here. These bachelors, I'm afraid, don't know all the little things we girls need."

Sybil looked at her narrowly.

"I don't need any 'little' things," she said. "Teddy gives me everything I want."

"Oh, of course," Millie agreed softly in the tone she used for Teddy's "queer" sister. "Your brother's a wonder, as we all know. But where would they be without us? Men, I mean. You should see my father trying to get dinner on cook's night out. He starts out bravely with a recipe for shrimps creole, but he always ends up with — yes, you guessed it — scrambled eggs and toast!"

She laughed the way Sybil imagined that débutantes in cigarette advertisements would laugh if they could — lightly, and with irrelevant tolerance, at things that weren't in the least bit funny.

"Teddy cooks better than I can," Sybil pointed out. "As a matter of fact, I can't cook at all."

Teddy was passing the cocktails, and Sybil, hearing from him that they were going to dine with Philip and Julia Anderton, decided that she would need several. She sat quietly and listened to the others, holding her glass out firmly every time Teddy came by with the shaker.

"Don't overdo it, Sib," he whispered to her. "These things have a kick."

She ignored his warning entirely, and by the time they had joined Philip and Julia for dinner in Charlottesville, she was feeling better about everything. She disliked Julia, but as the latter hardly noticed her she had no occasion to show it. Julia, with long, tawny hair, "leonine" as Teddy called it, and the big, handsome features of an Assyrian bas-relief, was the dominant member of the group. She assumed that all conversation was general, with herself in the center.

"Philip tells me you're always reading," she threw at Sybil. "Of course, I'm like Millie. I never read a thing." She smiled tolerantly at Millie. "I find that I absorb more by listening to people. You know, I crave people," she continued, turning to Philip. "They're my real hobby."

"Oh, I prefer books," Sybil said boldly, emerging from her silence. "You can take off their jackets and put them on shelves, and they stay there. You can use them to stand on to reach up to high shelves. You can hide money in them. You can use them as paperweights. You'd be surprised, Julia, how useful they are."

Julia looked at her with embarrassment. It was beginning to be clear to all that Sybil had had a good deal to drink. But Sybil saw that Philip was watching her. She cared about nothing else. The dance turned out to be one of those dances that people dress for and don't go to. Sybil's escort proved to be a useful character; he had a room on the lawn and suggested that it was too nice a night to be inside. Everybody agreed with him, so they drove instead to the rotunda and spread out blankets on the grass and brought ice and paper cups and whiskey. They were joined eventually by other parties. Julia kept finding friends, other New York boys from the law school; Teddy talked with Millie; the Southern boy was busy with the drinks and people, and Sybil was left with Philip, stretched out on the grass with pillows under their heads, drinking bourbon and cracked ice. They talked about girls, mostly girls whom Philip had known and taken out, which ones were "serious" and which ones were "fun," and which ones his family had liked and which ones had worried them and which most approached Philip's ideal of what a wife should be. Sybil listened and made suggestions and laughed and felt at ease with him for the first time.

"I'd like to know what you think of a girl like Julia," he asked, looking at her with his curious eyes. "She's as different from you as anyone I can think of."

She glanced over at Julia balefully.

"Julia?" she said, in a distant, speculative tone. "I suppose that under all that manner and that drawl and all that fear of living a single moment in the past, she may have a soul. But one doubts it. She makes up her own world. It will disappear with her."

But the information that he sought was more specific.

"Would she be capable, do you think, of marrying a guy for his money?"

Sybil surveyed him with her new detachment.

"You mean you, for your money?"

He was embarrassed, she could see, but he did not really mind.

"All right," he said. "Me. For mine."

"Is there any real doubt in your mind about it?"

"You mean," he said, with his nervous laugh, "that no-body could love me for myself?"

"Oh, I didn't say that she wouldn't love you," Sybil corrected him. "I was explaining what she would marry you for."

Philip had now gone as far as he cared to go.

"Well, there's no danger of her marrying me," he said shortly. "Tell me something else. What do you think of Millie?"

She lay back on the ground and looked up at the stars. When she turned her head she could see the dark mass of the rotunda and the gleam of white columns in the darkness.

"Think of living in a world with all this," she said, raising one hand toward the sky, "and having a mind like Millie's. Imagine knowing so exactly what you want. And wanting what she wants!"

"What does she want?"

"She wants Teddy, to begin with," she said slowly. "Not that he's a bad thing to want. Far from it. But she wants to cut him down to size and have a little house in Greenwich and raise two dear little children, only two, a boy and a girl, and send them to small, select cocktail parties that are undistinguishable from other people's small, select cocktail parties."

"But Sybil," he protested, "isn't that fundamentally what all girls want?"

"I suppose it is," she conceded. "But then I hate all girls. You see," she said, turning her head towards him, "I'm absolutely logical. If it kills me."

"I take it, anyway, that you don't like Millie."

"Oh, 'like,'" she sniffed. "What is there to like about Millie? She's one of those people who won't even cross the street when the light changes. She's always waiting for a greener one. A special one for Millie."

"Is Teddy going to marry her?" he asked, still in quest of the particular.

"Teddy wants to marry," she answered. "Or rather he feels it's expected of him."

"Expected? By whom?"

"Oh, by everybody. By you, for example."

"Why the hell me?"

She pulled up some grass beside her and tossed it away. "He admires you. He always has."

"But I don't care whether or not Teddy gets married!"

"Well, Teddy's rather odd at times," she said, unsatisfactorily. "He thinks people expect things of him. He hates to let them down."

He changed the subject, or, at least, one aspect of it.

"How about you, Sybil? Do you admire me?"

"Well, I don't think you expect things of me. If that's what you mean."

"No, no." He laughed. "But do you admire me?"

She hesitated.

"At times."

"Such as?"

"Well, the time you told your sister at dinner to shut up when she was teasing me. I thought that was admirable."

He looked disappointed.

"Hell. That was nothing."

"But, you see," she said, "we have different values. To me it was everything."

"Why were you so scared that night?" he pursued. "Was it Ma? She can be bad, I know. But when you get to be friends, you'll see how different she is."

Sybil reflected on the unlikelihood of this.

"I think it was because I'd had so little to drink," she said. "I'm just discovering alcohol. I recommend it. Perhaps though, that's not necessary."

"You know, Sybil," he said more seriously, "if you'd been at Ma's the way you are tonight, you'd have knocked them flat."

"That's what I'd like to have done."

"No, seriously, Sib," he persisted. "You've got all sorts of possibilities. You don't make the best of yourself. Take your looks for example. When you're not looking frightened, you can be almost beautiful."

She sat up and laughed.

"Oh, Philip," she said. "You put things so wonderfully!"

"Look, kid," he said impatiently, "I'm paying you a compliment. I'll thank you to take it seriously."

"But I do take it seriously, Philip," she protested. "I take you much too seriously. That's why I run away from dinner parties and make cracks about girls like Julia. Don't you see it?"

What he would have answered to this she was not to know, for the blond Virginia boy who had been her escort sat unsteadily down between them and joined in the conversation. But Sybil did not mind. She looked up at the sooty clouds that were passing over the stars and felt happy. Even if it doesn't last, she told herself, I have this. She knew that she would not again forget what he looked like.

Everybody began to get fairly drunk at this point except, of course, Millie. Sybil remembered afterwards noticing this. It was one of her few clear memories of the latter part of the evening. The full effect of what she had drunk hit her quite suddenly, and she had a vague recollection of everybody waltzing on the grass and then, unfortunately, a much clearer picture of herself being very rude to Julia in the car. They had all, apparently, crowded into Philip's Packard, and Sybil remembered pointing out not once, but several times, loudly and clearly, that there was no reason to drop Julia off last simply because she was staying the furthest away. They did drop Julia off, somewhere, and next the young Virginian, and then they went to the place where Millie was staying and while Teddy was seeing her in, Philip kissed her, and this time she made no objection. It was all incredible, and when she and Teddy got back to his apartment she burst into tears.

.   .   .

Very different were her feelings when she woke up the next morning. It was not only the hangover, which was severe; it was the flood of realization of all she had done and said. Teddy went for a walk while she sat glumly on the window seat and drank coffee. Every now and again one of her less tactful remarks of the night before would come to mind, and she would twinge. At noon there was a knock on the door, and Philip came in. He was dressed in riding clothes.

"How are you feeling?" he asked cheerfully.

The sight of him, so healthy, only accentuated to Sybil her inability to live in his world. She felt tired and suddenly cross. It seemed hard that she should have to be obsessed with a man who was so bound to lose interest in her.

"Terrible," she said glumly.

"Bad as that?"

"I made a fool of myself last night."

"Now, Sybil." He smiled, but she saw that he knew what she was talking about. "Don't go on that way."

"But I did," she insisted. "I tried to be something I wasn't. I tried to be gay and sophisticated. And I was a dismal flop."

She felt the tears coming and shook her head, as if to stop them. She was angry, positively angry with him, for having made such a botch of her life.

"Sib, you take things too hard."

"You *do* think I made a fool of myself, don't you?"

He laughed.

"No. Of course not."

"Oh, of course you do. And that makes me mad, too. Because I didn't really." She looked at him with sullen eyes, and then continued bitterly: "If you had any real standards, I mean, you'd see how unimportant all that is. How trivial."

He looked taken aback.

"But you're the one who seems to think it's important," he pointed out.

"Well, it is. To me," she continued illogically. "I can't play these games. I can't play any games," she finished hopelessly.

"Stop beating yourself."

There was a silence during which they stared at each other across the room. She had been right the first time, after his mother's dinner. To retreat with her thoughts to the gentle, irritating prattle of family life. Banging doors clanged through her brain.

"I don't think I can go on with this, Philip," she said solemnly.

He stared at her.

"On with what, for God's sake?"

"With you," she said, and she listened, almost with admiration, as the voice from her inner world spoke. "It's all right for you to take girls out and make passes at them and tell them things you don't mean. But I can't play that game." She paused and swallowed. "So what happens? I make a fool of myself. Everyone else sees it's a game, and there I am pretending it's real." She saw the sudden sympathy in his eyes and rebelled against it. "Oh, it's not that I'm sorry for myself," she protested fiercely, "or that I think my affections have been trifled with. I *loathe* girls who want to be taken seriously."

She looked at him defiantly.

"You mean you're in love with me, Sib?"

She almost despised him at that moment. She opened her mouth, but she was too excited to speak.

"Are you?" he repeated.

"Of course, I am," she said finally, in a lower voice, almost as if it wasn't anything that mattered. "That's all there is to it. I just am. It's not my fault," she added irritably. "And you're not expected to do anything about it. So don't worry."

His eyes were fixed on her with an intent stare that she could not read.

"There's nothing to worry about," he said firmly and paused. "It's the greatest compliment I've ever been paid," he continued in what struck her, even then, as a synthetic tone. "I'm not going to say anything about myself now. I think these things should be thought out. But it's not all a game with me, Sib. You're wrong there. Honest."

She caught the inflection of his every syllable. She could see perfectly how he strove to attain simplicity and became pompous in his striving. She wondered why love was ever called blind.

"No, Philip," she said unhappily, "you mustn't give it any thought at all. You see, I'm not the person for you. I'm full of moods and hates and depressions." She felt the tears again in her eyes. "I'm a strange thing, really, and not much of an asset. You ask my family. They'll tell you. You're a straightforward, objective person with the world at your feet. You need a straightforward wife."

She sounded to herself like a girl in a movie, sentimental and absurd, but as she looked away from him, out the window, and saw Teddy returning from his walk down the path to the front door, she realized the difference. He was not contradicting her.

"Tell me, Sybil," he said gravely, "why are you that way? What's wrong with you?"

She glared at him.

"I don't know," she said. "Everything, I guess."

And then the door opened, and Teddy came in. That afternoon they all went riding, and in the evening Sybil took a train back to New York. Philip did not revert to the topic which they had been discussing nor did he offer to drive her to the station. She had not, however, expected that he would.

Chapter

Eight

SYBIL HAD NEVER felt as low as she felt after her return from Virginia. There were moments when she could not help wondering if she might not have turned her back on a happiness that was being offered her, incredible as it seemed, on a silver platter. The very suspicion of this, of course, was enough to destroy the dream world in which she had hoped to live, and she would find herself, in her bedroom, or in the library, or while driving with Aunt Jo, gloomily preoccupied with the picture of what she might already have given up. She could no longer derive any consolation from Ellen's efforts to cheer her up. Their old game seemed painfully hollow. She haunted her mother's bedroom in the early morning, pale, restless and uncommunicative, while the latter was having breakfast. Esther regarded her with an amusement that was still sympathetic.

"Is it really as bad as all that, dear?" she asked one day when Sybil looked particularly drawn.

"What?"

"Whatever it is."

"You always think something has to be wrong, Mother," Sybil said crossly. "You never think people can be just plain depressed."

"Well, you see I never am," her mother answered. "I always have a reason."

"You're lucky."

Esther looked at her for a moment and then smiled.

"For a girl who's always objected to meeting boys," she remarked, "you seem to have developed a most complicated emotional life. We used to be afraid that you'd never be interested in anyone. I must say, we needn't have worried."

It was something that Sybil could never get over, this detachment that her mother could show, just at those moments when one might have expected that she would show concern.

"Didn't you ever used to worry about men, Mother?" she asked.

"I can't say I had much occasion until your father came along," her mother answered, drinking her coffee. "But, of course, I always rather imagined he would."

"Why?"

"Oh, they do."

"But, Mother, were you never in love?"

"Oh, love." Esther shrugged her shoulders as though it were a word that she sometimes thought she would never hear the end of. "A great deal of nonsense is talked about love. You'll have to go to your Aunt Jo for that. She's the romantic one of the family." She seemed to imply, with just a flicker of contempt that such things were the playthings of the rich and childless. "Which reminds me. She'd like you to go to the opera tonight. It's *Romeo and Juliet*."

Sybil smiled a bit wryly.

"I shall call her," she said. "I shall tell her that I'll be glad to go."

. . .

Uncle Stafford had owned an opera box jointly with his brother in the days when boxes had been privately owned; since that time he had rented his old box for Monday nights only. Aunt Jo loved the opera, or at least she loved the opera house. She loved the big, gold curtains and the red plush of the boxes and the long intermissions when she could chat with the friends and cousins who came to call. She had no patience with people who sneered at this aspect of opera; she believed that the prosperity of music was intimately connected with the prosperity of boxholders. The main season was now over, but the spring season, for new singers, had begun, and Aunt Jo, who hated to miss anything, was attending the first performance.

When Sybil arrived for dinner she discovered that, prompt as she was, she was the last there. Sitting in a semicircle in the living room and drinking the sweet rhum cocktails that Aunt Jo always served, were her uncle and aunt, Nicholas and two elderly women, of Aunt Jo's age, who occupied the principal armchairs on either side of the fireplace. Sybil had an uneasy feeling that she had met them before; she seemed to remember that they were sisters and old maids and somehow important. She hovered at the edge of the circle.

"Sybil, you remember Miss Emily Hilliard, don't you?" Aunt Jo was saying. "And Miss Harriet? They're Philip's aunts, you know."

Sybil murmured something indistinguishable and shook their hands. They were both big and stout and had square faces and long, unpowdered noses; they were even dressed alike, in velvet and lace, their feet in black pumps with bows. There was something incongruous about the magnificence of their pearls and of their sapphire and yellow diamond rings.

"Oh, yes, my dear," Miss Emily was saying to her. "I can remember you as a child at *Salome*. So intense and quiet. Though I didn't think, Jo," she continued, turning to Sybil's aunt, "that it was quite the opera to take a young girl to."

"Oh, Sybil and I have been to worse things than *Salome*," Aunt Jo said, smiling. "Haven't we, Sib?"

Miss Emily's penetrating look, directed again at Sybil,

seemed to take her in, up and down, in search of some trace of the after effects of such an exposure.

"One never knows," she said, with a rather bitter laugh, "whose head they will be asking for these days. Not John the Baptist's, anyway."

Sybil sat down, refusing the cocktail, hardly able to take her eyes off Philip's aunts. Any resemblance to Philip, however, except in the square chin, was not noticeable. Lucy Hilliard's children, it appeared, had all taken after her. Much stronger was the resemblance of the Misses Hilliard to Philip's father. They had the same thin, grudging line for a mouth and the same clear, suspicious eyes. She remembered that Philip had told her about them and how they lived across the street in his late grandfather's tomb of a house and watched disapprovingly from their windows the comings and goings of Lucy's friends. Lucy, apparently, had quarreled with them, almost openly, but she made her children go there at intervals to keep them in what she called a "testamentary" frame of mind.

"Your aunt was telling us that you met Philip this winter," Miss Harriet was saying to her. "At a ball."

"Oh, yes. I did."

"He was behaving himself, I trust?"

Sybil smiled weakly.

"I think so."

"Why, Harriet, doesn't he usually?" Aunt Jo asked.

Miss Harriet, who was the younger of the sisters, turned to Miss Emily for confirmation.

"What would you say to that, Emily?"

"Oh, I think he *behaves* himself," Miss Emily said, addressing herself to the others. "He's a good boy, really. Harriet, I'm sure, is thinking more of his opinions. He seems to have got his head full of radical notions somewhere. When he called on us last summer, in the country, he kept looking out at the lawn and talking about playgrounds for the poor."

"And we thought he was flip about taxes," Miss Harriet put in gravely.

"But he's not!" Sybil exclaimed, to her own surprise as well as that of the others. "You see, we've discussed those things," she said hastily when she saw how everyone stared. "He's terribly serious. He doesn't believe in a high income tax. For people who work, that is. He says it penalizes enterprise."

"Oh, indeed," Miss Emily said dryly. "And what sort of a tax does Philip believe in, if I may ask?"

"He believes in a high inheritance tax," Sybil went on unthinkingly. "And a high tax on income that comes from stocks and bonds."

Uncle Stafford, sitting apart in his armchair, very old and brown, with thick silver hair, chuckled.

"I've heard more radical things than that, Emily," he said, "in the heart of Wall Street."

The Hilliard sisters admired Uncle Stafford; he was one of the pillars of their world, but, like most men, he could never be trusted to be serious.

"I simply can't understand these young people," Miss Emily retorted, ignoring him. "They take everything and give nothing. I'm afraid, in Philip's case, that our sister-in-law has not done what she could to correct him. The atmosphere in that house is entirely too sophisticated. This is what comes of it."

"But you can't say that Philip gives nothing!" Sybil exclaimed. "He gives a lot. He's open and generous!"

She stopped, appalled at her own recklessness. She saw Aunt Jo smile and Uncle Stafford wink at her, and she flushed. The sisters exchanged glances, and Miss Emily, as the eldest, drew herself up in her chair.

"My dear young lady," she said severely, "we know all about Philip. He may be a charming young man, but he is still very young and very inexperienced. We would advise you to take his enthusiasm for this 'new deal,' as they still call it, with a grain of salt. Any new deal, remember, is always a new deal for spendthrifts. Harriet and I have had to learn, to our sorrow, that giving to people who don't work only creates ingratitude. You probably think we're two selfish old women. You're for giving away the moon, I daresay. And the stars as well." She waved a hand toward the ceiling and shrugged her shoulders. "The day will come when you will learn what we have learned."

"If Sybil ever gets her hands on a star, Emily," Aunt Jo broke in at last, in her brisk, smiling way, "she won't be giving it away to anybody. Take my word for it. Look at whose niece she is."

Sybil said nothing after this. The Hilliards, she reflected bitterly, were bound to treat her badly. All during dinner she kept glancing from one aunt to the other. She remembered that Philip had told her that they were like a married couple. Miss Emily, she decided, although the elder and more domineering, was the wife. She was the chatterer, the artist; one could make out in the heavy gestures of her thick arms and in her way of tossing back her head as she laughed, that she must have somehow conceived of herself as "floating." Miss Harriet, on the other hand, who was stolid and even stouter, without gestures, who sat in comparative silence, following her sister's conversation and now and again correcting some too extravagant statement, was the husband, the banker, content to sit back with a cigar and watch, indulgently and affectionately, the admired antics of his charming and otherworldly partner. It seemed a pity, even to Sybil, that they should have no outlet, except in conversation, for the political resentment that seemed so remarkably to obsess them. In another day and age they would have followed their monarch over the border and dedicated themselves to the drab formality of a court in exile. No Bourbon princess would have shown greater resolution or dignity. But to them, in an age stripped of such possibilities, was left only the dry remedy of complaint, of denunciation, of the shrill letter to the *Herald Tribune* and the lewd meanness of the Roosevelt anecdote. It was not enough.

"If you girls have finished with the government," Aunt Jo said at last, putting down her napkin, "we may as well go and hear what's left of the opera."

Sybil had hoped to sit alone in the back of the box and indulge in fantasies about Philip. But this was not to be. Aunt Jo, who saw that she was going to mope because Miss Emily had hurt her feelings, made a point of placing her in the front row between the sisters. Aunt Jo was not one to permit the self-indulgence of moodiness. She was irritated with Emily Hilliard for taking it upon herself to scold her niece in her own house, but she wanted Sybil to learn to cope with such things. During the first act Miss Emily and Miss Harriet made remarks to each other across Sybil in the almost normal speaking tone that so many of their generation habitually used in an opera box. To Sybil it was stifling. All her life she had been accustomed to being with Aunt Jo and her friends; she had slipped away from the hard circle of her demanding contemporaries to become a silent and unresponding figure in the background of her aunt's world. It had been a drugged existence, not altogether unpleasant. She had hoped after Charlottesville to return to it. It had not occurred to her that she would find even Aunt Jo too familiar. And too old.

The curtains fell, and the lights went on. The singers came out and took their bows. The Misses Hilliard applauded, but lightly.

"Isn't it incredible, Emily," Miss Harriet said, "the people you see in boxes today? The women especially. They look like trained nurses out of uniforms for the first time."

"But, they are, Harriet. They are, dear."

Sybil could not bear it. She was suddenly sure of that.

When Miss Harriet, smiling at her sister's wit, turned around to repeat the remark to Aunt Jo, she got up and slipped through the anteroom to the corridor. But not quite in time. She heard Nicholas' voice behind her, the sharp, clear voice of one who knows that the person addressed will stop. It was not an unkind voice, but it was firm and cousinly.

"Are you going for a stroll, Sybil?"

He waited until she came back to him. She knew that Nicholas, who took all his standards from his grandfather's day, or rather from what he imagined that day to have been, disapproved of ladies leaving a box during an intermission. That they should do so alone was so much the worse. That they should do so in order to visit the bar, as she intended, was unthinkable. The unthinkable, however, was just what Nicholas most anticipated. She could read her own intentions in his clear, blue, faintly mocking eyes.

"I don't care," she said desperately. "I had to get out of there. I couldn't breathe. Oh, Nicholas," she continued, almost pleadingly. "They're such old fossils, aren't they? You know they are. Dry, dead fossils!"

His expression did not change. Nicholas never raised his voice except to the multitudinous class of his social inferiors. His eyes seemed to smile the least bit more, as though all that one could ask of life was that the unredeemable should act unredeemably, and this, after all, was what was happening.

"Fossils are usually dry, Sybil," he said. "And I believe they're invariably dead."

"But you know what I mean!"

"I'm not sure that I do. As neither my father nor my stepmother, nor the Misses Hilliard are dead, I can only suppose that you are using the term 'fossil' in an abusive sense. Which simply means that *you* have no use for them. Your question, then, boils down to whether or not I agree with the fact that you have no use for them. Obviously I'm compelled to."

"But do *you* have any use for them?"

"What should I use them for?"

She stamped her foot in exasperation.

"Oh, Nicholas, why do you always act this way?" she cried. "Can't you see that I'm miserable and that I want to be alone?"

For a moment she saw in his eyes something that might have been solicitude.

"Sybil," he said more gently, "is there anything I can do to help? Would you like to go to the bar and have a sherry? I won't ask you any questions, I promise. But sometimes it helps to be with a member of the family."

It even crossed her mind to take him up on this and to tell him about Philip. But as she looked into his eyes and saw through the faint puzzlement to the faint alarm, she knew that she could never scale the high wall that he had built around his heart. He had sought refuge so long in formality that he had surely forgotten how even to listen to a story like hers without finding in it more than a confirmation of his belief that young ladies had ceased to be ladies. But it was not only with Nicholas that communication was impossible; it was with anyone. She was surrounded by the smiles of those who had destroyed their own ability to comprehend.

"I'm not your sort of person, Nicholas," she explained in a sharp tone. "That's what you don't understand. I could never explain it to you or to the Miss Hilliards or even to Aunt Jo. You all think I ought to fit myself into your sort of world. But I don't even know what it's all about. I haven't the remotest idea what any of you get out of it," she continued recklessly. "I don't even know what it is that I'm meant to enjoy or why I'm meant to enjoy it. Are *you* happy, Nicholas?"

His smile widened slightly with his embarrassment.

"I hope I am," he said. "My pleasures may not be of the violent variety that seem to be so popular today, but such as they are —— "

"Nicholas!" she cried. "I'm going up to the bar to order a drink. By myself. That's my kind of fun. That's the kind of person I am!"

He nodded gravely.

"You won't shake me in my opinion, Sybil," he said, "that whatever kind of person you are is a very nice kind of person to be."

She turned from him and hurried up the stairs to the foyer, her eyes full of tears. She skirted her way rapidly through the crowded tables in the foyer until she had found an empty one. She asked the waiter to bring her a brandy. The room looked as though it might be full of familiar faces, but she could not recognize any of them. She lit a cigarette and wondered what she would ever do but pitch herself against a world that could always annihilate her with a single reproach. Rebellion in a void. Against nothing.

When her brandy had come and as she was raising it to her lips she saw Philip, and it seemed as if everything that could pulse and pound within her had suddenly stopped. He was making his way through the tables towards her, and he was smiling. Then she felt blackness all around her and a roaring in her ears. But she did not faint. She did not even smile.

"I see that we're up to our old tricks," he said, sitting down beside her. "Solitary drinking. A slightly better bar, I admit, but the same thirst. Maybe I should have one too. Just for appearances." He beckoned to the waiter.

She still could not speak.

"I telephoned you this evening when I arrived," he continued, "and heard you were at your aunt's and were coming on here. So I got a ticket and I've been waiting for you. I knew you'd come alone, because I know your ways."

"Oh, Philip," she murmured. "Nicholas almost came with me," she added vaguely.

"Well, I'm glad he didn't. Who is Nicholas?"

She just managed to shrug her shoulders. He could never keep her family straight.

"When these people have gone," he said, "I have something to tell you. Do you mind missing the next act?"

She shook her head.

"Well, fine."

Then the bell rang, and she watched the big room gradually empty as the people returned to their seats. In only a few minutes she was alone with him amid the empty tables.

Chapter

Nine

PHILIP WAS NOT a creature of impulse; he thought things out carefully, particularly when they concerned himself. When he had finished this orderly process, however, he acted swiftly and logically upon his conclusion. He had talked to Teddy at length about Sybil's difficulties, which, after all, was only sensible, and Teddy, of course, had entirely reassured him, which was equally sensible. He had then addressed himself to the exact nature of the attraction which she had for him, and he had decided, clearly and definitely, that it was more intense than anything that he had felt before. He had then figured up how many law classes he could afford to cut and had taken a train for New York. The whole procedure would have struck Teddy as calculating, but Philip was always true to himself and was certainly not devoid of feeling. Under the apparent self-assurance of his Hilliard exterior lurked his own share of the universal craving for affection. Philip might have received a certain degree of love from his family, particularly from his mother, but theirs was not a demonstrative affection, and Philip, after all, was far from a subtle person. Without bitterness he was still inclined to wonder how many of his friendships were based on his position and money. Passionately literal, he had always yearned for a disinterested love that he could clearly recognize and classify as such. What had made him select Sybil, almost unhesitatingly, from the large number of more obviously attractive girls of his acquaintance was his strong sense, derived as early as their second meeting, of her devotion to him. When he thought of her, he thought of her brown brooding eyes and the pale intensity of her gaze. He felt, and felt correctly, that even her brusqueness was only the shell over her emotion. There was an enormous reassurance to Philip in this sense of a devotion that in no way depended on his future or even on his good character. With Sybil he could relax and be himself and still be loved.

She accepted him just as promptly and just as gratefully as he had anticipated and hoped. They had a strange and rather wonderful evening together. They sat in the bar until the next intermission, and then Sybil went back to the box to get her coat. She greeted the astonished looks of her aunt and the others with a brief smile and hurried off with the utterly inadequate explanation that she had "met a friend." They went to a night club and drank a bottle of champagne and walked back to Sybil's house and sat for an hour in the library. Sybil had never taken anyone into the house this way before. She listened to Philip and knew each time just what he was going to say. What did it matter? She could have listened to him forever.

They decided upon an engagement of only two months. It was then the early spring of 1941; he was to graduate from law school in June. They planned to get married immediately afterwards and take the summer off before he went to midshipmen's school on the U.S.S. *Prairie State.* They would take an apartment in New York where Philip intended to practice law after he got out of the service. He, of course, had planned it all out, and Sybil agreed to everything. Nobody could ever interfere with her again. She was in Philip's hands. Early the next morning, after a sleepless night, she went down to the dining room where she found her parents at breakfast. She announced her news triumphantly.

"Philip and I are going to be married," she said. "In the end of June."

Esther's hands fell upon the newspaper in her lap.

"Sybil, my child! Do you mean it?"

"Philip who?" cried her father. "Not Philip Hilliard?"

"We'll get an apartment," Sybil continued rather incoherently. "And he's going to midshipmen's school. You won't have to worry about us at all. And we want a small wedding. Very small."

Esther's eyes were now wide with concern.

"But, darling, we'll do it any way you want," she said. "You know that. But this is so sudden. You must give us a little time."

"There's a war coming," Sybil exclaimed defiantly, remembering what Philip had said. "We can't wait. We have to seize things while we can."

"War weddings may be too hasty," George murmured, feeling that he should say something.

"Just tell me one thing, dear," Esther went on, her eyes fastened upon her daughter. "Are you and Philip really sure? Do you really love each other? That, after all, is the only thing that matters."

Sybil stiffened. Whatever happened, she was determined not to allow the unbelievable happiness that seemed now actually within her grasp to be clouded by any association with her mother's household gods.

"What Philip and I feel about each other has got to be our own affair, Mummie," she said resolutely. "That's something that's terribly important to me."

Her father gaped at her.

"Are you two different from the rest of humanity?" he asked. "Are you somehow special?"

"Leave her be, George," his wife said sharply. She turned back to Sybil. "If it's important to you, dear, it's important to us."

Thus ended their first talk, the first of many. Esther, who had taken the unhappiness of her daughter's love affair with complete equanimity, was much more agitated by its sudden and joyful resolution. It was too quick, and Sybil was too excited. She had no faith in it.

"I know it must be fun for her to walk in and tell us that she's caught the most eligible bachelor in town," she told George afterwards. "Certainly. That puts *us* in our place. But is it enough to base a marriage on?"

George was provoked by his wife's way of regarding the whole problem as her own rather than his or even Sybil's.

"Do you think it's impossible that they might be in love?" he asked impatiently. "Can't you believe that anyone in your family can *ever* fall in love?"

George had been too surprised by Sybil's engagement to be entirely pleased. It struck him at first as almost unfair that a daughter who had always affected to despise anything that smacked of worldliness and who had resisted so passionately her family's least effort to make her appear in the social world, should now be engaged, without any apparent trouble, to the son and heir of the Hilliards. He was still smarting from a retort that she had made, only a few weeks before, in answer to his pointing out that she owed everything, her education and her bringing up, to the bank. "It was a mediocre education," she had actually had the nerve to say, "and a less than mediocre bringing up." He had always secretly hoped that she would marry a poor boy and learn about life the hard way, provided, of course, that

her Aunt Jo would allow it. And now, he reflected bitterly,
she would never understand. Still, when he considered, as
he soon did, the impression that the news, confidentially
dropped, would make on the fellow officers of his department at the bank that morning, he had to concede that there
might, after all, be compensations.

Lucy Hilliard, however, was far from conscious of any
compensations. Philip only stayed a few minutes with her
the morning after his engagement because he had to fly
back to Virginia. But the few minutes were enough for his
purpose.

"Darling, you're out of your mind!" she cried. "You don't
have to marry the girl because you think I was rude to her!"

"I thought you'd take that attitude," he retorted. "Everything's always a joke to you and Lila and Felicia. Laughs,
laughs, laughs. But this time I'm serious, Ma."

"So am I serious!" she exclaimed, pushing her breakfast
tray from her knees so roughly that the dishes spilled on the
bed. "Serious as hell! I've nothing against the girl. I really
haven't. But let's sleep on it. Shall we?"

"You sleep on it," he said. "I've got to go."

"It's just as I told Lila," she wailed. "You can't catch
these things too soon."

He left the room at this and did not come back even when
she shouted after him. Lucy was frantic. She telephoned
Lila and Felicia and got a certain amount of sympathy from
them. But sympathy was not what she wanted. She wanted
somebody to *do* something. In her desperation she even
turned to her husband. He was down on Long Island, but
she was driven there within an hour after Philip had left.
She found him at the kennels when she arrived, and they
talked it over as they stood by the wire netting and watched
the puppies barking. Mr. Hilliard was unenthusiastic but
undisturbed.

"I suppose this girl hasn't any money," he said.

Lucy shrugged her shoulders.

"I wouldn't care if she had millions," she retorted. "It's that mousiness that I mind. And all the hate underneath it."

Mr. Hilliard continued his train of thought.

"I know about George Rodman," he said. "I inquired about him that summer that Philip went abroad with Teddy. I understand he's not a bad sort of chap. On the cheap side, but gets around. His wife must have some money."

"No, no," she said impatiently. "They've been living off Jo Cummings for years. Everyone knows that."

Her husband brightened.

"I'd forgotten about Jo," he said. "This girl's Jo's niece, isn't she? I've always liked Jo, you know. I used to go around with her crowd before I married you, my dear. And Stafford is a very substantial citizen. They're one of our old families, you know."

Lucy stamped her foot. It was always this way with Seymour, as with his sisters, in any question of marriage. They reverted immediately to anachronisms.

"Old like the Third Avenue El," she snapped. "Old in a cockroach sense. How can you be so stupid about this, Seymour? And don't console yourself that this girl will ever see a penny of Stafford's money. It all goes to that stuffed shirt of a son of his."

"Oh. I'd forgotten about him."

"Well, he's very much alive," she retorted. "When Stafford dies, you'll probably have to take over the support of the entire Rodman family."

"That will be Philip's problem," he said dryly.

"Oh, Seymour, you *can* be exasperating."

"And you, my dear, take things too hard," he said severely. "The girl can't be as bad as you make out. I remember her at that dinner you gave. Philip may be able to make something of her. Who knows?" And then he went on to make a remark that showed how literally if not how feelingly he had kept abreast of modern thought. "And if it doesn't work out, my dear, how much have we lost? They can always be divorced."

. . .

The only person who accepted the engagement with unqualified enthusiasm was Aunt Jo. Philip's good looks and Sybil's obvious infatuation appealed to the romantic in her, and the fact that he was a Hilliard was simply the final touch that made it all perfect.

"Your mother doesn't think money's important," she told Sybil when the latter called on her with the great news. "And it isn't, of course, compared to love. But when you've got both, my dear, you've got a lot. The world is yours, and don't you forget it."

"But I wouldn't care if Philip didn't have a penny, Aunt Jo," Sybil protested. "In many ways I'd prefer it."

"I know you would, my dear," Aunt Jo said, leaning over to give her hand a little pat. "And that's fine, too. All I mean, child, is that everything about your engagement is perfect. Everything. Oh, wait till I see Emily and Harriet! Can you picture their faces!"

"Oh, Aunt Jo, will I have to tell them? I won't, will I?"

Her aunt burst out laughing.

"Look at the child! Scared already. No, dear, Philip will do that and take you to call. But you mustn't be afraid of people any more, Sybil. Remember that. You'll be a personage from now on."

After dinner that night Aunt Jo and her sister, Esther, met in the latter's upstairs sitting room, filled with pink pincushion stools and clusters of family photographs, for the first serious discussion of the engagement.

"You must be feeling triumphant, Esther," Jo said in her bantering tone. "To have married off Sybil so splendidly. And without even trying, either. People aren't going to be able to get over this one."

Esther shrugged her shoulders.

"It's funny, isn't it, Jo?" she said. "I always thought that Sybil would marry to shock me. An iceman, or something like that."

"Well, hasn't she?"

"Perhaps. But she doesn't know it. She's so dazzled by this man that she thinks we all are."

"I thought we all were," Jo said dryly. "Certainly George is."

Esther's silence conveyed the attitude of "Well, you know George."

"I can't make you out, Esther," Jo continued. "Or what it is that you really want for your children. You bring them up in the world and expect them to be hermits."

"I don't expect them to be hermits at all, Jo," Esther retorted. "It's simply that I don't want them to be taken in. And Lucy Hilliard is somebody whom a girl like Sybil might take seriously."

"And shouldn't?"

Esther hesitated.

"Well, Lucy may have her good points," she conceded. "But that's what makes her dangerous. That's what could take Sybil in."

"In? Into what?"

"Why, into her whole ridiculous life, of course," Esther said impatiently. "What else?"

"Sybil's young," Jo pointed out. "She may not find that life ridiculous. And if she doesn't, it won't be ridiculous for her. At the moment it's all fairyland. She's met her prince."

"But I don't approve of marrying princes," Esther said, shaking her head. "I'm enough of a snob for that. I'm all for people staying in their stations."

Jo laughed.

"You just don't like Philip, Esther," she said. "That's what you've got to face."

"I've never known the Philips of this world very well," Esther said reflectively. "They were the boys who never danced with me when I came out."

"We all have people like that in our lives," Jo said. "The people who make us feel inadequate. But is your Philip my Philip?"

"Certainly," her sister answered. "And he's Philip Hilliard."

"But if she's in love with him, Esther?"

"Is she?" This time Esther's shrug was monumental. "How can I take that chance?"

Jo stared at her. Even she was unprepared for the full impact of her sister's maternal egotism.

"I might point out, Esther," she exclaimed, "that it's not you who's taking it!"

Chapter

Ten

THE WEDDING itself, inevitably, reflected a blend of the moods of both families. Sybil, entirely conscious of the attitude not only of her mother but of her prospective mother-in-law and quite indifferent to both, went about her family's house in a dream and left the preparations to others. She would have preferred to have gone with Philip to a justice of the peace, and she would have suggested it had a fortunate instinct not warned her that he would have been shocked. Philip's liberalism, she was already aware, was confined to politics. The wedding, therefore, would come off more or less according to form, and Sybil, at first appalled at the prospect of the Hilliards being thrown together with her own parents, finally decided that it was perhaps, after all, only fitting that the long corridor of her childhood should come to an end in the stiff meaninglessness of a wedding reception. Beyond it all lay the garden of her adult years, and that, of course, was what counted. Her mother and Mrs. Hilliard and Aunt Jo could play, if they wished, with wedding cake and invitations, like parents who, under a Christmas tree, toy with the mechanical gadgets which they have given their children.

Lucy Hilliard, however, was having a considerably better

time with the gadgets than her former classmate at Miss Heely's School. To begin with, as mother of the groom, she had no direct responsibility for the success of the affair, and, secondly, she had decided that, as long as the die was cast, she might as well get all the fun out of the wedding that she could. She was intrigued by Esther and by her worries; she could not fathom the conscientiousness with which Sybil's mother weighed every name on her list and wavered between brands of champagne, a conscientiousness that defeated itself at every turn, for if Esther's first instinct was usually right, coming up as it did through the untroubled waters of her intelligence, her second, prompted by anxiety, was just as apt to be wrong. Thus her first list of guests, sensibly restricted to family, old friends and officers of the Cummings bank, became, after days of nervous contemplation, absurdly and hopelessly extended to include all the derelicts whom Esther thought it might be snobbish to omit, old maid companions of deceased aunts and odd, insecure women who might once have given Sybil piano lessons. It was as if Esther considered that the gods who watched her so jealously looked upon this wedding as the ultimate test of her salvation. Lucy had no sense of the agony of such decisions. If she had, she could not have indulged in her game of going over the list daily, as it grew, and adding, for each new name of a former trained nurse of Uncle Stafford's or an old tutor of Teddy's, the names of some particularly boisterous couple from her own tough crowd. Esther, of course, was in no position to object; she could only sit and chew her pencil and reflect sadly that in the end the party would probably not even fit into Jo's big house.

"You know, I have a kind of admiration for Esther," Lucy told Viola Paton over an after-lunch brandy at the small French restaurant where they always lunched. "Imagine caring as she cares. Do you suppose you go to heaven for that sort of caring?"

"Of course not," Viola answered. "It's not goodness on their part. It's the fear of doing wrong. 'Shall we have French champagne or domestic?' 'Will the little people criticize us or the great?' 'Will I have spent too much money for my husband or too little for my daughter?' Where do *you* think those people go, Lucy?"

"Hell?"

Viola shrugged her shoulders.

"They never know. They can't decide."

"Come to the wedding, anyway, Viola," Lucy urged her. "It'll be good for laughs."

But the wedding was not quite as odd as Lucy had thought it would be, for Jo Cummings, after all, was the person really in control, and nothing, even with Esther's fussiness, could go too wrong in her well-run house. It was hot, as only Easton Bay could be hot in late June, but it did not rain, and the guests were able to move about on the big lawn and drink champagne under the marquee. Sybil had no attendants except Millie. Teddy, two weeks before the wedding, had told her that he and Millie were now definitely engaged, and Sybil, full of her own happiness, had been able to rise to this gesture. Philip, however, had fourteen ushers, and with the exception of Teddy they were all large, self-assured Harvard athletes who walked on the balls of their feet. As she looked at them and at her mother, oddly overdressed, with big white feathers on a big brown hat and a drawn expression on her face, and at Teddy, perspiring and laughing and talking to everybody, and at her mother-in-law, pumping hands violently with an old friend further down the receiving line, and at Aunt Jo, smiling over a huge orchid and moving her arms in time to the waltz music, she felt dizzy at the juxtaposition of her old life and her new. This is how they celebrate, she thought; this is what they do, with their lace and their jokes and their champagne glasses and their kisses and their kindnesses; it's all very well for them, and I see now how nicely it's meant — *oh,* how nicely — for where I was wrong was ever to resent them, but it's not for me.

"Darling," she said in Philip's ear as she danced with him a few minutes later, when the receiving line had broken up, "it doesn't have anything to do with us, does it?"

"You mean it doesn't have anything to do with anyone else," he answered.

"I mean they couldn't know how I feel about you?" she continued. "They couldn't or they wouldn't look that way."

"What way, Sib?"

"Oh, the way they do. Like sheep."

"Are they like sheep?"

She smiled and shook her head. He was such a comfort to her already, this husband who was part of them, whom she knew so well and who knew her so slightly. His very failure to understand her was a consolation; she had a rôle to play now, and she would know how to play it, without the watchers who knew her and knew when she was doing things wrong. She could play the Hilliards' game and outplay them at it; she was suddenly sure even of that. It was not hard, after all, if one was on one's own. She looked confidently over Philip's shoulder at his two older sisters who were talking to each other in a corner. There was nothing, really, that she could ever mind again, except the loss of this turbulent love that filled her, a love that was her own property, a love that would not even depend, queerly enough, on how Philip treated her or what he felt about her. It was a love, she thought, as they circled the floor, that had come between the jagged edges of life and her own sensitivity like a mat, a love that had drained life of its fear and made it so much more than endurable. I'm happy, she thought in consternation; I'm actually, actually happy!

"Ellen, isn't it wonderful?" she said, going over to where

Ellen, with a very red face and a very shiny black hat, was proudly standing. "Ellen, darling, aren't you happy for me?" she asked, kissing her.

"Will you not be messing your dress, child," Ellen reproached her. And then, giving way to her emotion and hugging her, with tears in her eyes, she whispered: "Go back to the others, child."

"You'll come to me, Ellen, when I'm back, won't you? You'll look after my children?"

"You won't be wanting an old woman like me!"

"Promise me, Ellen! Please promise me!"

"Go on with you. I promise."

Then there was Nicholas saying good-bye to her, stiffly but very nicely, and Aunt Jo giving her an overdemonstrative kiss, and dressing upstairs with Millie, who was very sisterly and constrained, and when she finally came downstairs and looked over the bannister at all the faces and the small clump of her girl friends, if one could call them friends, waiting for the bouquet, she felt suddenly independent and sad at the same time, for the only face among the young people that she loved was Teddy's and without thinking and to the amazement of all, she blew him a quick kiss and threw him the bouquet.

. . .

Esther and her sister, Jo, sat smoking cigarettes on a weatherbeaten marble bench on the lawn, surveying the litter of strewn napkins and cigarette butts on the grass before them. Inside they could hear George speaking in a rather cross tone to the waiters, already engaged in the sorry task of reconstruction. Everyone had gone, and the sisters were drawn together by the great family bond that existed most intensely on the occasion of a wedding. For a few moments they could look together at Esther's offspring with the detachment of a united older generation.

"It'll all go smash, Jo," Esther said gloomily. "It'll all go smash and then what?"

"In the first place, it won't," her sister said, patiently and firmly. "And, in the second place, if it does, we'll start over again."

"If I only thought that the child had a chance," Esther continued, "I wouldn't mind so much. But she doesn't know what's happened to her. It makes me sick, Jo. Really it does."

"Esther, you're too extreme." Jo knew the strain that her sister had been under; she was doing her best to be sympathetic. "You keep talking about Philip as if he were nothing but a wooden Indian. I couldn't disagree with you more. I find him charming. But, after all, Sybil may like wooden Indians. You did."

Esther took this impassively.

"But how is the wooden Indian," she persisted, "going to like *her?*"

Jo, after all, had been under a strain herself. She was older than her sister, and she was tired. Her patience suddenly collapsed.

"You're the most ungrateful woman I've ever known, Esther Rodman," she said sharply. "We ought both to be down on our knees giving thanks that Sybil has found anyone half as nice as that boy to share her life with. And what are we doing? Talking about wooden Indians! The trouble with you, Esther, is that you're afraid to take a chance! You're afraid of life! That's what it is!"

"Whose life, Jo?"

"Your children's."

But as they sat there, side by side, the afraid and the unafraid, they looked extraordinarily alike.

Part Two

Chapter
One

SYBIL in the years afterwards thought of her marriage and the war as having occurred simultaneously, and each event in retrospect took on some of the emotion with which the other was colored. Their honeymoon in Canada lasted for the whole summer; in the early fall they moved to an apartment on the East River, and Philip went to Midshipmen's School. He had to live on the U.S.S. *Prairie State,* moored in the Hudson, but he had liberty one night a week, and that was always a night of celebration, ending up in prolonged visits to at least three of Philip's favorite night clubs. They were extremely happy. Philip treated her almost as a child, instructing her with elaborate detail into the mysteries of married life. He had a particular way of his own for doing almost everything, from mixing a cocktail to arranging shirts in a drawer, and it was necessary that she should learn these things. But she was a willing pupil. In fact, she followed him blindly. When she heard of wives who were rude to their husbands or who bossed them about, she could only surmise that such marriages were miserable. Like many intellectual women she found delight in submission, in doing things for Philip, particularly in thinking about him when he was away at the school. The Navy had added another coating to the glistening exterior of his masculinity, and when he appeared in the doorway on those longed-for Saturday afternoons, in his blue uniform, her heart would stop.

"Did you get the seats for *Holliday Pudding?*" he might ask.

"Of course."

"And reserve a table for six at the Crystal Roof?"

"Yes, Philip."

"And did you remember to telephone Ma about the underwear and pajamas that I left in Glenville?"

"I did."

"Good girl. You can have a kiss."

Philip was efficient; he liked to do a lot of things, and he liked to do them well. He liked to read the newspapers, very carefully, and talk about politics; he liked to exercise, and he liked to drink. He mapped out his days and nights with meticulous care and allotted his energy and his time neatly in accordance with his desires and ambitions. It was a simple matter for his wife to learn the pattern and, having learned it, to maintain it. With Philip beside her she was less shy at gatherings of his friends; she talked more easily and learned to eliminate some of the bluntness that had startled people in her old self. Only if her husband was criticized did she snap at people with anything like her former asperity.

"Don't let the big boy get the harness over your neck," Julia Anderton told her once. "Show him who the boss is. If you don't, he'll ride you."

"If he'd wanted a bossy wife, Julia, I assume he'd have taken you."

Julia stared.

"Taken!" she exclaimed. "What do you think we are? A harem?"

Her family gave her no trouble. Millie called occasionally and gushed over the apartment, but it was obvious that she did not really like it. It was too much larger than the one that she and Teddy were planning to take to be in the category of younger marrieds' apartments and hence could not be fussed about in the same way. Millie could be impressed by things a little bigger and better than her own, but not doubly so. Besides, Sybil and Philip had taken the apartment furnished because of the uncertainty of the future. They had stored all their wedding presents, so what could Millie admire? Esther and George were pleasant enough to Philip, and he was exceedingly polite to them, but they saw little of each other. George admired Philip's being an athlete and a "regular fellow," but, like Millie, he was a little too impressed with the Hilliards to relax with them.

The big event of the autumn was Teddy's marriage to Millie. All the family except Sybil considered her a "perfect" girl, and a great amount of enthusiasm was demonstrated. Millie was quiet and sweet and intensely feminine; it was assumed that she would be practical, too, and keep Teddy's head "out of the clouds," as George put it, without making him feel that he was missing anything there. She could be counted on, in short, to carry on the maternal good work and to see that Teddy, whose imagination had always seemed dangerously open to romantic ideas, became a lawyer, a father and a family man. Esther could turn her son over to this girl and receive, as the lawyers put it, a receipt and release. In the immediate future, however, it would be her duty to share Esther's burden of worry, for Teddy, like his brother-in-law, was a midshipman on the *Prairie State* and would, in all probability, be sent to sea. Worry to Esther was like a pagan sacrifice; the more relatives who joined in it, the more were the gods propitiated.

"I know you'll like her, Sib," Teddy told her, "when you get to know her better."

"Will I?"

"And if not, what of it? I'm not going to be one of those husbands who insists that everybody love his wife. You and I go way back, Sib. Nothing can break that."

She frowned.

"Does she like the books we like?"

"Lord no!" He laughed. "Does Philip?"

She had nothing to say to this. She had nothing, indeed, constructively critical to say about Millie at all. She could not bring herself to tell him that Millie, for all her feminine helplessness, real as well as assumed, had trapped him. For what could have been easier game for a seemingly helpless girl than Teddy who, under his high spirits and exuberant charm, was so impressionable and obliging? Even Esther confided to Sybil that she had a dim suspicion of this. She was always badgering Teddy with questions about his happiness. One day he turned on her with an unprecedented sharpness and snapped: "I'm getting married, Mummie. Do I have to be ecstatic too? Will you *never* be satisfied?"

"What do you suppose he meant?" Esther, appalled, asked Sybil afterwards. "Did I say something wrong?"

"I suppose he wanted to be let alone," Sybil suggested. "People can be happy and unhappy at the same time, can't they?"

"Can they?" Esther's voice was filled with dismay. "It sounds too queer."

If Teddy had his misgivings, however, Millie seemed to have none. She met each new friend or relation of the Rodmans' with an attitude of "I just *know* we're going to like each other," expressed with many smiles and a good deal of wriggling of her shoulders. When Millie shook hands, nervously and jerkily, she seemed to be pumping her desire to please into the other person. Even Sybil had to admit that if ever a girl had tried to be nice, it was Millie. And all she wanted, too, as Philip had once told her, were the things that every girl wanted: a home and children and the security afforded by a moderately industrious husband in an ordinary job. But Sybil wanted Teddy to have what she had; she resented as much as ever anything that smacked of compromise.

At the church she watched the ceremony with a lump in her throat, her arm under that of her husband to whom she had confided none of her doubts. Philip lived in a different world; it was up to her to meet him there and not drag him into the dampness of her worries. She was already pregnant, too, and bore his world within her. Yet as she listened to her brother's clear responses at the altar, she felt again the old urge to protect him from the world. It was too late.

After the wedding came Pearl Harbor. He and Philip were transferred to the west coast, and Philip was sent to the Pacific to join a light cruiser as a communications officer. The interminable war years with all their consequences and lack of consequence had begun.

Chapter

Two

PHILIP was in the Pacific for the first three years of the war. During all of this time, except for an occasional spell of shore duty in Pearl Harbor, he was at sea. He came home on leave only once, for three weeks, in 1943 and saw his son, Seymour, called "Timmy," who had been born in his absence. He was proud of the boy and glad, in his way, to see Sybil, but it proved, between them, to be a period of some constraint. When he flew back to the coast afterwards, it was not so much with a feeling of relief as with a feeling that he had not had quite the fun to which he was entitled. He was not, however, wholly clear in his own mind as to what this fun should consist of.

Sybil had been, needless to say, devotion itself, but Sybil had changed. She had changed, in many ways, for the better. The expression of intensity in her eyes was still there, as was the determination somehow inherent in her paleness, but one no longer was troubled by the sense that she had formerly conveyed, of a dog ready to snap. She was calm and even graceful. She was almost, in fact, serene.

Her evolution from the cocoon of her earlier resentments had, oddly enough, been quickened by Philip's long absence. She had missed him terribly, but she had learned to live with the emptiness. Had he been home she might have been submerged in his positiveness. As it was, she had the baby and her war work and was responsible only to herself. She went eight hours a day to the Red Cross information service and interviewed families who had not heard from their boys overseas. It was the kind of work that she would have been far too shy even to think of in the past. Esther observed her daughter's improvement with appreciation and skepticism. "There's nothing like a hero in the family," she pointed out to Millie. "Particularly when he's away."

Sybil's relations with her family-in-law had also taken a decided turn for the better. Despite the coldness of her initial reception, she had made a great effort with all of the Hilliards, even cultivating the maiden aunts to prove to herself how entirely she had merged her life with Philip's. She called upon Miss Emily and Miss Harriet every other Saturday and almost persuaded herself that beneath the perpetual fountain of their complaints was hidden at least the semblance of a human need to love and be loved.

"Do you suppose she really likes them?" Philip's sister, Lila, asked her mother. "Could anyone really like the aunts?"

"Good Lord, no!" Lucy raised her hands at the very idea. "Give her credit for something! She's playing a game. These quiet little girls are the ones that get ahead. 'All the rest, residue and remainder of my estate to Miss Mouse.' I wish I had a dollar for every time I've seen that in the papers." She nodded her head, in grudging admiration. "More power to the girl. She's got the right idea. You and Felicia are too lazy to go near the old dragons. For all you care, they could leave their money to a dog-and-cat hospital!"

"But you never go near them yourself, Ma."

"Well, they're certainly not going to leave anything to *me*," Lucy retorted. "Why should I be bothered? But you're their own flesh and blood, God help you. You might as well get something out of it."

Sybil found it far easier to get along with her sisters-in-law than she had anticipated. Lila and Felicia were big, handsome, indolent girls, without a trace of their mother's malice, who could spend the entire morning discussing nail polish and the entire afternoon shopping for it. Their husbands and children seemed to take up very little of their time, and they lunched or had cocktails with Lucy every day in the week. Oddly devoid of energy, they never demonstrated the least dissatisfaction with their rather inert existences. "They're like cows," Philip used to say disgustedly, "except they don't give milk." They looked upon Sybil, without envy, as an intellectual, and came to accept her point of view unquestioningly in every field that had not been previously covered by their mother's. Arlina, the youngest sister, who was still at school, a large, emotional, messy girl, was ecstatic to find a sister-in-law so quiet and sympathetic. She developed a crush on her and imitated her in everything.

It was with Lucy, however, that Sybil made her most important conquest. The war had given Lucy a needed outlet for her energies, and she was a changed woman. It was, of course, *her* war, but as even she could not be allowed to run it all, she chose prisoners of war as her specialty. She became the head of a large office that sent parcels to our soldiers and sailors in enemy hands; she worked indefatigably the whole day and often at night. All of her tumultuous abilities, long scattered in parties and travel and loose, easy, rough talk became centered in her job. She talked of nothing but the war and excoriated those who, in her opinion, were not doing their share, even to the point of shaming George Rodman into volunteering for one night a week of guard duty on the piers. In the flurry of her activity, she became increasingly impatient with the inertia of her husband and daughters, and Philip, her only child in uniform, seemed more than ever to her the only true child of her body. The least that she could do, while he was fighting in the Pacific, was to be nice to his wife, and in this way she made the discovery of Sybil's better side. She was delighted to find that her daughter-in-law, like herself, was busy in war work, and she began to include her in those daily lunches at the French restaurant which, even with all her new activity, Lucy never discontinued. Gradually she and her friend Viola came to discover the intelligence under Sybil's reserve and the dry humor that was beginning to take the place of her truculence. "But she's absolutely marvelous!" Lucy exclaimed after lunch one day to Viola. "I had no idea!" She was always ready to admit that she had been wrong. Lucy was not a small woman. "Did you really know you had a jewel, darling?" she asked Philip when he came home on leave. "Or was it blind luck?"

Philip, to tell the truth, had not known. He had not suspected it, either, from Sybil's letters which had made him slightly uncomfortable. He had been very conscious of their note of intellectualized sentiment; he had felt vaguely that they were unusual and had not altogether liked it. Sybil's devotion, when he was with her, expressed in her large, steady stare, was gratifying and reassuring; he could put an arm protectingly over her shoulders and continue easily talking to his friends. But Sybil's devotion expressed in her neat, concise handwriting and coming to him in never failing pages across the broad, hot Pacific seemed too set apart from the simple standards of the men around him. The letters of the sailors that he read as a ship's censor, filled with erotic, misspelled reminiscences of physical intimacy, seemed destined for wives very different from his. He was not sure in what vein he wanted her to write him, but certainly in an earthier one than the letter which he received when she heard of his shrapnel wounds.

"It is so unbelievable to me, my darling," she wrote, "that there could be people in this world who would fire on a ship that you were aboard. You tell me that it was nothing but a scratch, and I pray that you are not just trying to reassure me, but even a scratch — how could they *want* to? To do it to you? These are the things that it is impossible for me to believe as I sit in my office before my file cards, looking down on Madison Avenue and watching the people walk up and down, the people who aren't in the Pacific and who think of the war, if at all, with a shudder and then tell themselves that it isn't so bad if you're really *in* it, the way people who catch fish tell themselves it's all right because a fish doesn't feel. When it gets too bad for me I go across the street to call on your mother amid her ringing telephones and scurrying assistants, and I admire her activity and cherish the consolation that she gives me since we have become friends. I do return, however, wondering a little why so many men must die that Lucy Hilliard may be redeemed. Little Timmy is just like you and such a comfort. Please, please get well, darling, and come home. Without you I'm back in the darkness and understand nothing."

To this Philip answered that the shrapnel wounds had come from splinters of shells fired by his own ship and that they had not even been bad enough to keep him in sick bay. He had been relieved of watches for a few days and assigned to duty on the ship's court-martial board. The rest of the letter described this experience in the turgid style of the young lawyer:

"To think that I never expected to practise law and now find myself a judge! Not that you should picture me in the sober black usually associated with judicial garb. I sit, on the contrary, with two of my worthy brothers arrayed in khaki shirts open at the neck behind a simple wardroom table before which our trembling defendant is arraigned.

Has he been late relieving his watch? Or missed muster? Woe betide him!"

Sybil did not feel that such letters had very much to do with herself, and she noted the style even as she told herself that she didn't, but, still, he was writing from a new and wonderful world, *the* world, and if anything came out of it that did not tally with her standards, then *her* standards were the ones that would have to be changed.

When he came home on leave after a year and a half of duty in the Pacific and four major battles, with ribbons and stars, and only a little less hair and a little more weight, she was almost frightened at the intensity of her own happiness, even if she was troubled, deep down, at the prospect of having to work out a different relationship. For she was very much aware, and she knew from some of his letters that he was aware, too, how little they had really known each other before the war. She knew, however, that he would not want to be fussed over, and she knew that he would want to see his friends. She decided that it would be best if they did not go off alone, but if they spent his leave, instead, in New York and in Glenville where she could share him with Lucy and his sisters. This turned out, fortunately, to be just what he wanted. For the first few days there was an inevitable self-consciousness between them, but this was soon relieved by cocktail parties and dinners where Philip was featured, and after a bit they settled down to what seemed to Sybil their new relationship of his telling her about life on his cruiser and of her laughing at his jokes. Philip had really not changed at all. If anything, he had rather enjoyed the Navy, although, like all reserve officers, he would rather have died than admit it. She was still attractive to him, and he adored the baby. What then was wrong? Was it only the long months between, which, as everyone seemed to agree, made such reunions as trying as they could be wonderful? Or was it — as she uneasily felt — that she herself had changed, that she had become a more forceful, a more coherent and communicative person than Philip had known before, a person who could not quite be smothered even in their most intimate moments? She saw this person in the mirror on her dressing table as she was getting ready for dinner on the last night of his leave; she made out the new confidence in her eyes and in the face that loomed at her over the big stoppers on the perfume bottles, and she saw, too, the tears that appeared suddenly in her eyes, tears that she could not be once again the silent, clinging girl whom he had loved enough to marry, against all of his family. But she was growing up; it was a process that could not be retarded. She put on her earrings; she placed a drop of perfume behind each ear; she went to take a final look at the baby, and she was ready to go out.

Chapter
Three

WHEN PHILIP BOARDED his plane for the West Coast it was not with a feeling of unrelieved gloom. He knew that he would have to wait in San Francisco for his orders anywhere from a day to a month. He liked San Francisco, however, very much, and he had not told Sybil that he might be delayed there. He felt rather guilty about this on the flight out, particularly as she believed everything that he told her so implicitly, but he reasoned with himself that, after all, he might be there for only a day in which case she would have taken the trip for nothing. He knew, of course, that she would have been happy to take the chance, but then there was the baby to consider, and was it really such a good idea to leave little Timmy with Mrs. Rodman, who was such a fusser, or even, for that matter, with his own mother? Besides, there was himself to consider. He had been fighting the war and risking his life, and he was going back to do it again. A man in his situation needed more than the relaxation that even a devoted wife could give. He was fond of Sybil, of course; he loved her, indeed, but he had many navy friends in San Francisco, with their wives, and they weren't Sybil's type at all. They thought nothing of sitting up and drinking all night, and there were other things that they took a good deal less seriously than Sybil did. The long and short of it, he decided, was that Sybil was the perfect peacetime wife. But hell, this was war.

By the time he arrived in San Francisco he felt almost reconciled to his own rationalizations. There were several officers from his cruiser who, like himself, were awaiting transportation, and the life was very much what he had so cheerfully anticipated. His only duty was to report every morning at eleven to see if his orders had come, which gave to the rest of the day the pleasant quality of a possibly final day of grace. After the third day he telephoned Sybil in a fit of remorse and told her that she probably wouldn't be hearing from him again. He implied that orders were imminent.

"Oh, darling," she said. "To think that I might have had three days more of you. But anyway. Good luck, dearest."

On the fourth day he met Irene Hodges. She was quite a bit older than he, and her husband was attached to Philip's cruiser, but he was not in San Francisco. He was at sea. Irene was a large, graceful, blond woman with a perpetual smile and disconcerting eyes. She told Philip, not once but several times, that she and her husband believed that what one did while the other was away was none of the other's business. He always started his evenings at Irene's apartment, drinking a great many cocktails and listening to her calm and outrageous flattery. It pleased him even though he knew how often she used it on others.

"What are you thinking of, handsome?" she asked him one evening as he sat looking into his cocktail glass which he was holding between his knees. "About the dear little wife and the dear little boy back home? Oh, poor handsome. Poor lonely handsome. Let Irene fix him another drink."

She made no effort to move from the sofa on which she

always lay stretched, perfectly still. She never took her eyes off him.

He got up and poured another drink for each of them.

"As a matter of fact, I was just thinking that I haven't been thinking about them," he said. "Not enough, that is."

"And what good does thinking about a woman do her?" Irene retorted. "Can she tell whether or not you're thinking about her? Of course, she can't. If you want to keep her happy, write. That's the only thing that counts. Obbie always writes." Obbie was her husband, and her voice softened a bit as she mentioned his name. "The poor precious. I know *he's* not thinking of me. But I think he's a million angels to write. And I love him for it."

"He doesn't write such a hell of a lot," Philip pointed out.

She looked quizzical for a moment. Then she laughed. It was a long, easy laugh.

"Oh, you darling," she said. "You have to read each other's mail, don't you? Censorship. Of course. It must be so cozy. I can just see you, my handsome lieutenant, with all your Chelton background and your inhibitions about peeping, finally released into an absolute heaven of other people's business." She clapped her hands. "Oh, it's divine! You know it's divine!"

"We only read the outgoing mail," Philip said with dignity. "Not the incoming."

She laughed louder.

"Oh fiddle!" she exclaimed. "I'll bet you know what laxatives I take. And what side of bed I get out of in the morning. Why, *Mr.* Hilliard!"

They looked at each other and smiled. It was a long pleasant smile. She knew that he had turned the corner, at just that moment, and that their friendship was about to enter a new phase, the one towards which she had been slowly, and even lazily, directing it. He knew that she knew it, and she knew this too. There was no hurry. At the end of their smile she laughed again.

"If it doesn't matter what a man thinks," Philip pointed out, "it can't matter too much what he does. If his wife doesn't know, that is."

"No, Socrates."

"But it isn't really true that I don't think of Sybil," he said defensively. "I think of her a lot. Except maybe not in the right way."

"My poor handsome puritan," she said, shaking her head. "How you abuse yourself! Of course your wife's an angel. Of course, she's pining for you. Of course, she'd cry her little eyes out if she could peek into your big bad mind. But remember, my handsome, that she isn't going to have the chance. Unless you're more of a puritan than I think you are. Unless you tell."

Philip said nothing to this, but after a moment he moved over to her side on the sofa. There were still doubts, there were even inhibitions, but when he put his arms around her and sensed the quick, assured possessiveness of her response, he knew that he had left the quiet subtlety of Sybil's world for the world of the censored letters. It was his first infidelity.

When he left, ten days later, for the Pacific, his sense of guilt had already disappeared, and he was feeling as relaxed as, in his opinion, a serviceman was entitled to feel. Irene had been perfect and their affair without sentiment. When he had said good-bye, she had simply given him some embroidered handkerchiefs to take to Obbie on the cruiser. On the transport to Pearl Harbor he did a good deal of conscious and unconscious comparing of her with Sybil. He worked himself almost into the position of putting the blame on his wife for what had happened. A man, after all, expected something more than the submissiveness that Sybil offered. And why not? He had rather a desire, as Irene had foreseen, to write her about the whole thing. In this, however, he managed to restrain himself. She was a Rodman, and one could never be entirely sure how Rodmans would take things or what they would do.

Chapter

Four

TEDDY WAS SENT to the Pacific early in the war as was Philip, but because of the need of shore-based communications officers of his training, he was not sent to sea. He spent instead the first six months in Pearl Harbor and thereafter was transferred from atoll to atoll as they were captured. At first he was disappointed not to be at sea, like Philip, but Teddy's was a nature that turned naturally to the compensations around him. He even learned to enjoy the Quonset hut life on those small sandy islands surrounded by the shimmering blue of the Pacific. It was a regular and peaceful existence, with enough whiskey if one was an officer, in an atmosphere that was entirely youthful and masculine, with none of the problems presented by women and children, by old age and disease. He knew better, of course, than to write any of this to Millie who, like Sybil, was nursing her first child; his letters to her were carefully explicit as to his loneliness. To his mother, however, he once tried to convey some sense of the odd pleasures in the life that he was leading, but Esther, immediately and unreasonably seeing a threat to his marriage in such an attitude and terrified that Millie might in some way suspect their illicit correspondence, made no reference in her answer to any of his comments but inundated her letters instead with unsolicited details of Millie and the baby and Millie's dear little apartment and how much he was missed. Opening this letter and being greeted with the chill of its unwelcome domesticity Teddy was still able to smile as he traced the anxiety of his mother's scratchy handwriting and read between the lines her gentle reproach that he must not pretend to like the atoll existence, that New York was where his interests lay and would he please not forget it? Good old mother, he said to himself; she thinks I'll be a Gauguin, after all. And then he wrote her a proper letter, giving her full details of his health, and another to Millie, full of plans for their future, and after these he could let himself go in a letter to Sybil, who always understood.

"I never get tired of sitting in the evening outside my Quonset hut and looking down over the beach and the sea. Particularly if there's a squall coming up, for then as the clouds roll over and the sea becomes white-capped and the palm trees begin to blow I feel the exciting calm of being on a tiny spot in what seems an infinite sea. Why is it, Sib, that the men here have no sense of the immensity of the surrounding vacancy? I read Spengler and Brooks Adams and feel relieved at the sense of distant decline. Yet how they talk, all around me, of girls and home towns, of 'shoes and ships and sealing-wax.' Of cabbages but never of kings."

His life, of course, was not as inert as he made it sound. There was a great deal to do, and Teddy did things efficiently. His capacity for enthusiasm included even the military, and his sense of drama could feed on the picture of organized discipline and sacrifice in the Pacific. But the great difference in Teddy's life was the impersonality of the Pacific and the people fighting in it. He had brought himself up, after all, in the school of his own charm and its effect on people.

"It seems almost," Sybil wrote him, "as though we had

changed places in life. It makes me feel inadequate when I think how grateful the unhappy families who come to the Red Cross would be for even a touch of the kind of sympathy that you can give. And where are you? Marooned on a sea-girt atoll in the comparative solitude that was always *my* ideal! How will it all end, Teddy? Will you come home and lock yourself in your room and refuse to go to dances? And will I be everyone's favorite? And will either of us be happier?"

Teddy smiled at her unexpressed thought that the change in their positions was at least doing *him* good. They had never really trusted him. Any of his family. Sybil had always been afraid that he would become a philistine, and his parents had trembled that he wouldn't. Well, perhaps they were both right. At any rate, he couldn't be too concerned. The family seemed small and shrill from the vantage point of his Pacific isolation.

When Philip's cruiser was in Eniwetok he and Teddy met at the officers' club. They sat all afternoon at a board table under a thatched roof and drank beer. Philip described his life aboard his cruiser in great detail. He assumed that Teddy, being shore-based, would have nothing himself to say. Later, however, and after many beers their conversation became more personal. Philip, who was always naïvely candid, ended by telling Teddy the whole San Francisco episode. It was, perhaps, an odd confidence to make to a brother-in-law, but Teddy had always listened to him with sympathy in the past.

Teddy's reaction, however, was not what he had hoped. He looked at Philip in a very odd way.

"You're shocked," Philip said irritably. "I shouldn't have told you."

Teddy thought this over for a moment before he answered. The only thing that surprised him was that he was shocked.

"I guess I am, Phil," he said. "I guess I still feel protective about Sib."

"But this sort of thing has nothing to do with Sybil," Philip protested. "It doesn't affect her one way or the other. Or the way I feel about her."

Teddy nodded slowly.

"I've always gone along with you in these things, Phil," he conceded. "That's true. I've always gone along with all my friends. Maybe I'm just beginning to be stuffy." He suddenly laughed. "But do you know something, Phil? I *want* to be stuffy."

He looked at his brother-in-law, whom he had always so admired, as if he were seeing him for the first time. He had spent, it sometimes seemed to him, a veritable lifetime with no moral existence outside of his fondness for other people. If Philip was his friend, then Philip could do no wrong. No real wrong. But people had got him nowhere and never would get him anywhere. What, after all, was the use of them?

Philip, however, only blinked at him.

"You mean, you think I'm a heel?" he asked belligerently.

Teddy, looking at him, laughed again.

"Yes, Philip," he said cheerfully. "I suppose you are, more or less, a heel."

Philip grunted.

"I suppose you wouldn't cheat on Millie if you had a chance," he said nastily. "I suppose you'd be a little tin Jesus."

Teddy, looking out at what seemed the infinity of ships in the atoll, reflected that Philip was genuinely incapable of thinking that anyone was different from himself.

"I suppose I would, Phil," he said.

When they went back to their respective quarters that night Teddy was able to push another of his childhood gods off the mantel. His hearth, indeed, was now quite covered with their pieces, and he slept well. Philip, on the other hand, slept fitfully in his bunk and dreamed of Sybil fixing him with reproachful eyes. His mother was laughing, and so was Irene; there were many laughs in his dream. But Sybil was not laughing.

As he awoke in the morning to the clanging bells of the ship's general quarters and dashed to his station, helmet in hand, he shook off the dream with impatience and anger. It was a world of men and things in which he lived. The real Philip had nothing to do with the strange squeamishness of his wife's brother.

He wrote Teddy, weeks later, in a cheerful vein, after a good deal of postponement and after the cruiser had left Eniwetok, without mentioning their dispute. To mention it at all would have been to make too much of it. He received a pleasant answer, entirely noncommittal and full of Teddy's general thoughts about the progress of the war. Like many of the letters which he received from friends, even in the boredom of shipboard life, Philip never quite finished it. Not long afterwards he received an overdue transfer; he was detached from his cruiser and ordered to Washington for duty in the Navy Department. After three years in the Pacific this was welcome news, and he wrote Sybil and told her to look for a house in the capital and wait for him there. It was not impossible, he told himself, that he might stop off for a few days in San Francisco on his way home.

Chapter

Five

DURING THE LAST WINTER of the war Philip and Sybil occupied a small house in Georgetown. No effort had been spared by Lucy Hilliard to make Philip's life comfortable. As soon as the letter had arrived announcing his change of duty she had gone with Sybil to Washington to look at real estate. Having found no suitable house for rent, Lucy had promptly bought one.

"It's a good investment, anyway," she told her astonished daughter-in-law. "And what the heck? After three years out there he deserves it. Even if you live in it only a week. Give him fun, dear."

Sybil kissed her. Their relations now were very good indeed. When Philip arrived she was already settled in the house with Timmy, now three years old, a delicate, sensitive child who showed signs of resembling his uncle, Teddy. Much as Sybil adored her son, she was somewhat concerned that his existence had still not diminished, in any degree whatsoever, the intensity of her preoccupation with Philip. She did not see, at the moment, how she was to do justice to both of them. Philip, however, was delighted with everything, including his son, and Sybil could hardly bring herself to believe that it had really happened and that he was really home. Her cup, it seemed, was filled to overflowing. It was a pity that no Rodman could regard such a prospect without foreboding.

Philip was excellent at perfunctory things, and his manners were undeniably good. There may have been something methodical in his fairness, but nonetheless it *was* fairness. If he and Sybil, for example, dined one night with old classmates of his to reminisce about events in which she had no part, he was careful to suggest the following night that they do something that was fun for her. She never held him to this, and she suspected that she was not meant to, but, still, he made the offer, and it was only the offer that she cared about.

What Philip was actually doing, of course, was building up credit against the day when he might need it. He had resumed his relations with Irene on his return to the West Coast, and he had used up a week of his leave before coming to New York. It had all been fun, but it was over — at least for the time being — and it was obvious that he should now give some attention to his marriage. Philip wanted his home life to be independently fortified; he was learning to disconnect it in his mind from his occasional diversions. As a matter of fact, he even reasoned to himself at his desk in the Pentagon, the second phase of his affair in California had washed away the resentment that he had been developing against Sybil and had made their reunion a good deal easier than he had anticipated. Much of the strain on him had gone when he had lost his fear of being confined for life to one woman. Sybil, after all, was a good wife, by most standards, and the mother of his child; it was almost pathetically easy to keep her satisfied. If he got restless in the future there would be business trips and excursions and all that these implied. There was no reason to rock the boat.

He was not very busy at the Navy Department. Nobody expected too much of Pacific veterans. He was a lieutenant commander now and looked very impressive at his desk behind his ribbons and battle stars. When he got home a little after five he was still full of energy and wanted either to go out or to have people in. Sybil complied as best she could, but she knew nobody in Washington, and it ended with Philip's collecting a somewhat heterogeneous circle of navy friends and friends of his family's. The latter were largely New York businessmen and lawyers who were working for the government in a civilian capacity. Their wives, as might have been expected from Lucy's circle, were apt to be hard and thin and entirely sophisticated; they dazzled Philip who had always secretly admired his mother's world, even when he denounced it. Sybil knew this and could still be amused by it. She also noted that his "liberalism," his whole interest in politics, in fact, had melted with the first rays of a Pacific sun.

"You spent all last evening with Laura Ingraham," she pointed out one day at breakfast. "I thought you would want to talk to Alfred Kay about the paper he wants to start when the war's over. I kept trying to edge him over to you, but you were like a waiter. I couldn't catch your eye."

Philip was buried in the newspaper.

"I was looking at Laura," he said gruffly. "You'll have to admit that she's easier to look at than Alfred."

"Certainly. If that's what you want."

He glanced at her over the top of the paper.

"What do you mean, if that's what I want?"

She shrugged her shoulders.

"I mean if you'd rather look at Laura than listen to Alfred," she said. "I can't conceive of it the other way round."

He looked at her with a funny little smile.

"Laura, my sweet," he said, "is a very attractive woman."

She did not pursue the subject, but she was aware that the subjects were increasing that she did not pursue. She was just beginning, after the first months of their reunion, to realize what she had suspected even prior to his return: that they did not really have a relationship at all. The idea broke in on her gradually, and she refused to be panicked by it. If there was no relationship, it was up to her to construct one. She saw that he wanted her to be more sophisticated. She knew that she could never be bold and languid like Laura, but she could be quiet and controlled and could make her fewer words felt. She sensed that Philip no longer wanted her to be clinging, and she tried to affect a kind of brittle indifference except when they were alone. It was difficult, but it was absorbing, and it kept her from being what he called "sticky." She paid more attention to her clothes, and even Philip noticed this.

"You know you *really* look well tonight," he said to her once as she was coming downstairs in a new black evening dress. She could always tell when he meant something. "I'm proud of you."

"Do I look as well as Laura?"

"Like Laura's daughter."

"As old as that?"

He gave her a little tap on the chin with his fist. It was a small, playful gesture, but it was something that he had not done since before the war. She was suddenly trembling.

"Oh, Philip," she said and hurried past him into the car so that he should not see the tears in her eyes. It was only at such moments that she realized how far things were from what she had once visualized.

The spring came on and the summer and the unbelievable events of the atom bomb and the Japanese surrender. Philip got out of the Navy in the fall, and they went to Bermuda and then back to their apartment in New York. The house in Georgetown was sold, as Lucy had anticipated, at a profit, and the Washington interlude was over. Sybil was honest enough to admit to herself that the war had been something of a romance to her. She had been wretchedly worried about

Philip, of course, while he had been in the Pacific and lonely as even she had never been lonely before, but at least there had been exaltation. Whatever there was in her life now, there was certainly very little of that.

She was disappointed when Philip went to work as a vice-president of the family company which held the real estate in the city that comprised the bulk of the Hilliard fortune. He announced it to her only after the final decision.

"It's not a permanent thing," he explained when he saw her expression. "But I agree with Daddy that one might as well learn where the chips come from."

"But, darling, you won't even be using your legal training," she protested. "It seems so — well, so stodgy. And you're *not* stodgy, Philip."

"Certainly, I'll be using my law," he said, bridling. "Real estate's nothing but law. Evictions and rent control and sales and multiple-dwelling statutes. As a matter of fact, I doubt if I could handle the job if I weren't a lawyer. You just don't know what you're talking about, Sib."

Very likely she didn't. She was ready to concede this. It did, however, seem to be part of a pattern that he had once repudiated. She knew how irritating it was to be reminded of an outgrown idealism and said nothing further. But what was far more disappointing to her was that he did not want another child, at least not then. In Washington he had put it on the ground that he might have to go back to the Pacific and be killed, and he didn't want to leave her more tied down than she was. Now he claimed that it would be better to wait for a year until things had "settled down." Sybil minded this very much, but, as usual, she gave in. Lucy knew of her disappointment, for the Hilliards discussed everything among each other. She tried to cheer her up.

"Don't worry, dear," she told Sybil. "I know the Hilliard men. He'll come around. It's hard for us to understand how much the war has upset him. I know he doesn't look it, but it's still there, down deep. Where it doesn't show."

So Sybil resigned herself to their new life. When she found herself insufficiently occupied, for she had Ellen to look after Timmy, and a cook, she returned to her history, but she made it a more active hobby than before. She chose Frances Brandon, the mother of Lady Jane Grey, as the subject for an essay biography. The field was free from intrusion, and she spent many hours in the Public Library extracting what material there was on her rather shadowy subject and making herself an expert in the problems of the English succession. Her final result, ruthlessly synthesized, was a paper of less than fifty pages. Philip discovered it on the living-room table one night and read it carefully while she was out of the room. He had never heard of the subject, but he praised it in his extravagant, uncritical way and talked of taking it to a friend of Lucy's who ran a literary magazine. For once in her life she was abrupt with him.

"I must do these things in my own way, Philip," she said sharply, taking back the manuscript. "If they're not perfect, they're nothing."

She noticed that at cocktail parties Philip always singled out a particular girl to talk to, but as it was apt to be a different girl at each party it did not occur to her to worry. In fact, the idea that she might lose him altogether, as so many wives in the post-war period had lost their husbands, was inconceivable to her. There were no divorces in her family. Such things only happened to other people. Millie and Teddy, for example, seemed to have readjusted smoothly to each other. Millie had had her second baby, and Teddy was working in a large law firm and working very hard. But he seemed to like it and was even boring on the subject of his bond issues. They lived in a small house in Greenwich that Aunt Jo had bought for them. People worked things out. They were all adult now, Sybil reflected, a bit ruefully, and they had to solve their own problems. It was what life was.

Chapter
Six

THE BUSINESS with Julia Anderton started one evening towards the end of the first post-war winter while Sybil was in Greenwich spending the night with Teddy and Millie. She and Philip had been asked to one of Julia's cocktail parties, but that, needless to say, had been no deterrent to Sybil's excursion.

"Why don't you go anyway?" she asked Philip that morning. "After all, she was an old girl of yours. It would be kind."

"Oh, I imagine Julia's done well enough without me."

"She hasn't married," Sybil pointed out. "She's probably still pining for you."

It was, in fact, a surprise to everyone that Julia had not married. She was the adored only child of a timid, nervous couple who had had just enough money to give her the same disadvantages that richer girls enjoyed. Julia's coming-out party, in a few hours, had wiped out the savings of ten years. But she *had* come out, and there had been champagne and men to park the cars and inferior toasts and a dancing team from a night club whom nobody had watched. Julia herself had carried it all off with a commendable bravado. Since then her life had been anticlimactic. She had nothing, indeed, to show for it now but her manner, that rough and superior carelessness that went so well with her big limbs, her big but excellent figure, her large, firm nose and long, tawny hair. It may have been an overdose of this casualness, combined with the frankness and occasional unheeding vulgarity of her talk, that put men off. Julia had always been in the center of things, but wives, apparently, were chosen from the perimeters.

The cocktail party, at her parents' gloomy apartment, filled with shapeless stuffed chairs and dark lithographs, in a shabby building on Madison Avenue, like all of Julia's cocktail parties, was only the accumulation of her married friends. One should break away, she thought with discouragement, as she looked about her. There was no future in this. Life gave a girl only a few years in which to marry; afterwards she was swept on remorselessly in the ineligible company of her more successful contemporaries. She went over to confer with the old butler who had been hired for the evening.

"Less vermouth on the next round," she told him. "And don't keep giving people new glasses. Fill up their old ones."

How they jabbered, she thought irritably, as she turned back to the living room. Now that they had left their babies in competent hands and their apartments neat and clean, they could put on their cute little party dresses and join their husbands at Julia's, poor, dear, irresponsible Julia's, and drink too many cocktails. After all, it was all right for them; it happened so rarely and they worked so hard, but poor Julia . . . well, what *did* Julia do all day?

"What a nice apartment this is, Julia," one of them was saying to her; "it must be wonderful to live here. You know, I forget sometimes, since I've been married, how well our parents do live."

"Julia, you'll forgive me if I rush off now. Little Tommy has a cold . . ."

"When are you coming to see your godson, Julia? He keeps asking for 'Auntie Hoolia' now."

Damn them all, she breathed to herself. Were they *trying* to hurt her? They looked her straight in the eye and dared her to say that she was bored by their children. They knew she wouldn't. How well they knew! She saw Philip come in.

"No wifey?" she asked him. "Everybody here has a little wifey. You'll be quite left out."

"Sybil's gone out to Greenwich for the night," he explained. "She said to tell you how sorry she was."

"How sorry was that? But never mind. I'm glad she's not here. I need a man to myself. Grab a drink and come talk to me."

Philip had always enjoyed himself with Julia, and he liked the feeling of not being watched by Sybil. After a couple of cocktails he was having a thoroughly good time. Julia had abandoned her other guests and was sitting alone with him in a corner.

"I don't know why I give these ghastly parties," she said. "It's like some ancient fertility rite that goes on and on, long after it's lost its significance. Sybil's so wise to stay away. But then Sybil *is* wise."

"Why is Sybil so wise?" he asked.

"My dear, she managed to steal you out from under my very eyes. And nobody even suspected her, either. Until she walked off with the season's catch. Oh, she's deep, that girl. No question."

Philip laughed. He was pleased.

"Was I the season's catch?"

"Well, you know, I think you were." She looked at him critically for a moment. "Of course, you were thinner then. More hair, too. I was mad for you."

"And now I've lost my charm?"

She laughed.

"Listen to him!" she exclaimed. "How you eat it up! But not from me, boy. You've got your Sybil. Let her butter you up. She's paid for it."

He laughed again.

"Why aren't you married, Julia?"

"Oh, go to hell."

They kept being interrupted by couples arriving or leaving, but he stayed by her side. The Julia of whom he had vaguely disapproved in his law-school days, a Julia who had seemed a small-scale replica of his mother and her friends, was now a person in keeping with his post-war point of view. Her air of jaded superiority intrigued him. She made him feel, but not unpleasantly, like a young boy whom, for the moment, she fancied.

"How about dinner tonight?" he suggested.

She looked at him with more interest.

"After the party?"

"No, now. Let's get out of here."

Julia made a rapid calculation. Most of the people had left, and her parents could be trusted to look after the hangers-on. If she stayed, for manners' sake, she would be left to sup coldly on the remainder of the hors d'oeuvres. It was the kind of decision that she made quickly, but one could see that she was making it.

"All right," she said. "Let's blow."

In the taxi he suggested Truro's, a particularly expensive restaurant, before she had to. Her only worry was whether she would have to pretend it was her birthday to make him order champagne. This turned out to be unnecessary.

"Let's pretend it's somebody's birthday," he suggested when they were seated at their table. "And order a bottle of champagne."

Really, he was perfect. Julia quite cheered up.

"How nice to get away from that stuffy party," she said, settling back in her seat and lighting a cigarette, "and to be taken out by somebody else's husband. What else could a girl want?"

Philip laughed, but he was busy ordering the dinner. She

didn't have to make any suggestions as he ordered all the most expensive things.

"You know it's fun to take someone out who really likes good food and champagne," he began.

"They must be so hard to find, too."

"Well Sybil always likes to dine at home," he explained. "Not that that isn't fun, of course," he added cautiously. "But a guy likes to go out every now and then. The Rodmans are great ones for reading aloud and things like that. Sybil and her mother, that is. And Teddy." If Philip had something on his mind he came to it directly, regardless of what other topic might have been offered. He was anxious, in his way, to be loyal, but it was impossible for him to keep off his own affairs.

"I know what you mean," she said. "I used to play with Teddy as a child. While Sybil hid upstairs. He was always thinking up games about being Elizabeth and Essex. Of a deadliness, my dear. You can't imagine. Or can you?"

He nodded.

"Did Aunt Jo play too?"

"Did she!" Julia raised her eyebrows. "I'll say. She was Arty, the life of the party. She'd even dress up." She finished her cocktail. "But leave us draw a decent curtain over that. They're not bad old things, Mrs. Cummings and Mrs. Rodman. If you like the type. Which I don't."

Philip had never heard Sybil's family so freely discussed, even by his own mother.

"If Sybil could hear you!" he exclaimed.

"It wouldn't surprise her in the least," Julia said coolly, taking out her compact and going to work on her lips in the deliberate way that she had. "She's always disapproved of me. Because I wasn't nice to Teddy. Or was it because I was too nice to him? I never can remember. Of course, she's always been incestuous about Teddy." She pursed her lips as she applied the lipstick. There was something infinitely assured and arrogant in the way she turned their table into a ladies' room. "I wonder you're not jealous."

But Philip had no desire to explore new and ill-considered theories about Sybil and Teddy. The most·that he required of his friends was that they should confirm his own presuppositions.

"Do you ever get the impression, Julia," he asked more probingly, "that Sybil is just a bit . . . well, flattened?" He swallowed. "As if she'd been sat on when she was little?"

Julia gave a peal of laughter.

"Sat on!" she exclaimed. "You mean run over by a truck! Of course! By Mrs. Rodman. And just as she was dragging herself out of the road, poor creature, Aunt Jo came by and knocked her out for the count!"

At the pop of the cork Julia transferred all her interest to the bottle that the waiter was now pouring.

"She's so tense," Philip continued, preoccupied. "She wants everybody to have such feeling about things."

"Probably because she hasn't any herself," she said, taking a drink from her brimming glass. "That's usually the way, isn't it?"

When she turned to look at him, she was struck by his seriousness, and it occurred to her for the first time that he might be something more than the bored husband to whom she had become so drearily accustomed. This was a possibility that shed a very different light on things. Julia was not a person to discard a solution to her problems, particularly when that solution was tossed in her lap. She had not made her remarks about the Rodmans from any ulterior motive; it was simply her usual way of talking. Now, she decided, she would have to concentrate.

"Phil," she asked suddenly, "are you and Sybil splitting up?"

He was shocked. But not overly so. Philip was crude; he was relieved by directness.

"Gosh, no," he protested. "What makes you say that?"

"The fact that you want to buy another woman champagne," she said, shrugging her shoulders. "So you can complain to her about your wife."

"But you're sympathetic, Julia," he said, smiling. "You have no idea how sympathetic you are."

"For a bottle of champagne and a dinner at Truro's?" she retorted. "You're darn right I'm sympathetic!"

"And I thought it was all because I was such a handsome guy," he said, pretending to look hurt. "Are you sure it's only the champagne, Julia?"

Somewhat to her surprise, for it was early in the evening, she felt his arm stealing around her back. Decidedly, it was too soon. Firmly, decisively, but not humiliatingly, she removed it.

"Don't be so sure of yourself, Philip Hilliard," she said coolly. "There are a lot of things I'm interested in, and looks happen to be only one of them." She smiled at him as the waiter fussed with their plates. "Even looks like yours, dear."

She had not been unfair. It was not her fault if her candor should have been, of all things, the most intriguing to him. She had never studied people, even young men, closely enough to determine their preferences. They had a long talk about the difficulties of mismated couples, and in the taxi going home she was able to make him keep his distance with little more than a gesture. Decidedly, she had not done badly. When she got out he begged her not to tell anyone what he had said about Sybil.

This she passed off lightly.

"I wouldn't dream of telling a soul, Phil," she said with mock gravity. "Except your Aunt Jo. And Mrs. Rodman. And dear Nicholas. Of course, I tell *them* everything."

Chapter
Seven

SO, ANYWAY, it started. It would not be fair to say that Philip went home that night infatuated, but he had certainly decided that he wanted to be, and by the following morning he had decided that he was. Julia had become overnight the main interest in his life. He began planning, in his orderly way, how best to go on seeing her. The traditional way, always the way that would appeal to Philip, was to plead business as an excuse for staying out at night, so he devised a series of fictional real estate operations to engage his spare time for at least a month. Sybil believed him implicitly, and his scheme derived a totally unexpected support from his father, who told her, for no reason at all, that Philip was working too hard. Mr. Hilliard had a way of picking up impressions without any basis of fact and of stating them so firmly that others were convinced of their accuracy. It was now late spring, and Philip solved the summer problem by suggesting that Sybil go to Aunt Jo's in Easton Bay, where he could join her for weekends. Easton Bay was within commuting distance of the city, but he had always made it clear that he would not commute. Sybil was not enthusiastic; for the first time her feelings were really hurt.

"I thought you didn't like Easton Bay," she pointed out. "And, darling, I'd be away from you all during the week."

"Oh, I like Easton Bay all right," he said hastily. "That was just a pre-war prejudice."

There was a pause.

"Darling, was *I* a pre-war prejudice?"

He kissed her, with sincerity, in anticipation of the success of his plan.

"I want you to get Timmy out of the heat," he explained. "If you want to be cool you've got to move. It's as simple as that."

"We could go to your mother's in Glenville," she said, more doubtfully.

But Philip had no idea of allowing his wife and mother to combine forces. Any such combination, under the circumstances, was sure to be against him.

"It's as hot there as in the city," he said decisively. "Besides, I feel more independent at Aunt Jo's."

Sybil, as usual, was obedient, and by the end of June he was spending every evening from Monday through Thursday in Julia's company. This, however, was not altogether plain sailing. Julia had no qualms about breaking up a home; she had every intention of becoming the second Mrs. Hilliard. To her the whole matter of marriage and divorce was so completely a game, in which no holds were barred, that she found it actually difficult to understand people who felt otherwise. But acquiring a married man was a harder business than acquiring a bachelor, and Julia was not endowed with the discipline needed to maintain a pose of being pleasant, even when everything that she most cared about depended on it. She disliked, for example, staying in town after the middle of June. "It's all very well for you," she would tell Philip. "You have your job. But what am I expected to do all day?" She disliked even more his reluctance to discuss the question of divorce. She had shown no squeamishness about becoming his mistress; she had decided, and rightly, that he was not the kind of man whose interest would increase with frustration. She had joined with him, however, in taking every precaution to make their affair a discreet one. Sex to Julia was primarily a business matter in which one could never lose sight of the ultimate goal.

"When are you going to tell Sybil?" she asked him one night as they sat at the bar of Truro's. It was one of what Philip called their "free" nights, when, because of their habitual caution, they thought they could afford to be seen dining together, as old friends, in a restaurant where they were apt to see people they knew. "Do you think you're being entirely fair to her?"

He looked uneasily away.

"It'll keep," he said. "Wait till the fall."

"You might as well know now, Philip Hilliard," she continued in a more irritable tone, "that I have no idea of going on with this Back Street life indefinitely. After all, I didn't go to Miss Heely's school and bust my family coming out in order to end up as a kept woman."

"Now, Julia."

"I know it's going to hurt Sybil and all that," she went on, "but, after all, it's got to come sooner or later. You can't go on indefinitely being married to someone you don't care about."

"No, but you don't understand, Julia. It's so difficult to tell Sybil. She's so . . . well, it sounds conceited to say so, but she's so wound up in me."

Julia shrugged her shoulders.

"She'll get a good settlement," she said. "She'll be all right."

Philip did not like this at all. He did not like to have Julia assume so easily that any woman whom he abandoned would ever again be "all right," and, like a true Hilliard, he loathed the idea of having to make a settlement.

"Sybil doesn't care about those things."

"Well, she'd better learn," Julia said crossly. "These moony, impracticable girls make me tired. They make the rest of us seem so mercenary. But I notice that they always seem to get what they want in the end. After all, she landed you."

This was what Julia could never forget. Sybil had not been Philip's "type." It had not been in Julia's scheme of things that he should have liked her. Therefore, it was a perfectly proper thing to supplant her.

"I know it's hard on you, darling," Philip said more soothingly. "But leave it to me. I shall know when to act."

He really meant this. Julia's temper had not yet diminished his infatuation. In fact he found it rather a relief after the almost cringing quality of Sybil's submission. Julia, like himself, was of the world. She understood him, and she did not mind his understanding her. He would rather have continued on the existing basis with her, but if this was not to be, he was willing to take the steps required. There would be consequences and more consequences, scenes and more scenes; he would have to face his own family as well as Sybil's, but in the end he would have corrected his early error and started life again with a wife of his adult choosing. He was almost thirty and knew his own mind. Divorce, after all, was not the worst thing in the world. His sister, Lila, was in Reno at this very time.

Chapter

Eight

AS AUTUMN APPROACHED, Sybil at last began to feel uneasy. Philip had come down for only four weekends during the entire summer and had taken no more than ten days' vacation. She had heard twice from solicitous friends who had seen him with Julia Anderton. She had not mentioned this, but he had seen fit to explain to her that when he was lonely in town he sometimes took out an old girl friend and "gave her a whirl." Her mother, who was also at Aunt Jo's, took a poor view of his non-appearances, and questioned Sybil closely about the nature of his real estate work.

"I thought all he had to do was collect rents," she said.

"Oh, it's much more than that," Sybil explained. "You have to buy strategically and get control of corners and that sort of thing."

"Do you do it on weekends, too?" Esther asked bleakly.

"I suppose you must."

One Saturday after lunch she was sitting on the terrace by the rhododendrons reading aloud a Burgess story to Timmy. Aunt Jo and the others were upstairs resting, in the true Easton Bay tradition of how best to spend an afternoon in the country. Philip had telephoned to say that he was coming down for the weekend, and she was waiting for the sound of his car on the drive, hoping to catch him alone for a few minutes before he went off to play golf at Glenville with Felicia's husband. Timmy, however, did not allow her attention to wander; he sat beside her on the canvas-covered sofa, one hand on her knee, peering intently up into her face as she read. He had not turned into a Hilliard. At least not yet. He was four and a half now and very thin, with spindly arms and legs and wide, cheerful blue eyes. Sybil loved him in her own tense, concentrated way; she worried about his being an only child and being too much with her and Ellen, but she had no definite idea what to do about it. He seemed, despite her worry, robust for a child so thin and unexpectedly outgiving.

"Sammy Jay was certainly sorry that he had said what he had said to Blacky the Crow," she read aloud. "Yes, sir, Sammy Jay was very sorry indeed. In fact, he was the sorriest jay —— "

She heard the roar of wheels on the drive from the other side of the house, and stopped.

"Don't stop, Mummie."

She stared out over the lawn, ignoring him. Then she heard the screen door to the front hall slam.

"Mummie, please go on. Please go on, Mummie!"

"Darling, I think I hear Daddy."

Philip came out on the terrace, the evening paper folded under his arm. He leaned down to kiss her and put his hand on the back of Timmy's neck.

"Darling," she said. "It's been a long week."

"Terrible." He sat down on a chair opposite and reached over to pick up Timmy and put him on his lap. "How are you, old man? Been looking after Mummie?"

"Mummie was reading to me about Sammy Jay," Timmy explained in his high voice. "Do we have to stop now?"

"Just for a bit," Philip answered. "Then Daddy's going off to play golf."

"Philip," Sybil said timidly, "I know you can't tell ahead of time, but I was wondering if you had an idea . . . any idea . . . how long this period of night work was going to last."

He put both arms around Timmy and looked down at the top of the boy's head.

"Hard to say. Why?"

"I thought I might move back to town."

He looked up at her.

"And roast this kid in the city?" he demanded. "I wouldn't hear of it."

"Oh, Timmy could stay here," she pointed out quickly. "Heaven knows there are plenty of people to look after him. Mother and Ellen. To say nothing of Aunt Jo. You wouldn't mind, dear, would you," she continued, speaking to Timmy, "if Mummie left you here with Grandma and Ellen for a few days?"

Timmy was playing with Philip's fountain pen which he had taken out of his pocket.

"I wouldn't mind," he said.

Sybil looked down at her clasped hands. She was ashamed to be so hurt by a child. Was she going to be like her own mother? She looked up and smiled.

"You see, Philip," she said, "what I mean to you all."

Philip gave the boy a little shake.

"Don't say that to Mummie," he said. "Of course, you'd mind if she went away! No, Sib," he continued to her, "it's out of the question. It's perfectly absurd for you to be running into town every time I'm held over at the office. That's kid stuff. I won't have it."

"But, darling, if I *want* to be in town?"

"Sybil, for Pete's sake, can't you drop it?" he said irritably, getting up. "You make too much of things. Hi there, Aunt Jo!" he said eagerly, as the latter appeared in the doorway. "How have you *been*? It must be swell to be out here all week. It's hotter than Hades in town!"

Sybil resolved to go into it again with him later that afternoon, but she found him evasive and, when she finally
cornered him, positively angry. This frightened her, and as
she did not know what to do, she did nothing. She cultivated
a desperate hope that if she ignored the whole problem, it
might turn out not to exist. The end of August and September passed. It was her sister-in-law, Millie, who finally
compelled her to face the facts, shortly after Sybil had
moved back to town for the winter.

She and Millie got on as well as could be expected, considering their basic lack of congeniality. Millie herself
would have liked to develop the relationship. She would
have enjoyed the rôle of older sister and the long, intimate
chats in which her extra year of age and social experience
might have given her a lead. But this was not to be expected
with a sister-in-law who cared nothing for the little things
that filled Millie's life.

"She doesn't think the way other people think," Millie
used to protest to Teddy. "I always seem to be saying the
wrong thing to her and putting my foot in it."

What provoked Sybil about Millie was the way that she
exploited her own helplessness. Millie might always be in-
viting the world to admire the excellence of her domestic
arrangements, but these arrangements were rarely the ac-
complishment of the gentle, poised creature who so proclaimed them. Behind the pretty backdrop of Millie's independence labored the unseen stagehands who made it possible for the show to go on. There was primarily, of course,
Teddy, infinitely patient and attentive; then there was
Esther who saw to it that the maid was kept and the cleaning woman sent in, who took the children when Millie was
"tired," and sent supplies and arranged for repairs; there
was Uncle Stafford who supplemented Teddy's income and
Aunt Jo who gave Millie parties and bought her novels and
took her to the opera. And it was all done, too, with the

sense that if it wasn't done, Millie, at any moment, might simply collapse on her pretty pink-coverleted bed and never get up, for that was the way Millie would do it, if she ever did it. Without warning. Not that she had ever threatened this or anything like it. But one knew, if one was her husband or aunt or mother-in-law, that Millie's motor was a small, delicate, one-cylinder affair, like a machine in a child's toy, not really designed to move its vehicle forward except, once in a while, over a smooth carpet, before admiring eyes. If Millie were to be kept moving, as life seemed so remorselessly to require, through emotions and events hardly fitted for her, it would only be by grace of the pushing and pulling that had to be carried on, unseen of the audience, by wires leading to and from the wings. And it had worked, at least so far. Millie moved gracefully across the stage and seemed, indeed, to put her sister-in-law in the shadow. She was Jo's and Esther's masterpiece.

Millie called Sybil on the telephone after the latter's return from Easton Bay and suggested that they go shopping. It was the kind of excursion that they usually made together once a month. When Sybil went to their club to meet her at the appointed hour, she found, as usual, that Millie was late.

"Darling," Millie said when she finally appeared at the door of the waiting room. "I'm miserable to have kept you. But my cleaning woman's had to stay with that son of hers who's always getting sick. I had to call Mrs. Rodman to get me someone."

"Poor Mummie."

"Don't be silly, dear. She *likes* being efficient."

Sybil put down her magazine, and they started forth. Before counters heaped with gloves Millie tried on pair after pair, holding her hand out in front of her and turning it this way and that; in front of glass shelves bearing little bottles and enormous powder puffs she sniffed and made faces. Sybil showed what interest she could, but Millie did not need advice. She only wanted to have her disinclinations confirmed.

"But you haven't bought a thing for yourself, Sybil," she protested during the absence of a salesman in search of a black silk slipper with a pinker bow. "And that's what I really had in mind for this morning."

"Oh, I have plenty of things."

"Sybil, that isn't so." Millie became very serious on the subject of clothes. It was the only field in which she could assert authority over her sister-in-law. "You've got plenty of those plain suits that you always wear. They're good for that boyish note you like, I grant. But has it never occurred to you, my dear, that you're getting just a wee bit old for that?"

Sybil laughed.

"Maybe so, Millie. I wasn't trying to be boyish. I just hadn't thought about it."

"But shouldn't you think about it?"

Sybil looked at her more attentively. Millie never kept the conversation away from herself unless she had something significant to say. Something, anyway, that Millie regarded as significant.

"Does my appearance embarrass you, Millie?" she asked in a different tone. "Please tell me if it does."

Millie immediately became warm and confidential. She patted Sybil's arm.

"Of course, you don't embarrass me, darling," she said. "Don't be so prickly. But people who are always reading books and thinking big thoughts sometimes forget the little things in life that help. There's nothing wrong with your being an intellectual, dear. I'm all for it. But you can be intellectual and buy a new hat, can't you?"

"What shall I buy, Millie? You be the judge."

"Something feminine," Millie said promptly. "And winning. Something that's helpless without being helpless. If you see what I mean."

"Winning?" Sybil repeated. "Whom do you want me to win, Millie?"

In the pause that followed Sybil realized for the first time that Millie was embarrassed.

"Maybe I should have said — win back," she answered in a low voice, looking down at the floor affectedly. There was a long pause. When Sybil broke it, it was on a dry note.

"I didn't know my troubles were so public," she said. "Do you think, Millie, that Philip is a man to be won back with a hat? If he's lost, that is?"

"Certainly I do!" she exclaimed, obviously relieved that she had not been the one to bring up his name. "Anything that catches his eye. And makes him look at you differently. What does Julia have to offer him, I'd like to know? If you lose him to Julia, darling, it will be a case of default. Pure and simple."

The atmosphere in the long pink room of evening slippers and jeweled buckles, of round bottles of perfume in glass cases, of silk stockings draped over French dolls, the sense, in short, of an overwhelming femininity was suddenly stifling to Sybil, as if her nose had been buried in a huge powder puff. They mocked her, these things; they seemed to say with a sneer: Do you think we don't know men, Sybil? After all the centuries? And did you really think you could defy *us*?

"Oh, Millie," she said miserably, "I'm so ignorant about these things. Does he really like Julia? I didn't know. Millie," she continued, putting a hand on her arm, "what shall I do? Am I going to lose him? Does he really see her all the time?"

Millie was overwhelmed by this sudden flood of appeal; it was more than she had bargained for. Luckily, at just this moment, the salesman returned with her slipper. Raising her finger to her lips and detaching her arm from Sybil's grasp, she continued the conversation as though they were discussing a mutual friend.

"But I thought you knew about her, my dear," she said. "He's been taking her out all summer."

Sybil's head reeled.

"I knew he saw her," she murmured. "But not like that. I didn't really think it was that sort of thing."

"It's *always* that sort of thing," Millie said decisively. "Always. No, that's still too big," she continued to the salesman. "And too pink. Have you anything with a lavender bow?"

"I'll see, ma'am."

"The thing to remember, darling," Millie continued hastily, before Sybil could break down again, "is that it won't take much to beat her. I'm not really worried about you, to tell the truth. But you've got to brighten yourself up a bit. Julia's too disagreeable to hold any man for long. She's bound to hang herself, given enough rope. But if I were you, Sib, I wouldn't give her any rope at all."

"But do I want to fight for Philip?" Sybil protested. "Has it come to that? And if it has, should I?"

"Nonsense, my dear," her sister-in-law retorted. "Any woman must fight for her man." Millie had become a character in any, in every play. "You mustn't be a doormat," she continued. "Doormats are what men step on on their way to other people's houses."

Sybil stood up. It was unendurable that Millie should know more about her life than she did.

"That all may be quite true, Millie," she said with as much dignity as she could muster. "But it may also be that some things aren't worth fighting for."

And turning, she went swiftly out of the hated shop.

·　　·　　·

She walked for three blocks without thinking of anything and turned into Central Park. Then she tried to think that she was stunned; she was even conscious of her own disappointment that her mind should be functioning as clearly as it was. Could one be overwhelmed or even disappointed when one was alone? Did human relations have only to do with humans in company? And then it all came over her again, and she had to sit down on a bench. My God, she said to herself, I want to die. I really do.

When she arrived at her mother-in-law's table at the restaurant where Lucy always lunched, she found her with Viola Paton drinking vermouth cassis. Lucy took in her paleness and her stare and knew what was wrong.

"Have a drink, child," she said. "You look as if you needed one."

Sybil sat down between them.

"Thank you," she said.

"Have you been shopping?" Lucy continued. "Or have you just seen a ghost? Viola, my dear, you've scared the child. It's that dreadful powder of yours."

But Viola raised her hand.

"Lucy, I think she's ill."

Sybil shook her head.

"It's only that I'm not modern," she said in a level voice. "I heard just now that my husband is in love with someone else. We're brought up to take these things in our stride. I should be able to keep my chin up. But I can't."

Lucy and Viola exchanged a quick glance.

"You're not jumping to conclusions, I hope," Lucy said sharply, "because he's been seen out once or twice with Julia Anderton?"

"I know all about it, Mrs. Hilliard," Sybil said.

Viola showed tactful signs of leaving the table, but Lucy shook her head abruptly. She wanted her to stand by for possible emergency duty. Lucy, like a true admiral, never underestimated the gravity of a situation. She was ready, as at the clang of a general quarters alarm, to take her station and assume command. For this was not to her a minor matter, like Lila's shedding of her inconsequential husband. This was different. This was Philip.

"You know all about it, fiddlesticks," she said in her rough, kindly tone. "You don't know a thing about it, my dear. You probably think this Julia is the first. But if I know my Hilliard men, and I'm afraid I do, she isn't. Oh, I know how you feel. Like lying down and giving up. And nobody could blame you for a minute. Phil's been a bad boy, and we're going to give him a bad time. But it isn't the end, Sybil. Not by a long shot."

"Please, Mrs. Hilliard . . ."

"Let me be, dear. I know best. Now, Viola, you stay here with Sybil and order her a double something. I'll be back in a minute."

Lucy got up briskly and went to the manager's little office. "I shall need your telephone, Henri, for about five minutes. It's important."

"Certainly, Mrs. Hilliard."

He moved quickly about, fussing, getting her an ash tray, cleaning off his desk. Then he left the room, closing the door softly behind him. Lucy checked her little red hand book and dialed Philip's business number.

"It's Mrs. Hilliard. I want to speak to my son," she told the girl who answered.

"I'm sorry, Mrs. Hilliard. He's on another wire. Can I —— "

"Cut him off," she said abruptly. In a few moments she heard Philip's voice. He sounded peeved.

"What is it, Ma?"

"Look here, Philip Hilliard," she began firmly, "I'm here at Henri's with Sybil. She's found out all about you and that Anderton girl, and she looks ready to jump in the river.

I want you to put your hat on and come around here as fast as you can and tell her that you're through with that woman once and for all."

There was a silence, heavy with his consternation.

"What do you know about me and Julia?"

"Whatever there is to know," she retorted. "You're so damn naïve, Philip. You're like a smug little goldfish that doesn't know we're all watching you. Everyone's known about you all summer except Sybil, poor creature."

There was another silence.

"Why didn't you tell me?" he demanded.

"Because I thought you'd be over it by now." Her tone relented as she sensed his confusion. "It's nothing but damn nonsense. I know that, and you know it. But Sybil cares so terribly. Why don't you come over now, dear, and reassure her. The poor child thinks her marriage is on the rocks."

She heard him take a deep breath.

"But I can't reassure her," he said. "I was going to tell her this week, anyway. I want a divorce, Ma. Julia and I are going to get married."

"Are you crazy?" she almost shouted. "Do you want to make yourself a complete laughingstock?"

"You're just going to say something you'll regret," he said, anger taking the place of his surprise. "You always do, you know. Remember how you were when Sybil and I were engaged?"

"That was then," she snapped, "and this is now. That girl's made you a perfect wife. Do you want to throw her over for some tart who's after your money?"

"Mother!"

But when Lucy was angry there was no stopping her.

"Well, there won't be any money, my fine sir," she continued explosively; "that's what you'll find out. If you think your father and I are going into the business of supporting tramps ——"

"You seem to forget that I have my own money," he said frigidly.

"Then it's all you ever will have!"

Philip would have hung up except that he wanted to give her a message for Sybil. Besides, he had had enough experience with his mother's temper to know how quickly it could come and go.

"This is not dignified, Mother," he said. "Will you kindly allow me to handle my own life and be good enough to tell Sybil that I shall come to the apartment to see her as soon as she's through with you?"

"I'll bust that trust I set up for you," Lucy continued wrathfully. "I'll sue you and get it back!"

This time he did hang up. Lucy returned to her table, trembling with anger, but aware that she had allowed her temper to interfere with her strategy. She was almost shamefaced when she took her seat between Sybil and Viola.

"There's nothing to worry about," she said; "it's going to take a little time, that's all."

Sybil had not said a word in her absence. She was still numb; she had a curious, almost intriguing feeling of being isolated, without being able to communicate, behind the frozen wall of her own pain. But when she saw the discomfort in her mother-in-law's eyes she roused herself.

"You've been talking to Philip?" she asked.

"Yes. But just for a minute. As you saw, my dear."

"He wants to marry her, doesn't he?" she continued.

"Darling, he's got some crazy Hilliard notion in his head," Lucy admitted nervously. "But it doesn't mean a thing. Wait till I've talked to him, really talked to him, and wait till his father has ——— "

"But he *does* want to marry her?" Sybil pursued.

"Well, he thinks he does. Now."

"If he wants to," Sybil said clearly, "he shall."

She listened impassively to Lucy's and Viola's protesta-

tions. When Lucy finally told her that Philip was going back
to their apartment to see her, she got up and left the restaurant to meet him.

At home she sat in a chair in the middle of the living
room to smoke a cigarette and wait. She realized, as her eyes
roamed over the walls and furniture, that it was not a good
room. Most of the things in it had been wedding presents or
loans; the Chippendale chairs had come from Lucy; the
eighteenth-century flower prints along the walls, slightly
faded, belonged to Aunt Jo; an Aubusson carpet, unhappy
in its surroundings, had been the gift of the Hilliard aunts.
Her own things, books and prints and photostats of docu-
ments, were scattered about, but not in a way or of a nature
to pull the room into any sort of coherence. She had not
cared about coherence. Maybe Millie was right; maybe such
things mattered. It was Millie's world and Philip's world
and even Julia's; there was no point resenting it. If they all
wanted it their way, why should they not have it? She heard
the rumble of the elevator doors and then Philip's key in
the lock.

"Sybil?" he called from the hall.

"In here."

She watched him as he came into the room. He looked
self-conscious and embarrassed, but his eyes did not try to
avoid hers. He sat down on the sofa and lit a cigarette.

"I understand Ma's spilled the beans," he said.

"Millie told me."

"How did Millie know?"

Sybil only shrugged her shoulders.

"There's no point in my saying I've been a heel, Sib," he
said. "That's too obvious. There really isn't much point in
my saying anything, I suppose. We were probably too
young when we married. Now I want to marry Julia. That
seems to be about it."

As she looked at him and heard him actually say it she

felt the tears that she had determined to hold back.

"Oh, Philip."

"I'm awfully sorry, Sib," he said unhappily.

She put her hand over her eyes.

"You needn't be," she said. "I always knew that I wasn't the person for you. I wanted to be. God knows I wanted to be." She paused for a few seconds to keep back a sob. "But I wasn't. I knew you, and you didn't know me. So I was the guilty one. I've had several happy years, and that's all I have coming to me. If you want Julia now, you should have her."

He got up and went over to her to stop the flood of self-abasement. He put his arm around her shoulders, but she even kissed his hand.

"Sib," he protested. "For Christ's sake!"

"I trapped you into it, anyway," she continued wildly. "You can have your divorce! Of course, you can have it!"

She had forgotten her lines; she had collapsed entirely. She could only bury her face in her hands and sob without pretense of control. For she knew, even in the darkness that was engulfing her, that she had reached the nadir of her humiliation; she knew that she had embarrassed and disgusted him beyond hope of repair. But if it was too late, why should she care? Was she not already beginning to feel, deep down, an odd, resentful satisfaction that she should be acting so exactly as he must have expected her to act?

Chapter

Nine

PHILIP MOVED OUT of the apartment that same day and took a room at his club. The following morning the separation and the proposed divorce became generally known. Feeling ran high and was largely antagonistic to Philip. Lucy Hilliard carried on her campaign against Julia by announcing as publicly as possible that all of her sympathies were with her daughter-in-law. Sybil's refusal to fight disgusted her.

"It seems rather hard that nobody should be lifting a finger to save your marriage except myself," she told her crossly.

"You're very kind, Mrs. Hilliard," Sybil said firmly. "And I can't tell you what it's meant to me. But I have to do what I believe is right, don't I? What does anything else matter?"

Next to Lucy, Aunt Jo was the person most upset by the news. It filled her with disappointment and remorse that the handsome and eligible young man whom she had so recommended to her sister should turn out as Esther had predicted. She was very snappish with the Misses Hilliard when they insinuated that their nephew might not be the only one at fault. This suspicion had its origin not so much in their partiality for Philip as in their general distrust of his whole generation, a distrust which they cherished suffi- ciently to find the news about him and Sybil not totally dis- tasteful.

"The way children are brought up today," Miss Emily said sadly, when she and her sister called on Aunt Jo, "one can't really expect anything else. They marry whenever they choose, whomever they choose, and at the first little snag — poof! — they're off to Reno."

"I might point out that Sybil was not brought up that way, Emily," Aunt Jo answered in a voice that had a slight tremble. "Nor is the home atmosphere at my sister's in the least comparable to the atmosphere at Lucy's. Sybil, it seems to me, has been a good wife by the standards of any of us."

"Of course, Jo."

"Nobody was criticizing Sybil, you know."

All heads nodded, and the subject was changed.

George Rodman did a great deal of blustering about his son-in-law's reprehensible conduct, but he did none of it to Philip. Teddy seemed the least surprised of the family and said almost nothing, while Millie went about telling her friends how different things would have been if "poor Sybil" had only listened to her. Philip's sisters were distressed, but they did not take divorce seriously. Arlina Hilliard, the youngest and Sybil's particular champion, squeezed all the drama out of it of which she was capable.

"My sister-in-law," she would whisper to her friends darkly at débutante parties, "has had to put up with things that I could never have put up with. *Never!*"

Esther was the person who accepted the matter with the greatest resignation. Her concern had always been over future catastrophe; she could show commendable calm when faced with the actual event. As long as she had made her sacrifices, as long as she had put in her quota of worry, did the ultimate decision really concern her?

"It may be difficult for you to see it now, dear," she told Sybil in her wisest tone, "but this could be one cloud that really has a silver lining. I never thought you were made for that Hilliard life. I know it's painful for you to admit that, but we might as well look at the bright side of things. If there is one. You are what you are."

"You mean I am what you've made me," Sybil said dryly.

"Perhaps." She had no patience with any of them. The mist of convention that covered the termination of her marriage seemed as thick and cloying as the mist that had covered its commencement.

Philip had told her that she must have a lawyer and to everyone's surprise she had turned, not to Teddy, but to Nicholas. His impersonality was a balm after so much family solicitation, and underneath it she felt an unexpressed sympathy which was the only kind that she wanted. When she went to consult him in his office downtown, he listened to her story, his large eyes fixed upon her, without saying a word. After she had finished he twisted his big gold signet ring around a long finger. Then he moved an ivory paper cutter from one side of his desk to the other.

"So you propose," he said, "to go to Nevada and get a divorce there. You propose further to accept any settlement that the Hilliards may offer. And, finally, you propose to have a loose, informal arrangement about the custody of your child. I see. There's only one thing that I don't quite understand."

"And what is that?"

"What you need a lawyer for."

She looked at him blankly.

"But aren't there papers and things to be drawn?"

"Not for unconditional surrender. Let the Hilliards draw them."

"Oh, I know it seems terrible to you, Nicholas," she said, "but I can't be technical with Philip. I know it looks as if he's behaved badly, but there's more than one side to every picture —— "

"Is there enough on Philip's side," he interrupted, in his clear, legal voice, "to justify your having to commit perjury in Reno for his sake?"

"Perjury?"

"Exactly that." He looked at her gravely. "You will be obliged to state under oath that you intend to reside permanently in Nevada. I am assuming that this will not be your intention. What is that but perjury?"

It was never possible, in arguments with Nicholas, to know what moral significance he gave to facts.

"Suppose I get the divorce in New York?" she suggested.

He nodded immediately.

"Much better," he said. "Then it will not only be honest but airtight." He paused for a second to watch her. "Of course, we will have to prove that Philip has committed adultery. But from what you have told me, I don't anticipate much difficulty with that."

Sybil flushed.

"Oh, Nicholas!" she exclaimed. "You know that's out of the question!"

He raised his eyebrows inquiringly.

"I fail to see why," he said coolly. "As a formula it fits the facts. Miss Anderton may not like it, but I can't imagine why we should consider her feelings. The divorce, when granted, would be valid beyond question, and, as I would handle it, instead of a Reno lawyer, it would cost you nothing. There might be a few disagreeable articles in the tabloids, but I can't see why we should care. Certainly the Hilliards can rise above a little publicity."

She shook her head.

"I couldn't do it, Nicholas," she said. "You know I couldn't. There must be some other state."

"You have this idea, Sybil," he said severely, "that it's

proper for a wife to give her husband a divorce for the asking. Unfortunately, that is not the premise on which the laws of divorce are based."

She sat back patiently.

"What *should* I do then, Nicholas?"

"I would suggest, to begin with," he said, as they turned at last to the practical remedy, "that I draw up a separation agreement to be signed here." He stared over her head at the gloomy print of Chief Justice Taney on the wall behind her. Nicholas had all the mannerisms of his profession, the steady stare, the occasional nod, the alternating slow-fast tempo of speech and the precise, almost defiant enunciation of legal terms. "This agreement would provide for a substantial property settlement, and it would give you absolute custody of Timmy. Philip will sign it. He's hardly in a position not to. This will not mean, of course, that he can never see the child, but it will place the matter in your discretion."

Was it resentment, she asked herself. Was it that which made him so anxious to penalize Philip, to disgrace him? She wondered if everyone, like herself, really envied the Philips of the world.

"When all that has been arranged," he continued in the same metallic tone, "but not a minute sooner, we can entertain the question of divorce. But I can see no reason why you should go to Reno. Let him go. *He* wants his freedom. Let him perjure himself."

There was a moment of silence. He had had his fun now; he had finished.

"I know you're the best friend in the world, Nicholas," she said, "and I know that you've given me the best advice. I knew, of course, that you would." She stood up. "But my hands won't be any cleaner for not going to Reno. It's all part of the same thing. If I have to be a perjurer, I have to be a perjurer. I've told Philip I'll do what he wants. And

I'm sure that you'll help me no matter how much it goes against the grain. I'll call you when his lawyers are ready to come and see us."

After she had gone, he sat there alone, still looking at the picture of Chief Justice Taney. Of course, she was right. He *would* do as she asked. But he could not help wondering, as he shook his head, if he would ever learn to understand the different elements that went into the make-up of his stepmother's niece, or what in the world she had ever seen in a man like Philip Hilliard.

Towards the latter, whom he had always disliked, his bitterness was not allayed by Sybil's generosity. He allowed Philip and his lawyer to come to his office, at her request, and he listened to them with a formal politeness. He then, rather grimly, went to work on the necessary papers. But there were certain things that he would not even try to be polite about. He was walking through the bar of his club, on a night that happened to be ladies' night, on his usual lonely course to the dining room, when his eye fell on Philip sitting with Julia Anderton and another couple in a corner. He passed straight on without nodding, but as he was about to enter the dining room he heard a step behind him and felt a hand on his shoulder.

"Nicholas, I'd like you to meet a friend of mine, if you've got a moment," Philip said in his friendliest tone. "Come on back, can you?"

Nicholas looked at him coldly.

"Who is your friend?"

Philip flushed for a second, but only for a second.

"Julia Anderton."

"I have met Miss Anderton in the past," Nicholas answered in clipped tones. "I see no necessity for our being introduced a second time."

Philip's mouth fell open. Was it an era, after all, when anyone refused to meet anybody?

"Oh, Julia's all right," he said cheerfully, putting his hand again on Nicholas' shoulder. "You'll like her. Once you get to know her."

"Possibly," Nicholas conceded. "But why should I get to know her? She's your mistress. Not mine."

Philip took his hand off the other's shoulder and turned very red.

"You'd better watch your step, Cummings," he said ominously. "You're talking about the young lady whom I intend to marry."

But Nicholas simply continued to fix him with his chilly stare.

"It's hard for people to know that, isn't it," he inquired, "when you're still married to my cousin?"

There was a weighty pause.

"Well, anyway," Philip said heavily, not knowing what honor might require in so awkward a situation, "you'd better cut out those cracks about Julia. Unless you want your block knocked off."

Nicholas, however, was remorseless.

"Do you regard the term 'mistress' as a 'crack'?" he demanded. "I'm sorry. I had thought it accurate. You're not going to deny that she *is* your mistress, are you? Because I should tell you that as your wife's lawyer, although in no way at her instigation, I have made it my business to find out exactly what your relationship with Miss Anderton is. The word 'mistress' appears to cover it exactly. Can you suggest a better? At any rate, I must insist on my right so to describe her whenever I have occasion to discuss your affairs with those who may be concerned. If you object, you are at liberty to seek redress, either legally in a slander suit or illegally, as you threaten, in an assault upon my person."

Philip's breath was now coming in pants. There were no rules for handling a person who so boldly defied the most elementary precepts of good fellowship.

"Would you like to step outside," he demanded, "and settle this thing like a gentleman?"

"I most certainly would not," Nicholas replied. "I have not come to my club to give you an opportunity to start a brawl in the street."

Philip stood there for a moment more, looking at him uncertainly.

"Oh, go to hell," he retorted. "God damn lawyers," he sneered as he moved away. "Shysters. All of them."

Chapter

Ten

NICHOLAS MAY HAVE been committed to Sybil's plan
of action, but he certainly stalled for time. He took what
Philip and Julia regarded as an eternity to prepare the details of the separation agreement, and he absolutely refused
to be hurried. The delay, combined with his rudeness to
Philip at the club, made Julia uneasy. She did not relish the
idea of being advertised by Nicholas as Philip's mistress,
and she began to suspect a plot on the part of Sybil and the
Rodmans to delay the divorce in the hope that Philip would
tire of her. As she could not be sure that such tactics, if
adopted, would not be successful, she decided, without consulting Philip, to see his wife.

"Sybil, couldn't we get together and talk things over?"
she asked nervously, when she got her on the telephone.
"It seems so artificial for us never to see each other."

There was a pause of several moments.

"You mean what they call a 'civilized talk'?" Sybil's voice
came back at her, cool and distant.

"If you want to put it that way. Is there any reason why
we shouldn't?" Julia hesitated. "Except, of course, I know
you've always disliked me."

"That is correct."

Julia had been brought up on the theory that no matter what she herself felt about the world, the world was bound to love her. Even under the present circumstances so marked an exception to the theory struck her unpleasantly.

"Well can I come or can't I?" she asked, rather crossly.

"Come around now, Julia."

Sybil hung up when she had said this. Timmy had just come into the room with Ellen; they were bundled up for a walk in the park.

"Who was that, Mummie?" he demanded.

"A friend of Daddy's, darling."

"What's his name?"

"His name is Julia," she said grimly.

"You haven't been speaking to that woman, Mrs. Hilliard!" Ellen exclaimed. "You haven't so lowered yourself!" Since her employment by Philip, Ellen had insisted on calling Sybil by her married name, but their relationship otherwise had retained its old informality. "That brazen hussy! I remember when you were a child and she came over to play with Teddy how your Aunt Jo used to say: 'That's a bold girl, Ellen. Keep your eye on her and don't let her take any of the children's things!'"

"Thank you, Ellen," Sybil said coldly, "but I think I can run my own life."

"You should have hung right up on her. That's what you should have done!"

"Why should Mummie have hung up on her, Ellen?" Timmy cried. "Why?"

"Ellen, will you please take Timmy out now," Sybil said sharply.

The delay in the divorce proceedings, now of several weeks' duration, had had its effect upon her also. It had not been, as Nicholas had hoped, to stiffen her into demanding better terms, but rather to make her reconsider, as Julia had feared, the very question of divorce itself. Deep down,

Sybil had expected more recognition from Philip of the generosity of her surrender. She had allowed herself to picture a sublimation of their relationship into a selfless release on her part and a lasting gratitude, coupled with a faint, nostalgic regret, on his. However crushed, she could yet sustain her dignity by sensing the drama of her own annihilation. It was not that she required pity from Philip, or from Julia, for that would have been galling to her in the last degree, but she had expected that they would at least face the gravity of what they had done to her and contrast it with what she was doing for them. Philip, however, had not even communicated with her since he had left, except for three telephone calls on purely legal details. When Julia, therefore, came into her living room that afternoon with an air of defiant, if elaborate, casualness, Sybil greeted her without rising, and only with a nod.

"It may not be in the best taste for me to be here," Julia began, sitting down, uninvited, on the sofa opposite Sybil's chair. "And I know it's a deplorable situation and all that, and I know you won't believe me when I say I'm terribly sorry."

"I won't."

Julia swallowed.

"However, as I see it," she continued, "if we've all got to bow to the inevitable, we've got to bow."

"Apparently."

"I mean it's to everyone's best interests," Julia pursued, "to get the darned thing worked out once and for all."

"You think, then, that there *is* a solution that can satisfy everyone?"

There was a pause.

"Certainly. A divorce." Julia cleared her throat. "How else can anyone be satisfied?"

"Must they be?"

Julia began to be irritated. She wondered if her worst

suspicions were not about to be confirmed.

"What I'm getting at, Sybil," she continued, "is this. When are you planning to go to Reno? I think I have the right to know that much."

What Sybil minded most, more even than Julia's insolent practicality, was her attitude, so faintly concealed, that these things were routine and rather boring, that the least that could be expected of an unwanted wife was that she should remove her dreary self from the picture and let young love take its course. Sex, to Julia's mind, apparently had its own duties and obligations; the discarded should take their phlegmatic stand in line before the gas chambers without complaint.

"I'm not sure that I'm going," she said tersely.

Julia stared.

"You mean you're going to stay here!" she exclaimed. She suddenly paled. "You don't mean you're going to divorce Philip in New York!"

Sybil shrugged her shoulders.

"Why should I get a divorce at all?" she asked. "After all, I'm not the one who wants it."

Julia crossed her legs and settled back on the sofa with an air of relief. The brief vision of being named co-respondent had not been pleasant.

"I shouldn't think it would be much fun to be married to a man who wanted to marry someone else," she said casually. "What sort of a home does it make for Timmy?"

The arrogance of this left Sybil speechless for a moment.

"I'll make my own decisions about my own child, thank you, Julia!" she exclaimed finally, in a rush of anger. "At least I can make a better home for him than you ever will!"

Julia, before answering, paused to light a cigarette.

"Don't get mad, Sybil," she said calmly. "Nobody wants to take Timmy away from you. I simply thought that you and I could discuss the whole thing like two rational beings."

"Why should I be rational?" Sybil demanded. "I don't

feel rational. I've never felt rational about you."

Julia shook her head several times, wearily but patiently, as though she were arguing with an angry child.

"You're not making things any easier by acting this way," she observed. "I know it's hard, but you ought to be more realistic. If you don't get the divorce, Philip will. It'll be better all around if —— "

"Let him!" Sybil cried defiantly. "Why should I do everything? Why should I humiliate myself by going to some shoddy divorce mill full of dressed-up cowboys? Do you know what I think of practical people, Julia? I *loathe* them!"

Julia paused for a moment and then shrugged her shoulders.

"Well, stay here then," she said, "if you must. Philip can go. It seems rather hard that he should have to leave his job for that long a time. Particularly when you're doing nothing. And as far as shoddiness is concerned, it's six of one and half a dozen of the other. You'll have to consent to the thing in any event."

"Why?"

"Because, my dear," Julia said, almost condescendingly, "it won't be legal if you don't."

"Who cares?"

Julia's eyes widened.

"You mean you're going to refuse the divorce?"

Sybil hesitated. She had reached the point before she realized it. But in the sudden, startling void that surrounded her, she groped for this new direction. As she stared at Julia and the almost comic surprise on her features she felt her anger subside.

"I'm not going to refuse him anything," she said more calmly. "I'm simply not going to do anything in the least bit dishonorable. Not for your sake, Julia."

"But what's dishonorable about consenting to a divorce?"

"I'll tell you," Sybil said, suddenly coherent. "Nicholas told me. Philip would have to perjure himself. He'd have to swear that he meant to live in Reno. If I consented I'd be joining in the lie. Compounding a crime, or whatever you call it."

Julia's mouth had fallen open. Never in her long career of self-aggrandizement had she been blocked by a scruple so blatantly squeamish.

"But, Sybil, everyone does that. They expect you to, in Nevada. It isn't what you think at all."

"He'd have to swear, wouldn't he?" Sybil persisted.

Julia threw her arms in the air.

"But it's not a real oath."

"Then what is it?"

"Oh, my God, Sybil!" Julia exclaimed angrily. "You can't be serious! You're doing this to spite me. How else could you and Philip get a divorce?"

"In New York."

"But you just promised you wouldn't!"

Sybil even managed a smile. She was not above feeling a certain pleasure at the sudden change in their positions.

"I said I wouldn't do anything," she said firmly. "And I meant it. I'm not practical, Julia. I'm not going to perjure myself for you. Or divorce Philip in New York. I'm simply going on with my own life. With as much dignity as possible. If Philip wants a divorce, let him get it where we live."

"But you'd have to commit adultery!" Julia cried despairingly.

Sybil actually laughed.

"Now you're really asking too much, Julia," she said. "I don't think I can arrange to commit adultery for you and Philip. No matter how happy it would make you. You're most unreasonable, Julia. You want me to make myself a dishonest woman so Philip can make you an honest one. If

you love him, live with him. Why must I consent? Or give
you my blessing?"

Julia had jumped up and was walking back and forth
across the room.

"Don't be naïve, Sybil," she snapped. "Things have to be
definite. One way or the other. I have to know where I
stand."

"What do you want for your money?" Sybil retorted.
"And when have you spent more than a nickel on anything
you've wanted?"

Julia stopped and faced her.

"I suppose this is one of your clever tricks," she said.
"You probably think you can get a better settlement out of
Philip by making things tough."

As Sybil stared back at her she felt whatever small satisfaction there had been in defeating Julia ebb away. She felt
degraded and tired. But she did not regret what she had
said. Of this she was sure. She had been too passive. That
she had lost Philip for good she would have to face. But
that she would rescue him, however reluctant, from the fate
of being married to Julia might still have its consolation.
There was even a fierce, grim exaltation as the prospect of
standing, an adamant rock of courage and resolution, in the
center of the raging sea of their desired union.

"Your own dirty thoughts are your own, Julia," she said.

They both realized at the same time that someone was
watching them. Philip was standing in the doorway, looking
in dismay from one to the other. He had called to pick up
his squash racquet which he had left behind in the hall
closet and had heard the angry voices in the living room.

"Sybil!" he exclaimed.

She turned on him with a sudden fury that he had never
seen in her before.

"I don't care what you say, Philip!" she cried. "I know I

haven't any hope of getting you back! You've decided to go your own pigheaded way, and nothing in God's world will stop you! But as for my helping to let this gold digger cut you in pieces, that's out. I tell you it's *out!*" She was on her feet and standing in front of him, glaring up in his face. "If you can get a divorce, get it! I may even give you cause. *Good* cause. But I won't do your dirty work, Philip Hilliard! Not for one solitary moment more will I do it. God!" She turned and gave Julia a look of withering contempt. "To think I could ever have thought of helping that slut to marry you! I'm no better than a pimp!"

Philip said nothing in answer to her onslaught. He stood dumbfounded, staring at her, and then suddenly put his hands on her shoulders, as if to hold her back. He could feel her trembling; the intensity in her slim frame conveyed itself like an electric shock through his hands. He took them off her and turned to Julia.

"Let's go," he said briefly. "Leave her be."

Outside the apartment house, as they walked down the street in search of a taxi, Julia found her tongue.

"I tell you I think she's nuts," she said. "Seriously. They're all queer, you know, that family. If you hadn't come in when you did, she'd have thrown something at me! I hope she doesn't have a gun. I tell you, Philip, I'm actually scared of her. I mean it!"

But Philip was not following her expostulations. The Sybil of whom he had had a new vision, quivering and taut and ready, like a black panther, to spring, was more the Sybil whom he remembered from their first meeting. He was already wondering if he really wanted to abandon so fiercely loyal a pet. When she was angry, he was thinking, there was a quality about her that made Julia seem petulant and coarse.

"You shouldn't have gone there," he said sharply. "I told you to leave all that to me."

"Oh, all right." She shrugged her shoulders peevishly. "Except you weren't doing anything about it. You'll admit that, I suppose?"

But he didn't answer her, and they walked on together in silence.

Chapter
Eleven

SYBIL CRIED most of that night, and by morning she was in a state of great emotional tension. She maintained her resolution, however, and went downtown to see Nicholas and tell him that under no circumstances would she consent to a divorce. When she had got this out she felt better.

"I owe it to Philip," she kept saying, "to save him from her. One day he'll thank me. You'll see."

"Are you sure, Sybil?"

"Well, if he doesn't, he's a fool!"

"All right." Nicholas raised his hands. "Don't get mad at me now. I'm on your side."

When Lucy Hilliard heard the news she clapped her hands.

"She has some spunk, that girl, after all!" she told her husband. "Now we can turn the heat on that philandering son of ours."

Which she proceeded immediately to do. Lucy was too pleased to allow herself to lose her temper at Philip again. She was casual, almost subtle with her favorite child, whom she had been seeing steadily in spite of their fight and in spite of her refusal to meet Julia. It was understood in the

Hilliard family that violence was never resented for more than a day.

"The hell of it is," he told his mother a few days after the scene with Julia and Sybil, "that anything I do is going to be hard cheese on someone."

"Except on you, Philip, dear," Lucy said with some asperity, as she gave the cocktail shaker an extra shake. "Nothing's going to be hard cheese on you."

"I think in some ways it's harder on me than anyone," he said peevishly.

For her answer she poured him a Martini.

"The question before the house," she said in a business-like tone, "is how we get rid of Julia. Isn't that it?"

"Now, Ma!"

"Look, Philip." She settled back on the sofa, glass in hand. "Sybil bores you. Conceded. Julia is exciting. For the moment. Conceded. But what you don't see is that any wife is going to be boring some of the time, particularly to a man like you. And getting rid of them is a dreadful chore. Now Sybil's someone we all like. She's a good mother to little Timmy, and she didn't make any fuss about this Julia business until you started talking divorce. For God's sake hang on to her. It's a million times easier to change girl friends than to change wives."

Philip was not shocked. He looked at his mother admiringly. She was the arch-sophisticate, the original of the type that had always dazzled his less subtle mind. Now that his infatuation for Julia was dissolving into something more casual, he looked to Lucy to show him how to withdraw.

"Julia wants me to get a divorce in Reno," he pointed out. "Even if Sybil won't consent. She says that Sybil will never attack it in New York."

"Don't be too sure. She might do anything in the mood she's in now. Besides, how can you take the chance? There's the question of Timmy and alimony and who your heirs would be if you died. Julia knows that people in our position can't afford to take chances. She's been around."

He nodded as he took this in. Then he turned to the next problem.

"She says we might buy a ranch in Nevada and live there," he said. "Then the divorce would be valid even without Sybil's consent."

"Can you afford a ranch in Nevada?"

"Not if I have to support Sybil here. Unless you help out."

Lucy simply laughed.

"You know what you can tell Julia to that one," she said.

"Julia says she's given up everything for me."

There was another pause. Then they both laughed. It was the hearty laughter of his surrender and her victory.

"Darling, it's all so simple," she pointed out. "You tell her that your hands are tied. She took her chances at the start. She knew you were married and had obligations which you might not be able to get out of. Okay. So it hasn't worked out." She reached for the shaker. "It's been what I believe they call an interlude. A beautiful interlude."

Philip applied this formula with exactness the very next day. He had never been one who could brook delay. Julia, he had to admit, took it all in better spirit than he had anticipated. She was too much of an egotist not to recognize when the game was up.

"In another minute," she said sarcastically, when he had finished his little speech, "you'll be telling me that it's been an interlude."

He said nothing.

"One thing I'll say for Sybil," she continued. "It wasn't she who put you up to this. It was that mean old mother of yours."

"I wish you wouldn't speak of my mother that way, Julia,' he said with dignity.

She laughed derisively.

"What an utter cad you are, Philip," she said, almost admiringly. "You have a great big cake in front of you, intact. And crumbs all over your face from eating it."

"I don't know what you expect of me," he said.

"Oh, I expect nothing," she said with emphasis. "Nothing at all. Your women will always get you out of jams. And pick up the pieces. And take the blame. God! Run on home to your sniveling little Sybil and be faithful to her for a whole month!"

Philip left at once, very much relieved at having got off so cheaply. He could not even wait to get back to his club; he telephoned Sybil from a booth.

"Can I take you out for dinner tonight?" he asked. "To any place you want?"

There was a startled pause.

"What's happened?" she inquired. "Julia's night off?"

"She's at her family's," he explained. "Alone."

She still gave him no answer.

"Well, what about it?" he persisted. "Or maybe you have a date," he added, politely and conscientiously.

"No."

"Well?"

"Why not?" But her voice was not enthusiastic. "What have we got to lose?"

.   .   .

He looked very handsome, and he ordered the dinner with his usual care, making the waiter repeat each suggestion in painfully comprehensible English.

"I want everything to be just so tonight," he explained to her. "You see, I have something particular to talk over with you. Something quite particular."

Her mind wandered vaguely over the different possibilities. He was capable of asking her opinion on the most unseemly topics. He was capable, indeed, of asking her what sort of apartment he and Julia should rent.

"I suppose it's something legal about the divorce," she said. "But you know how I stand on that. If you want it, go and get it. I won't attack it. But leave me out of it. I'm not interested."

He breathed a sigh of relief that she had not, in her recent scene with Julia, revealed even this degree of co-operation.

"It's not about the divorce," he said.

The cocktails arrived, and Sybil reached for hers, he thought, with an unbecoming eagerness. She drank it quickly.

"I saw Julia this afternoon," he said, after quite a pause.

"Really."

"We had a long, serious talk," he continued. "I've also had one with Mother."

"Well, marriage is a serious business," she retorted. "Or at least it can be."

He ignored this.

"I know you've never liked Julia," he said. "You've always said she was discontented. Do you think she'll always be discontented?"

Sybil finished her cocktail and caught the waiter's eye. She raised her empty glass.

"Julia eats people," she said in a rather bored tone. "Everyone that she can. And she doesn't even have table manners. She chews them with her mouth open and misses all the best parts. She never knows where her next meal is coming from, so she eats them even when she's not hungry. But why should I care?" She picked up the new Martini that the waiter had brought her. "I'm not marrying her."

"Darling, you're bitter," he said reproachfully. "You haven't been bitter before. Not this way."

"Haven't I?" She shrugged her shoulders. "It's not the easiest thing in the world to lose a husband. Even if it does happen every day."

"Sybil, do you still love me?"

She didn't even look at him. She sipped her cocktail and stared across the table at the little orchestra in red coats that was playing Victor Herbert.

"You know I do." Her voice was hard in sudden contempt for her own sentimentality. "Some people, I suppose, only love once."

"Let me tell you something about Julia," he said immediately. "Something you may be glad to hear."

She looked at him inattentively.

"Has she had a stroke?"

He laughed, rather too loudly.

"No," he said. "As a matter of fact, it's not really about Julia. It's about me."

"Oh?"

"It's just that I agree with you."

"About love? Of course, you do. You've always been a determined romantic."

He shook his head.

"No. About Julia."

She stared.

"You mean you're not going to marry her?"

It was his turn to signal the waiter.

"I mean just that."

Sybil's head swam for a moment. Then she found refuge in a laugh.

"I hope you don't want me to break the news to her," she said.

"No, I've already done that," he said in a pleased tone. "Can you imagine being nagged by Julia for the rest of one's life?"

"But it wouldn't be for life, Philip," she pointed out. "Not with Julia."

He put an arm suddenly around her shoulders and started talking in her ear. But the only thing that she was aware of was fear, fear growing with an amazing circular speed and surging back and forth through her body.

"I've been crazy, Sib," he was saying. "Out of my mind. Call it the war or the post-war or what you will. But it's all right now, darling. It's going to be all right, too. For keeps. If you can only bring yourself to forgive me. Can you, Sib? Nobody could blame you if you couldn't. But can you?"

When she opened her lips no words came out. Too much was happening in her mind for any thoughts to be formulated. She was conscious only of trying to drive something down, of sitting on it and desperately spreading things over it to keep it from sight, of pushing and jabbing at it and all the while knowing that it was rising around her, encircling, enveloping, overwhelming. She knew that she must not give in to it; she knew dimly how much the love for which she had fought was threatened. Desperately she reached up and caught Philip's hand on her shoulder.

"Oh, Philip," she heard herself say in a strangled tone, "one doesn't forgive Hilliards. One accepts them. That's all."

Chapter
Twelve

AND SO it all began again. When they got back to their apartment that night they went to separate rooms, but the next morning, without further discussion, it was recognized that the future, to some degree or other, was to be a joint undertaking. To Philip such decisions were simple; he had made up his mind, and he saw no reason why she should have any difficulty in making up hers. Indeed, why? Surely it was not he who had been moving like a wraith about the town, a dim, pale figure announcing to all and sundry, as clearly as though the words had been splashed in red on her wide brow, that she had been wronged? He could not even understand it when at breakfast she told him that she wanted, at least for the time being, to keep her own bedroom.

"Well, sure." He shrugged his shoulders. "Anything you say. Except I thought you wanted me back. Really back."

"I do, Philip," she said unhappily. "It's just that I need time. It's all been so unexpected. One can't change one's attitude so suddenly," she said, looking up at him, "without some loss of breath."

He picked up the newspaper.

"You work it out your way, dear," he said in the tone of even kindness that he adopted when his mind was made up. "I've treated you like a heel, and I have no right to expect anything."

She counted the minutes until he left for the office. Then she went into the living room and sat in a chair by the window looking disconsolately out at the East River. Later she took Timmy for a walk in Central Park, watching for friends and turning away when she saw any. What had happened was that she would not let herself think; there were ideas, as she had felt at the restaurant, that had to be kept down. And what a thing it was, she reflected dismally, as she stared up at the statue of Fitz-Greene Halleck in the Mall and shuddered at the autumnal bite of the air, to feel a fool and to have no scapegoat but oneself. I am as these people, she reflected oddly, as she gazed about. I am not, after all, unique.

When she came home there was a message on the hall table to call Teddy. He had already heard the news. Philip, of course, would have methodically notified the whole family. He would have called them, one by one, and used the identical statement to each, not so much because he had prepared it in advance as because his mind, set in a formula, could repeat itself without limit.

"Sib, isn't it fine?" Teddy exclaimed when she called him. "I knew that he'd come to his senses. In the end."

"You're always right, Teddy," she said a bit dryly. "I depend on you."

Her mother was less radiant than Teddy when Sybil went to see her that afternoon, but then Esther was not a radiant person. There was never enough breathing space between the end of one complication and the beginning of another; satisfaction to her was a state of mind that only invited disaster. She had the intelligence, abetted by the superstition, to see danger in the fulfillment of any articulated wish. And Sybil had certainly wished for Philip's return. She gazed at her daughter now over the tea tray with eyes that seemed to be searching for the problem that must be lurking under the square fabric of her son-in-law's solution.

"This must give you great satisfaction, my dear," she said at last. "Particularly when you think what a good thing it is for Timmy."

Of course, Sybil reflected, Esther would think first of Timmy. What was marriage but a stock that paid dividends in a sense of achieved responsibility? Joy? What was joy to Esther?

"I don't know how much it matters to Timmy," she said gloomily. "There are so many divorced parents nowadays. It can't make as much difference as it used to."

Esther shrugged her shoulders expressively.

"I know it isn't going to be easy, dear," she said. "You can't mend a broken life in five minutes. Don't be impatient if it's not whole by tomorrow."

Esther's consolation had in it the same note of worried superiority that Sybil had resented in the past; she was still the Cassandra who smiled sadly at the collapse of ideals that she never sponsored. Yet to Sybil, who had felt, and for the first time, a rebuff in Teddy's lack of comprehension, it was oddly welcome to feel that her mother shared her own sense of deflation.

"Of course, I won't, Mummie," she began hesitantly. "It wouldn't be reasonable, would it? And yet — when I think how happy I was and then how miserable I was, I don't altogether see — Well, there's no reason why I should see."

Esther looked at her carefully.

"I imagine that one would have to love Philip very much," she said, "to be entirely happy with him."

Sybil looked up.

"Why?" she demanded. "Because he's so awful?"

But Esther only shook her head.

"No, dear," she said gently. "I know it's fun to misinterpret, but it's hardly fair. What I mean is that Philip has mannerisms and ways of doing things, very particular ways, that are lovable — well, if they *are* lovable."

"Isn't that true of any man?"

Her mother smiled.

"More so of Philip," she said.

Sybil had nothing to answer. She knew too well what her mother meant. But had Philip not been meant to stride, barefoot and heroic, through the sluggish, shallow waters of her mother's fears to rescue her from the family sand bar? Was he not to have been Esther's final and complete rebuttal?

"What would you do about him, Mummie?" she asked tensely. "Leave him? As he left me? Can I leave a man for being a fool?"

But at this Esther looked grave indeed.

"My dear child," she protested, "you can't expect me to make a decision like that for you!"

"You mean I've made my bed," Sybil said bitterly, "and now I can lie in it."

Esther, however, had no answer for this. She had turned her attention to pouring the tea.

Chapter
Thirteen

PHILIP WAS THE SOUL of consideration. At least outwardly. He seemed to find plenty to do at home without
bothering her, and he never asked friends to the apartment
without consulting her first. He suggested that she take a
trip alone, to think things over, or, if she wished, that they
take one together. He was very polite to her family and
agreed to dine at Aunt Jo's whenever she asked him. As she
still persisted in having their reunion a thing in name only,
he sometimes did not come home until very late, and on such
occasions no excuses were asked and none given. There
was a tacit agreement between them to regard his schedule
as dictated by extra work at the office. She knew that she
had no valid basis for complaint, and she knew that he
knew it. Yet it irked her that he should so take for granted
that his physical needs had to be taken care of; she would
have preferred to have him dedicate to her a period of
abstinence. Philip so obviously did not really think that he
had wronged her, or at least that he had done anything for
which his frank assumption of guilt and offer to return had
not handsomely compensated. She had wanted him back,
and he had come. Could a man do more? She did not like
to consider that what she may have wanted was penitence

and abjection, nor when she considered it, did she, in all honesty, feel that this was the case. Truly, she did not know *what* she wanted. She didn't want Philip to take her for granted and she didn't want him to pay her too much attention. She found that she was always observing him, about the apartment, with a sharply critical eye; she was increasingly preoccupied with the elaborate methodicity of his habits. She followed his mental check-off list, when he selected ten records for the Victrola before settling down in his armchair with two small cushions at his back, a whiskey and soda in his hand and four cigarettes, his evening quota, laid out on the table beside him. His habits seemed to reject her as complex and neurotic; they seemed to say: Look at me, after all. I'm fine. What's all the fussing about? What indeed?

She spent a good deal of time with Aunt Jo who, if less perceptive than Esther, was more sympathetic. Aunt Jo seemed to take it for granted that Sybil should not be immediately reconciled to her husband's return. She was a highly moral woman, and Philip's misconduct had been a grave disappointment to her. As a realist she was ready to forgive in the end, but she required a period of probation before the slate was wiped clean.

"As long as he's back to stay and sorry," she told Sybil one morning, "we may as well see what we can do with him."

Sybil had never thought of herself, however, as being able to "do" anything with Philip. That had never been their relationship. All she had wanted from him was to be allowed to love him. For it was love that was to have rescued her from the meanness of her father's world and the compromise of her mother's. It was love that was to have been her triumph and Teddy's failure. It was love, her own love, that was to have made the world so petty that she could despise it. And it was all of this that she had tried to see in her feeling for Philip. She could even smile now, dryly, at the realization of this, for had she not always known, ironically enough, that his was not a pedestal to sustain her image of him? Well, the foolish drama was over. She was not, as Prufrock said, Prince Hamlet. She had foundered in muddy waters, and the soft, thick sand that she could feel under her bow was part of the same parental shores from which she had resolutely turned her sails in the vivid past of an angry childhood. Very well. She would disembark. She would leave Philip and the cherished illusion that had never truly been an illusion. She would learn to live among the people whom she had despised, people who talked about love and what it meant to them, people who were always pretending that their love was deep and abiding even as they changed from one object to another. For it was true, after all, that she was one of them.

That night Aunt Jo gave a family dinner and took them, in her usual fashion, to the opera. It was a rather stiff occasion, being the first meeting between Philip and Nicholas since their unfortunate encounter at the club. Everybody, however, behaved well. When the curtain fell on the first act of *Siegfried*, Sybil clipped her arm under Nicholas' and took him for a stroll to the lobby. She brought her fur cape with her.

"There's been a war and millions of people killed," she told him, "and I guess even the ladies of our family can walk between the acts now."

"It's very commonly done," he observed. "But does a thing's being common make it right?"

She looked up at his fixed countenance.

"If you only believed in something, Nicholas," she said, "I wouldn't mind its being old-fashioned. But you don't. You don't believe in anything."

"What do you believe in, Sybil?"

"God knows."

They had reached the foyer and found a table. Sybil

opened her purse and took out a memorandum pad and a small stubby pencil.

"I'm going to write a note to Philip," she said. "Which I want you to take back to him for me. Then I'm going home. Alone."

She gazed at him for a moment, but he simply nodded.

"It doesn't surprise you?" she asked.

"Nothing that you do at the opera surprises me, Sybil."

She bent over the table to write her note.

"Philip, dear," she wrote, "I've gone home. Please go back to your club or to your mother's tonight. If you want to come to the apartment, of course, you can, but this is to let you know that I have made up my mind that the whole thing will never work. I can't go back. Any more than you can. I can't even face the next two acts tonight."

She folded it and gave it to Nicholas. He nodded again. Then she put her wrap around her shoulders and hurried out of the foyer and down the stairs to the main door.

Chapter
Fourteen

WHEN LUCY HILLIARD called the next morning at Sybil's apartment she found her daughter-in-law sitting in the living room waiting for her.

"What's all this nonsense about, Sybil?" she demanded. "Philip's just been over to see me. He's in a terrible state, poor boy. You can't be serious about this."

"Perfectly serious."

"What has he done now? Is there another girl? Already?"

Sybil shook her head.

"No, Mrs. Hilliard. This time it's me."

Lucy stared.

"You mean *you've* found someone?" she asked, almost incredulously.

"No." Sybil smiled at her tone. "No, it's simply that I'm through with Philip."

Lucy could only gape at the set expression of her unpredictable daughter-in-law.

"Simply that you're through with Philip!" she exclaimed. "After he's given up this Anderton girl and gone back to you! After he's turned over a new leaf!" A note of injured maternal pride crept into her tone. "What do you want him to do? Go down on his knees?"

"No. I don't want him to do a thing."

"Didn't you want him to come back? Isn't it what you and I have been waiting for?"

"I had thought so. But I was wrong."

There was a painful pause.

"What is it that you want, Sybil?"

"I want a divorce."

In a quick, involuntary movement Lucy raised her hands to her cheeks.

"But my child," she protested, "I thought you loved him."

Sybil shook her head.

"I never really loved him," she said. "And now it's worse. I don't even like him."

She looked at Lucy as the expression of hostility that she had been expecting filled her eyes. She had seen this hostility on other occasions, with reference to other people. She knew that once aroused, it could not be put down. If Lucy was loyal in her friendships, she was not the less unforgiving in her enmities. A person had a trial before her bar of justice, but the verdict could not be appealed or the sentence mitigated. And Sybil was pleading guilty.

"You don't *like* Philip?" she was saying in a harsh tone. "And may I ask why?" But then she paused. "We shouldn't really be discussing this today, Sybil. You're tired. One doesn't get divorced because one's husband goes to sleep at the opera."

It was a chance, a last chance for redemption.

"Mrs. Hilliard," Sybil said in a clear voice, "you don't appreciate my resolution. I can't blame you. You've had no warning of it. But I can assure you that I will never go back to Philip."

Lucy frowned.

"You might at least tell me what he's done."

"He has done nothing," Sybil answered. "Absolutely nothing. You see, Mrs. Hilliard, I want to be entirely honest with you. You have always been so with me." Lucy made no acknowledgement of the compliment. "I have always seen Philip through rose-colored glasses," she went on. "The other day I took them off. That's all. Philip to me is now a man with whom I have nothing in common. I couldn't possibly live with him again." She folded her hands in her lap decisively. "I'm not going to tell you that I'm thinking of anyone but myself, because I'm not. I'm not going to say that I want a divorce for Timmy's sake, because I don't. I'm leaving Philip because I lack the will power to stay with him."

It was a relief to have said it, a relief to feel the door so firmly closed to redemption. She had always been afraid that her mother-in-law, who had been in recent years so extraordinarily kind to her, would have been less kind had she known more about her. Lucy's character, like Philip's, was lacking in subtlety, and Sybil couldn't but feel that if she had been accepted at all, it was because she had concealed a large part of her true nature. Now there was no further need to fear. To Lucy she must have seemed indeed contemptible, nor would this contempt be mitigated by her frankness. Frankness of her sort, in fact, would strike Lucy as unfamiliar and "queer."

"I couldn't be more surprised, Sybil," her mother-in-law said in a hard voice. "I always thought that you had a great deal of will power. It seems to me that you don't choose to employ it."

Sybil said nothing.

"You haven't mentioned the word 'duty,'" Lucy continued. "I know, of course, that it is not fashionable among the young. But I had thought it might mean something to you."

Sybil felt a flash of resentment. It was hard that a woman like Lucy should talk to her about duty.

"I thought it would be simpler if I told you what I was

going to do, Mrs. Hilliard," she said. "I see no need to go into the list of duties violated."

This terminated the period of their negotiations. Lucy nodded, rather grimly, and changed her tack.

"I wonder if you've really thought this out," she said. "You've lost your grounds for divorcing Philip, you know. There's a defense in the law which I believe they call condonement."

Sybil felt a little shudder through her shoulders and her spine.

"Would Philip refuse me a divorce?" she asked.

"You refused him one."

She nodded slowly. Lucy's remark, which so brutally snapped the last chord between them, might only be the prelude of further and less familiar conflicts, in courts and before lawyers, publicized, unbearable. She closed her eyes for a moment.

"Of course, I shan't want any money," she said. "I couldn't take a penny of Philip's money."

"What will you live on?"

"I can go home. Or to Aunt Jo's."

Lucy snorted.

"She'll like that," she said. "And what about Timmy?"

Sybil looked at her in sudden fear.

"But Philip always said I could have him!"

"That was when Philip wanted the divorce."

"I see," Sybil said in a low voice. "But I'm sure we can work something out, can't we? Of course, I wouldn't want Timmy not to see his father. Or you. That's the way it should be."

Lucy was almost touched, though weakness rarely moved her.

"Give it up, my dear," she said in a final appeal. "You weren't made for this sort of row. You see what it's done to us already. And it'll go on this way. You'll suffer for it,

Sybil. Little by little you'll turn into a smaller person. Because you were never meant to be a divorced woman. Never. With some women it doesn't matter. But not with you, dear. Believe me."

There was so much in Lucy's appeal that Sybil could not answer her. There was even a hidden note of apprehension that Philip himself was the person who would really have the most to lose in a divorce and an appeal to Sybil to return, if only to save him from something worse, an appeal which contained, in a curious way, a tacit recognition of how little Philip had given her and an odd little bribe that if she would only return, Lucy would somehow find happiness for Philip and for her. For just a moment she felt on equal terms with the incomparable Mrs. Hilliard; for just a moment she actually pitied her. They were closer than ever before on the very brink of their separation. For Lucy seemed to be saying: "You're a funny, intense, not unlikeable creature, and Philip hasn't the sense to appreciate you, but if you'll only stay, *I'll* make it all right. And when I make a promise I keep it. If I die in the effort." Sybil's eyes filled with tears as she looked at her mother-in-law and slowly shook her head.

Part Three

Chapter
One

IT WAS ARRANGED between Sybil and Philip that Timmy should go to the Hilliards' during the summer months after the first winter of their separation. Philip and his sisters always used the family place in Glenville as a base of operations from June to September. One grandchild more or less was hardly noticed, and Lucy Hilliard, knowing that Philip wanted the sense of being a dutiful father with the least possible restriction on his activities, saw to it that Timmy was comfortably merged with her other grandchildren under the supervision of a joint nurse. Sybil's spirits were very low after leaving the boy there. It had not made it easier that Timmy so clearly regarded a visit to his paternal grandmother in the light of a vivid and desirable change. As she drove away she wondered if he would not turn out, for all his sensitivity, to be a true Hilliard.

Without Timmy she was more than ever at loose ends. Philip, coached by his mother, had stipulated a year's separation before the divorce should again be discussed, and she was finding the interim a painful period. Aunt Jo had asked her to spend the summer with her, and she had accepted. Easton Bay had the advantage of being a half-hour's drive from Glenville; she could go over to see Timmy whenever

Lucy allowed it. Her parents usually stayed with Aunt Jo
for their vacation, but this summer they had gone to a hotel
in Quebec. The reason for this unprecedented step had been
communicated to no one, but Sybil had guessed it. Her
father, uncomfortable at best with the Cummingses, found
Easton Bay intolerable when she was there as well. George
and his daughter had grown further apart since her marriage,
and his increasing tendency, as he aged, to contrast, loudly
and dogmatically, his own rough and ready Americanism
with the "pallid" intellectualism of his wife and daughter,
had done little to bridge the widening gap. George knew
that Sybil, silent as she was, observed him with a merciless
clarity; he knew that she was noting the increase in his
drinking, in his loudness, in the scatological content of his
anecdotes. At the golf club in Easton Bay, on spring and
fall weekends, she would glance in his direction as she
passed the bar and take in, acidly, the small group of
younger men bored by him, held there by the tyrannical spell
of his dirty jokes, a spell that owed its power to the belief
of men like her father that a failure to respond in guffaws
was a failure in virility. Oh, yes, she saw it and saw it with
the completeness of a child who had been watching him,
detached, from her earliest days, nor was she for a minute
unwilling to speculate on the failure of virility in himself
that made him so shrilly assert his masculinity in the consoling company of his own sex, at bars, with tales of the
unachieved. His conversation with Sybil when she left
Philip, for all practical purposes, finished things between
them.

"You mustn't be too hard on Phil because he's got a wan-
dering eye," he told her, hoping that on this point at least
he could speak with authority. "It's the way most young
fellows are. As a matter of fact, the wanderers often make
the best husbands. You only have to look around." He
winked at her. "A girl who wants a faithful husband can

always marry a man like Nicholas." He gave a loud laugh. "And what girl in her senses would want that?"

Sybil, however, only stared back at him.

"I think *I* might want that, Daddy," she said coldly. "I think there's a great deal to be said for faithful husbands. Like Nicholas. And like you."

It was not surprising, after this, that George should have persuaded his wife to try a summer in Canada, leaving Sybil, for the first time in years, the only representative of the Rodman family at Aunt Jo's. She loved the place; it was more home to her than anywhere else. The house itself was not remarkable; it was like any other big Long Island house of its era. It was large and square and of dark, dead brick; it had too many small windows, a long blue gravel driveway and a series of decaying outbuildings in the surrounding woods and fields. There was a barn with two ancient horse carriages, a playhouse built for Teddy and Sybil as children, and a garage, also of brick to match the big house and marred by a clock tower with a clock that did not tell the time. But the woods were green and full in summer and austere and melancholy in autumn, and Sybil could walk in the fields in the daytime and spend her evenings alone with her books.

Aunt Jo, as always, was sympathetic. She rarely made any reference to Sybil's domestic problems, yet she seemed to concede by her very silence that things were basically wrong. She even managed to imply, with a consoling gleam in her eye, that if things got too bad, she would bestir herself and find the remedy. Sybil was willing to sit by for the moment and allow herself to be sucked gently into the hum of activity that surrounded her aunt. It was as if her mind and body had taken on some of the paralysis of her heart, and she looked about the Easton Bay scene without distinguishing or caring to distinguish between the different individuals and events. She had lost her faith, her faith in whatever had kept her going as long as she had been going, her faith, presumably, in herself. It was only to be expected that, sensing the void that was opening beneath her, she should cling, for whatever reassurance they could give her, to the brightly polished railings that surrounded the orderly park of Aunt Jo's existence. Not, indeed, that she had any faith in the pattern of life that Aunt Jo and her friends exemplified, but at least it was a pattern. It held things together, and without it what would happen to them all? What, without even their pattern, would happen to *her*?

She went out driving in the afternoon with Aunt Jo, and each drive always ended in a call. Then there were lunch parties and card parties and even, from time to time, cocktail parties. Sybil did not play bridge, but she could sit quietly by the card table, doing her needle point, and listen to the busy chatter of Aunt Jo's friends. On and on it went; she marveled at its inexhaustible flow and at their faith in the particular, the concrete, their distrust of the universal. Sometimes it amused her to think of Aunt Jo, with her incessant cigarettes and her card games and her appreciation of the mildly risqué, as an eighteenth-century character, a marquise from a Thackeray novel, with red heels and a powdered wig, taking snuff at the whist table, but the picture would soon blur with her memory of how Aunt Jo's features would stiffen at the mention of certain topics, or of how she drew herself up before entering a drawing room, or of how she reveled in inferior, moralistic fiction, all true indicia of the intervening century which, with its pharisaism and its fatuity, had also its imprint upon her. Aunt Jo was never consistent with any picture that one might draw of her, but then Aunt Jo was far too sensible to care about consistency.

The Misses Hilliard had always been among Aunt Jo's close friends, and the opportunity of keeping an eye on their erring niece-in-law was not a thing to diminish the frequency of their visits to a house where the best company was kept

and the best bridge played. Aunt Jo knew all about their
peculiarities and the oddness of their point of view, and she
would sometimes mimic them in private for Sybil's amusement, but she never forgot that they qualified as "personages,"
the highest category in her varied classifications. Sybil's
attitude towards them, however, like her attitude towards
so many of the people in Philip's world, had changed from
passivity to bitterness. It was as if something within her
were seething and boiling, trying to escape. When she
meant to be simply critical this something would unaccount-
ably burst forth, and she would find that she had been rude.
At a lunch party given by Aunt Jo for Philip's aunts, she had
an attack of nerves that she was unable to conceal. The ladies
were discussing her old friend, Howard Plimpton, who had
recently left his Mabel, whom he had married during the
war, thrown up his job and was now living and painting
over a garage in Easton Bay. Sybil had hardly seen him
since her marriage, and she listened with interest to what
they had to say.

"Well, I suppose if you're successful you can get away
with anything," Aunt Jo was saying. "Take Gauguin. But
the thing about this Plimpton boy is that they say he can't
even paint."

"You don't mean, Jo, do you," Miss Harriet put in, "that if
he could paint, it would be *all right?*"

Aunt Jo smiled.

"No, Harriet," she said. "But it would certainly help."

"It all goes to show that you never can tell," Miss Emily
observed. "I understand that he was considered a very nice
young man. Polite and considerate. And now suddenly —
boom!" She raised her hands to indicate the completeness
of Howard's disintegration. "I don't know what else we
should expect. The young have no discipline today. When
they're bored with a responsibility they drop it. Why not?"

It was evident from the tremor in Miss Emily's voice and
the aversion of her eyes, in whose direction her speech had

been aimed. The atmosphere around the table became suddenly uncomfortable.

"Maybe the poor boy will get it out of his system this way," one lady, old and white and very soft, suggested placatingly. "And then they'll patch it up. She hasn't gone to Reno, has she?"

"Reno?" Miss Emily repeated meaningfully. "Mabel Plimpton doesn't have to go to Reno for her divorce. Not from what I hear."

Sybil's mind was suddenly filled with the image of Howard as he had been before the war, at their dinners together, when he had talked so angrily and yet so passionately about Mabel.

"Maybe he couldn't live with his wife, Aunt Emily," she heard herself say sharply. "Maybe she was hateful to him."

Miss Emily did not turn to her, but continued to look across the table at her sister. She and Miss Harriet always did this when in conflict with others. They appeared to be carrying on a debate between themselves, and only the light in their eyes and the tense, questioning note in their voices showed that their remarks were intended for a third person.

"Some of us believe he might have thought of that before he married her," she said. "What's more, I hear that he doesn't even support her. He won't send her a nickel."

"But he's always been poor," Sybil retorted, watching Miss Emily's profile. "And Mabel has her own money."

"Would any self-respecting man allow his wife to support herself and their children?" Miss Harriet demanded, apparently of her sister.

"Why not?" Sybil swallowed hard. Her heart was pounding violently. "What possible right do rich, spoiled women have to be supported?"

The conversation, as though at a given signal, broke into several smaller conversations. Sybil found herself deserted.

"My dear child," Aunt Jo said to her afterwards, in a grave

voice, "it's a great mistake for you to talk like that."

"Why? What did I say?"

"It wasn't so much what you said. It was your tone."

"But I can't bear them, Aunt Jo!" she burst out resentfully. "They're so *mean!* They goad me into being that way. You know they do!"

Aunt Jo shook her head.

"You know that I love you and Teddy," she said sadly. "You're like my own children. And you know how I care about seeing that you're provided for. I, thought my worries were over when Philip came into the family. But now, my child, be practical. Your mother and father have almost nothing to leave you, and your uncle's whole property is in trust for Nicholas. I've saved what I can out of income, but it's very little. You see, dear, you can't afford to be rude to the Hilliards. It's as simple as that."

Her aunt's big eyes, full of sympathy and kindness, were fastened on her own half-averted face. She was touched by the sudden revelation of solicitude, by the note of appeal in Aunt Jo's voice, by the sense of love and devotion behind all her worldliness. Yet, at the same time, she could be almost irritated at the lateness, the very irrelevance, of the appeal.

"Girls don't need money the way they used to when you were young, Aunt Jo," she said sullenly. "I'll be all right."

"But there isn't any point deliberately alienating people," Aunt Jo reminded her. "Particularly people like Emily and Harriet." And even though she knew that it was not an argument that would appeal to Sybil, she couldn't, with her own overwhelming sense of its importance, quite avoid it. "Remember, dear, that Timmy is the only male Hilliard in his generation. And each of the aunts alone is as rich as Philip's father!"

But Sybil could only cover her face with her hands.

"Oh, Aunt Jo," she protested. *"Please!"*

Chapter

Two

THE EPISODE with the Misses Hilliard had the effect, at least, of turning Sybil's attention to her own generation, and she began to go to the beach club in the mornings. This club, like everything else in Easton Bay, was a very special club. The beach was small and made up of more gravel than sand; from time to time it was unusable because of the smell of dead fish. The clubhouse was a ramshackle, shingle affair with two wings of bathhouses that had canvas tops and a bar that served soft drinks and beer except on Saturday nights when there was whiskey. The bay lay before it, small but pretty, filled with sailboats and surrounded by green hills with the roofs of the oversized summer cottages looming over the tops of the trees. Unlike most clubs on the island the beach club cost very little to run; it could afford to select its members, as carefully and as slowly as it wished, from its long and patient list of applicants.

Sybil used to go there in the morning with a book and a pair of dark glasses. The weather was hot and damp, and she had no desire to do more than sit on the sand, alone, in the shade of an umbrella and gaze out over the bay. There were other people on the beach, her contemporaries, with their children, people whom she had known as personalities

rather than friends in the distant grey summers of her un-
social youth when she had been sent over to their houses,
reluctant and shy, by an aunt whose faith in the healing
powers of group activity had been infinite. She knew them;
she still spoke to them, but their presence brought back some
of the old fear and the old hostility, and she was not in a
mood to go on with it. Most of them had grown up in the
tradition of Easton Bay; they were nice, plain, rather domi-
nating women who had married young lawyers and lived in
made-over garages or superintendents' cottages on their
families' old places. They seemed harassed by the problem
of raising their many children; Sybil had the sense, as they
drove up to the beach club in their battered station wagons
filled with offspring, with favorite pails and shovels, with
dogs and balloons and unrelinquishable dolls, of things being barely under control. Yet they were all engaged, as she
would remind herself, in the serious business of living. If
they were sure of their husbands and the direction in which
they were going, if they were able to proclaim in their very
messiness, however aggressively, the satisfaction of their
own adjustments, was she in a position to cast stones?

The only person in Easton Bay whom she wanted to see
was Howard Plimpton. She had thought of him frequently
since the day of the lunch party when she had defended him
against Philip's aunts. Surely, whatever had happened, he
and she would still have something to say to each other. If
their earlier conversations had been about how to acquire
Mabel, they might now discuss how best to get rid of her.
She had seen him in the village twice since that day; each
time he had been sitting in the car of the cousin on whose
place he was staying, waiting for the latter to finish her
morning call at the grocer's. He never, apparently, went to
the beach club. He looked exactly as he had always looked,
surly and removed; his hair was just as thick and just as
short, and he had the same scowl on his square, rather rigid

face and the same large, clear, blue eyes. Yet he had stared right through her as she passed the open car where he was sitting, in shirt sleeves and navy khaki trousers, stared, not insolently, but as if he had not seen her. When she had turned, uncertainly, to speak to him, he had looked away.

She had not been offended, simply disappointed. It was evident that he identified her with Aunt Jo's world, that he assumed that she would be on the side of a society whose basic principles he had violated. It was not, of course, as she well realized, the fact that his wife might have to divorce him which constituted this violation. Divorce had become, indeed it had been for twenty-five years, an accepted, a respectable thing. Howard's offense, in the eyes of Easton Bay, lay in his apparent indifference even to the necessity or fact of divorce, in his refusal, by leaving his wife and business, to bother himself with the neat tying up and crating of discarded things that constituted, to one degree or another, some recognition of their value. Howard had simply walked out. One could do anything in the world but that. Easton Bay, without really acknowledging him, spent much of its time discussing him. He was proof that one scandal, unlike a swallow, could make a summer.

"Whatever code you live by," Aunt Jo told Sybil one day in an argument about Howard, "there *are* responsibilities. That you can never get away from."

"But, Aunt Jo," she protested. "You beg the very question that he's putting!"

"You mean he doesn't believe in responsibilities?"

"I mean he doesn't believe in anything."

If she was to see Howard, anyway, it was evident that her only approach would be through Edith Kellogg. Edith was Howard's cousin, and it was over her garage that he lived and did his painting. She was five years older than Sybil and had been one of the people in Easton Bay who had most terrified her when she was little, but she wondered now if they could not be friends. For the Edith whose sophistication and blatant knowledge of things that no one else knew had made the other children of Easton Bay feel so inadequate, this Edith whose speedy ruin had been confidently predicted by the irate nurses of little boys and girls whom she led into bad habits, had become, in her early thirties, after an unhappy marriage to a South American dancer, a warm and sympathetic woman, of whom some people in Easton Bay might disapprove, but whom no one could really dislike. She had resumed her maiden name and returned to Easton Bay, childless, to occupy the large, ugly shingle house of her now deceased parents, and to make it a social center for the small artist colony at Mog Beach, so near and yet so infinitely far from Aunt Jo's world, and for those of her old friends, of whom there were several, who, because of business failure or marital discord, found her milieu a welcome change from what they were used to. Edith's world was a casual, formless world of small and endless cocktail parties dominated by the tall, bony, trousered figure of the hostess, constantly smoking, stalking about the old-fashioned living room that had now been inadequately modernized with a handful of Eames chairs, the contrast of which with the false, very dark Jacobean paneling was so bad that she claimed it was intentional. She went occasionally to the beach club, and one morning she sauntered up to Sybil's umbrella.

"I hope you don't mind my butting in," she said, looking down at her and inhaling the smoke from her cigarette. "After all, we grew up together, didn't we? We share the same neuroses. And I've had to shed a husband myself. It's no picnic. Come around this afternoon for a drink, why don't you?"

Sybil went and had several drinks and enjoyed herself. She liked the casual friendliness with which she was received by Edith's group. Those who had known her before looked

at her with a new interest. She was the little girl who had
so unexpectedly caught and so unexpectedly abandoned a
Hilliard. Gone was the hostile shyness that had once re-
pelled them; they viewed with approval her better clothes
and better style. They were curious, but not articulately so,
to find out what had happened to her marriage. Howard
was there, in a white shirt, open at the neck, and khaki
pants, and she had the courage, after two cocktails, to go
over and talk to him. He stood apart from the others, near
the piano where the drinks were, helping Edith.

"You wouldn't speak to me in the village the other day,"
she reproached him. "You looked right through me,"

"You didn't speak to me," he said briefly. He was looking
away from her, across the room.

"Did you think I wouldn't?"

He shrugged his shoulders.

"That was your affair, Sybil."

"Did you think that I would turn my nose up at you?" she
persisted. "Did you think I would say, There's that terrible
Howard Plimpton?"

He turned and gave her a level stare. It was curious, his
stare, full of intended defiance, as if he were trying to prove
to himself that, however he might dislike it, he could outface anybody whom he wanted to outface.

"I didn't really care," he said roughly. Then he shook his
head, with a quick, nervous movement, as if, almost impatiently, to check his own rudeness. "I don't mean that I
wouldn't care what you thought, Sybil," he said. "I mean
I wouldn't care if you thought that."

"But you used to dance with me when nobody else did,"
she continued. "How could I ever think badly of you after
that?"

"Certainly I used to dance with you," he agreed. "As I
remember, you were a nice little girl."

"You mean I was sympathetic," she corrected him. "I
listened to people when they told me their troubles."

"Oh, yes." He nodded. "You could do that."

"Thank you." She made him a little bow. "I see you're still a gentleman."

"Are you still a nice little girl?"

"I can still be sympathetic," she said.

But something in her tone made him stiffen.

"I don't know why you should think I need sympathy," he said abruptly. "Unless you have more than you need for yourself."

There was a pause.

"It's true what they say, then," she said dryly. "You've lost your manners."

"Well, it's my loss."

"You probably don't believe you ever had them," she continued. "Or that they mattered. But you did. And they did matter. They happen to have been one of the nicest things about you."

Saying which, she left him, with the feeling that her departure was without effect. He made it so unnecessarily obvious that he had no need of her, that nobody, in fact, had any proper need of anyone else. She went over to Edith to say good-bye.

"You see we're not poison, Sybil," the latter told her. "Why avoid us? Join the gang."

"I'm not sure that Howard wants me."

"Howard?" she asked. "Has he been cranky? But, never mind, dear, he's cranky to us all. I adore him, but he can be a pest. Particularly when he's toting that log on his shoulder."

"Why does he come to parties, then?"

"As a matter of fact he hardly ever does," Edith replied. "But even a lone wolf gets lonely, I guess. Sitting over there on top of the garage."

Sybil, encouraged by Edith, started to drop in at her house in the late afternoons. There were always people for cocktails, and occasionally she would stay on for a late cold supper. Aunt Jo's disapproval was obvious but inarticulate. She did not like to lay down rules as to where her family could go and not go, but she felt that it was a singular perversity that made Sybil choose for steady companionship the only questionable group in all of Easton Bay.

"I suppose your aunt thinks you come here for orgies," Edith remarked to her.

"She's right, too," Sybil replied. "I'm only disappointed that you haven't provided them."

"Well, hang on. The summer's still young."

Edith had been right when she said that Howard rarely went to parties. At least, he rarely went to hers. The men at Edith's were inclined to be more talkative than Howard and shrill. There was Frank Bayswater, for example, one of the perennial Easton Bay community, a long, thin, blond bachelor who, as Aunt Jo's friends put it, had never "found himself." Frank had a little money and no job; he tried to make an existence, if not a life, out of a diminishing supply of the quality that he insisted upon regarding as his charm. He believed, extravagantly, in his prowess with women and bored the younger men at Edith's with unsolicited tips in the art of making love. He was very stupid, but Edith liked him, and her group, highly tolerant, accepted him. They were amused when he singled out Sybil for his particular attention. He assumed, so obviously and so ludicrously, that her air of detachment only meant that she was in love with him.

One Saturday night, at the beach-club dance, Frank and Sybil were sitting alone on the terrace drinking whiskey and watching the ripple of moonlight on the surface of the bay.

"Do I presume too much in wondering if it has struck even you, Sybil," he asked her, with the affected pompousness which he believed to be a component of wit, "that our relationship, beautiful as it is, may be due for a change?"

She looked up in surprise.

"Oh, no. Why?"

"I wonder if even the strictness of your background can wall in your feeling for me."

"That feeling," she said, smiling, "is like Edith's toy poodle. I keep it at my side. With only a string for a leash."

There was a pause while he looked down, rather dramatically, to the ground.

"You are schooled in cruelty."

She laughed.

"I like you, Frank," she said. "I like people to affect emotion. It makes everything nicer."

"It does, does it?"

"I think so," she said. "Most people make a cult of sincerity. I used to." She leaned back and looked at the stars. "What a mistake. From now on I'm going to live in the eighteenth century. I'm going to be a happy hypocrite."

"You don't have to tell me that, you know," he said insinuatingly. "You needn't try to fool old Frank. Do you think I was born yesterday?" His sneer was suggestive. "Why do women have to dress up natural things in fancy clothes? You know what you want. You all want it, too. Particularly the ones who've been used to it."

She looked at him coldly.

"Is there anything quite so boring, Frank," she asked, "as loose generalities about sex?"

To her astonishment she felt his hand suddenly on the back of her neck.

"Try this on for a generality," he said roughly.

He pulled her forward, almost out of her chair, and kissed her on the lips. She wrenched herself loose. She stared at his face for a second and then slapped it viciously.

"Damn you!" she cried. "Damn you for a clumsy lout!"

Even Frank had to recognize that this was not coyness. He held a hand to his cheek.

"What the hell?"

"Does that convince you I'm not one of your clichés?" she demanded.

There was a pause.

"What sort of a girl are you, anyway?"

"An Easton Bay girl," she retorted.

"And what the hell sort of girl is that?"

But Sybil had already regained her calm. She was looking out over the bay, her arms stretched out on the arms
of her chair.

"A girl who doesn't believe in fundamentals," she said
tersely. "Or in sex. Those things don't exist here. That's
why I like it." She paused. "But you, Frank, were the serpent in the garden. You had to be cast out."

He looked at her as though she was out of her mind.

"And you believe that crap?" he asked in amazement.
"That there's no love in Easton Bay?"

"If I feel there's none," she said coldly, "then there's none
for me."

Frank complained the next day to Edith that Sybil Hilliard was "nuts." He explained to her what had happened,
but to his irritation she only roared with laughter.

"I suppose any woman who resists you is nuts, dear boy,"
she said mockingly. "Sybil was taking you for a ride."

"Oh, she wasn't kidding," he said, rubbing his cheek. "I
can promise you that."

"Well, anyway, it's perfectly natural," Edith continued.
"She probably hates the very idea of sex. I was that way
after my husband left me."

"Yeah. For twenty-four hours."

She gave him an oblique look.

"It's a phase," she said. "She'll get over it. What she needs
at the moment is something with pants that can take her
out without molesting her."

"And where," he sneered, "are you likely to find that?"

Edith shrugged her shoulders.

"She'll find it," she said. "And without any help from
you."

Chapter
Three

JUNE WAS FOLLOWED by July, and the real summer heat descended on Easton Bay. It was a damp, dead heat, and the big trees around Aunt Jo's house drooped. Even the well-raked blue gravel on the drive lost its luster. People began to disappear to Maine and Bermuda and the Cape, and Aunt Jo and Uncle Stafford went off for a month to stay at a large, airy clubhouse on the dunes at the Hamptons. When Sybil kissed her aunt good-bye in the front hall, the issue between them was voiced for the first time.

"I suppose you'll *live* at Edith Kellogg's while I'm away."

"Not quite."

There was a pause during which Aunt Jo gazed at her with a funny, hard little smile. Sybil suddenly realized that it was an embarrassed smile.

"I hope you don't go there to see Howard Plimpton," she said.

Sybil laughed in sheer surprise.

"Howard?" she asked. "What on earth gave you that idea?"

"It was just a thought. Or should I say a worry?"

"Maybe a worry of yours, Aunt Jo. Hardly one of mine."

She found after they had left that she missed them. The

emptiness of the big house, bereft of her aunt's energetic presence, served to intensify her own loneliness and irresolution. She dined in the evening with Nicholas in a rather stately way. He sat in his father's place and she in Aunt Jo's, and they regarded each other gravely over the gleam of the silverware while he talked, slowly and interminably, about his law cases, about the store in London where he still bought his shoes, about the unfortunate state of repair of the other big houses in the neighborhood and the sad deterioration of the north shore of the island in general. He seemed to know that his conversation was of no interest to her, but he never blamed her. His large serious eyes, slightly mocking, seemed only to suggest that if she did not care to contribute to the subjects of their conversation, she would have to be content with the humble fare that he offered her. It was, after all, his best.

She was less amused by Edith's parties after the incident with Frank Bayswater. It was not that she held this against Edith, but it had somehow discolored the atmosphere of her house, taking from it a part of the brightness and gaiety that she had found before. She was even becoming a bit bored with Edith herself who, after six or seven bold and striking mannerisms of speech, seemed to have exhausted the rather meager supply of her charm. She was an admirable person, Edith, brave and bighearted, but what struck one after even a brief acquaintance was the surprising fact that she was dull. As Sybil looked about Edith's living room, she began to wonder if this were not also true of her friends. Were they not fundamentally like Aunt Jo's? Didn't they have the same basic need for a handful of oversimplified premises? She felt at times that her remarks had the same jarring effect on them as they did on the Hilliard aunts, that the bleakness of her own loss of faith could be as isolating in one milieu as the other. And why not? If anyone was in the wrong, it was she.

Her feeling persisted that she and Howard were somehow in the same predicament. She had not seen him since their brief encounter at Edith's, but she knew that Aunt Jo had guessed correctly and that her real reason for going there was her hope of seeing him again. It was only when she had given up all hope of meeting him coincidentally that she made, for the first time, a morning call on Edith. She found her and Frank Bayswater playing backgammon on the porch.

"Hi!" Edith called to her, as she moved four men on a throw of doubles. "Fix yourself a drink. We'll be going to the club in a minute."

Sybil sat down and watched them. Twice she opened her lips and closed them again.

"Do you know where I can find Howard?" she asked finally.

Edith looked up in surprise.

"Now what's he done?"

"Nothing," Sybil said quickly. "I wondered if he would let me see his paintings."

"He'd probably be delighted," Edith said, throwing her dice again. "Amateur painters don't have that commendable reticence that amateurs in the other arts are blessed with. He's outside on the lawn."

When Sybil left, Frank looked up at Edith and winked.

"I suppose Howard won't molest her," he said, sarcastically.

"Whatever Howard may be, Frank," she said meaningfully, "he's not clumsy. Of that, my dear, you may be quite sure."

Sybil found him standing before an easel on the part of the lawn from which, through a vista in the trees, he had the widest view of the bay. He turned around as she came up and nodded. It was his own particular nod, more of an acknowledgment than a greeting. It committed him to nothing.

"Do you mind if I sit here and watch?" she asked. "I don't mean the picture," she added. "I mean the process."

He looked back to his canvas.

"Not in the least."

She sat down on the grass and looked out at the bay.

"Do you mind if I talk from time to time?" she asked. "You don't have to answer, you know."

"Sure. Go ahead." He turned to her and almost smiled. "This isn't one of my serious jobs."

"But there are serious ones?"

He shrugged his shoulders.

"Serious to me. Not to anyone else."

"Oh, come," she protested, to keep him talking, "Edith tells me you're good."

"Edith knows nothing about it," he said flatly.

There was something restful to her in his concentration, in the very fact that it *was* a bad picture and that he didn't care. When he stood still, he was very still; his thick, muscular frame seemed integrated with the heat of the day. If he moved his arm, he moved it quickly, almost impatiently, as if in deprecation of the petty human work of picturization that he was engaged in. The sweat stood out in beads on his round, unshaven cheeks; it glistened on his temples by the roots of his hair.

"Why do you paint?" she asked.

"Because I like it. Why does one do anything?"

"Why indeed?"

He looked around, as though to see if she looked as fatuous as she sounded.

"Why do you sit there and ask me questions?" he asked.

She pulled up a clump of grass and scattered it beside her feet. She was not going to let him make her mad again.

"Because I'm bored," she answered. "And because it's hot. And because I find you interesting."

"Why interesting?"

She pondered.

"Maybe because I feel that nothing that I could ever say would shock you."

He turned again and looked at her more inquiringly, taking her in, in his blunt, unapologizing way, for the first time that day.

"Are you going to tell me that you find me attractive?" he asked. There was no sneer in his tone.

"Would you like me to?"

He turned back to his canvas.

"I accept situations," he said tersely. "I don't make them."

"You mean women run after you?"

"How like a woman," he muttered, "to put one in the wrong. No, I'm not claiming anything, Sybil," he continued. "I get along. That's all."

"Well, I'm *not* going to tell you that I find you attractive," she said decisively. "I'm tired of attractive men. I married one."

He started to work on the sky in his picture.

"Do you find Philip attractive?" he asked. "Still?"

"Don't you think he is?"

"I never do much thinking about people like Philip," he said carelessly. "What's there to think about?"

For all her effort, she felt a stab of resentment.

"Who are you to look down on Philip?" she asked. "What have you done with your life to be so superior?"

He shrugged his shoulders.

"If you're still so protective about the guy," he asked, "why don't you go back to him?"

"That's my business!"

"And I have mine," he retorted, turning back to his landscape. "If you'll let me get on with it."

Her irritation collapsed.

"I'm sorry," she said lamely. "I seem to get wrought up over nothing. It must be the heat."

"Skip it."

"It's silly of me to take on so about Philip," she continued. "Particularly when, deep down, I feel the way you do."

Howard stood looking at his landscape, but she could see that he was not concentrating. She had apologized and she had done it handsomely; it was up to him now, with all his indifference to convention, to say something.

"It's not that I have any particular feeling about Philip," he explained, rather awkwardly. "It's the whole group of which he's part. They play little rôles they think have been assigned to them. It's harmless, really."

"You mean he's a stuffed shirt?"

"That's your phrase, Sybil. Not mine."

She sighed. There was something in the unchallengeable sincerity of his tone and the broad coverage of his remarks that made other standards seem inadequate. He had stepped over the border and was grazing placidly in the empty fields of his own emancipation. She had a longing to implicate him, to make him share her responsibility.

"What should I do, Howard?" she appealed. "Should I leave him?"

"Haven't you?"

"I could go back."

He turned to his pallette and mixed his paints.

"Do you want to?"

"No."

"Isn't that your answer, then?"

"Is that the only standard?" she asked. "What we want for ourselves?"

"What else? What other people want for us?"

She brushed this aside.

"You don't think," she persisted, "that I have any obligation to stay with Philip?"

"I don't think anyone has any obligation to stay with anyone."

"Not even for Timmy's sake?"

"Who's Timmy? Oh, your son." He reached into his box for another paint. "Well, I don't believe in sacrificing everything for children. They can take their chances with the rest of us."

"Your children," she retorted, "seem to be taking theirs with Mabel."

He turned and looked at her for a moment. His blue eyes seemed to be draining the spite out of her question, considering any residue of interrogation that there might be left. Yet in the very steadiness, the very blueness of his stare she became for the first time aware of a resentment that *he* might be feeling, a resentment against the world from which he appeared to have cut himself off.

"My children, as you say, are with their mother," he said evenly. "Your son, I take it, is usually with you."

"But he's with the Hilliards now," she cried. "And I hate it!"

He turned back to his picture.

"I have no place for the children," he said. "Mabel has. Besides, she's going to marry again. After the divorce."

"You don't mind her supporting them?"

She could hardly believe that she had said it. It was as if the spirit of Philip's aunts had suddenly descended upon her and was speaking, like a ventriloquist, through her lips.

"Money is money," he said briefly. "I don't worry about source."

"Oh, Howard, I've hurt you," she said, jumping up and going over to him. "I'm a bitch. But it's because I'm all upset inside. When I see anyone taking these things in their stride I want to strike out and hurt them. But you can make allowances. Can't you?"

He put down his brush and folded his arms.

"Are you trying to reform me, Sybil?" he asked. "What's this all about?"

She shook her head violently.

"You're wrong, Howard," she protested. "It's quite the contrary. I want you to reform *me*. I'm tired of pros and cons and wondering what I should do. And what I should feel. I want to learn to live with myself. Will you help me?"

For the first time that morning he came out of his isolation. He frowned, and then, quite suddenly, there was a relationship between them.

"I can't help you, Sybil," he said. "I can't help anyone, really. Look at my own life."

"But it hasn't got you down, Howard! That's the point!"

"Hasn't it?" He put his hands in his pockets, and walked a few paces off from her. "Well, anyway," he said, turning around and dismissing the note of introspection, "we can be friends. And that, in Easton Bay, is something. Already."

Chapter

Four

HOWARD WAS ONE to accept a situation readily, and after their conversation on Edith's lawn he took it as a matter of course that Sybil should come over each day and talk to him while he painted. In the evening they would drive to a local roadhouse and drink beer. Edith was quick to sense that their relationship was special; she decided to leave them to themselves. She could see that Sybil was intrigued by Howard, but she had more difficulty in making out what he thought of her. He was not articulate in personal matters.

"She's all mixed up, poor creature," she told him one day. "I hope you'll be nice to her."

"I'm mixed up, too," he retorted. "We're *all* mixed up."

"All the more reason to be nice to her."

"What makes you think I won't be nice to her?" he asked irritably.

"Because you're so damn theoretical, my dear."

It was certainly true that Howard was theoretical. It made him, even to Sybil, a frequently exasperating companion. There was no axiom that he was willing to take for granted, no idea, however casually brought forth, that he was not ready to explore by the standards of his new emancipation.

"Why do you say 'I ought'?" he was continually asking, or "What do you mean when you say a person is 'good'?" Sometimes, when she was anxious to get on with the discussion she found this trying, but she was always humble. She had enrolled, after all, as his pupil, and it was to be expected that the course would have its trying moments.

Howard, when he got started, which was not an easy thing for him, was apt to hold forth on what he considered the errors of his own bringing up. He was particularly bitter on the subject of Chelton School which, as he put it, was so full of false values that a lifetime was needed to slough them all off. He compared himself to a person who has been saved by an extensive surgical job, but who is incapacitated thereafter for normal life. "They got the Chelton out," he would say, "but the patient almost died in the process." Sybil, of course, had no partiality for Chelton, the school that had separated her from Teddy, but it was nonetheless a part of the nostalgia of her childhood, and she remembered her visits there in the springtime with a certain swelling of heart. She was not willing to throw quite as much into the junk heap as he. There were things, even in the Hilliard world, to which she still clung, and it often occurred to her that he might be going too far. One by one, painstakingly and conscientiously, he seemed to be jettisoning every principle of their joint background. Some of them came out easily, and some required digging, but all received the same careful treatment. His only fear was that he might miss one. Yet despite all he could do there was a certain hard core of the unreconstructed Cheltonian that he could never entirely obliterate. He was like a man sitting in a crowded street car, refusing, for some odd principle and greatly to his own discomfort, to give up his seat to a woman.

"But everybody in the older generation isn't a hopeless case," she protested one night. "My Aunt Jo, for example. She's a snob, I grant, but that's not the whole story. She's warm and kind and generous to all of us —— "

"Like the Pharisees."

She looked about the smoky little room with its four other tables, its stained red and white tablecloths, its nickelodeon that never worked. She reflected how stubbornly he always refused to go to the other roadhouse, the nicer one, because the summer people went there. It was really a night club, he used to say scathingly, that only masqueraded as a roadhouse.

"If she was *your* aunt, you'd see what I mean," she said.

"It's not a question of whose aunt she is," he said. "I know your Aunt Jo. I've known her all my life. She thinks that caring about who she sees and what sort of a car she drives and how the lawn looks are the minor things of life. Minor, but rather charming." He shrugged his shoulders. "But she's eaten up with them. They all are. Her whole group. They'd be nothing without them."

There was a long pause as she took this in.

"I think that's very rude of you, Howard," she said finally. "You know how much I care about her."

He put his elbows on the table, holding his beer level with his eyes and stared at the glass.

"I thought you wanted to talk about things the way they are," he said in an even tone. "If you want to go out with people who tell you nice things, why don't you? I'm not begging you to stick around."

She breathed deeply and picked up her cigarettes to put them in her bag. She pushed her chair back, as if to get up.

"I wonder if you realize what you're doing to yourself, Howard," she said. "When you said that about Aunt Jo, you knew it was going to hurt me. You didn't really want to say it, either. I know that. Fundamentally, you're soft as an old pillow. But you made up your mind that it was foolish of me to have illusions and foolish of you to respect them. And you *made* yourself say it."

He turned and gave her his most deliberate stare.

"Isn't that what you wanted of me, Sybil?"

"Not at the risk of your hurting yourself," she said. "You count for something, too, you know."

"Don't worry about me."

"I do, though. Is that forbidden?"

He shrugged his shoulders.

"I guess that's your business."

There was a long pause.

"You must be very bored with me, Howard," she said dryly. "It's been good of you to give me so much of your time."

He moved uncomfortably in his chair and then, looking up at the waiter, signaled for two more beers.

"I'm sorry, Sybil," he said brusquely. "I haven't been very nice. But I like you." He glanced at her and smiled with embarrassment. "You're a good girl. You really are."

It was the first compliment that he had ever paid her, and she was almost too pleased to speak.

"What do you mean by 'good'?" she asked, and they both laughed.

For the rest of that evening they talked pleasantly about painting and Edith and Easton Bay, and she even made him laugh with a description of the routine of Nicholas' day. When she got home that night she walked up and down the terrace alone, smoking and considering their relationship.

She had made up her mind earlier that year that she could never again fall in love. She had felt that such an event would be not only impossible but immoral. Now she was less sure, at least as to the first. Underneath the exhilaration that his grudging compliment had given her there was a disappointment in herself that after what Philip had meant to her she could still feel exhilaration at a compliment, but this, surely, was only the price that a person like herself should have expected to pay. It was all very difficult, but when had emotion been easy? She idealized Howard, and she knew that it irritated him, but she was not going to give it up for that. If she could enjoy seeing the polite and inhibited boy who had been so independent of his contemporaries in the truculent man who took her to the roadhouse, was that a pleasure to be foregone? Oh, she knew what people said about women in her position, that they were likely to tumble into anyone's arms, and she supposed there was some truth in it. But what was love and what was honor and what was loyalty — well, she was tired, and it was all beyond her. When she went to bed that night she took a sleeping pill and made her mind a blank.

The next evening, however, the issue of their relationship was presented in a different light. At the roadhouse, as they were getting ready to leave, he suggested that she spend the night with him. His expression was very serious; there was no implication that he took such things lightly.

"Oh, Howard, I don't think so," she said nervously, inadequately. "I really don't. Though I suppose I should have expected this."

His eyes were fastened on her.

"What else could you possibly have expected?" he asked. "I thought you liked me. I know I like you. What other relationship is possible?"

She looked miserably around the room.

"I suppose I thought we could be friends."

Howard, however, could be extremely doctrinaire in questions of sex. As he had once told her, satisfaction in this was the nearest thing to a duty that he recognized.

"We've been friends, Sybil," he explained. "Now we come to the point. It's rather futile if we don't. Perhaps you think I'm cold." He gazed down into his beer. "But I'm quite sure that I could satisfy you. I think you can trust me in these matters."

"Oh, it's not that, Howard," she said, putting her hand on his arm. "Or that I don't like you. No, I assure you, it's not that." She closed her eyes in a sudden seizure of giddiness.

"It's very much the opposite. But I'm not versed in these things the way you are."

"You mean you're afraid?"

She shook her head, her eyes still closed.

"Maybe. I don't know."

If he had only put his arm around her or even put his hand on hers, or addressed one kind word to her, she might have given in. She knew this now, and her head throbbed with the knowledge. But what made the whole thing so utterly hopeless was her sudden sense, as she opened her eyes and saw him look away, that *he* knew it, too. It was not that he was too cold or too indifferent to play his part with more feeling; it was his own deliberate choice to be that way, to take no advantage, to avoid even the tiniest cloud of sentiment on the wide, clear sky of his realism. She sighed and took out a handkerchief to wipe her nose. The gesture ended the scene between them.

"Do you have much success with women, Howard?" she asked. "Seriously. Edith intimates that you do."

She had never actually seen him blush before.

"Edith ought to keep her mouth shut."

"But do you?"

He shrugged his shoulders angrily.

"I get along. What the hell, Sybil? What's it to you? Obviously, I'm not going to have success with you."

"You don't try very hard," she observed dryly.

"You mean I don't talk pretty?" he retorted. "No. However much I may have bored you, at least I've spared you that."

She closed her bag as if preparing to leave.

"A pity," she said.

He put his change down on the table by the check and pushed his chair back.

"It wouldn't do any good if I started now, would it?" he asked.

She hesitated. Just for a moment.

"No, I don't think it would," she said.

On the drive back they talked very little. Howard made a few remarks about his cousin Edith and speculated on whether she would marry Frank Bayswater whom he described, with his usual charity, as an ass. Sybil looked out into the night and reflected that Frank at least believed in something. Even if only in his own fictional popularity.

The next morning she ran into Edith at the grocer's, and they talked, as they rarely did, about Howard.

"I'm delighted, you know, that you and Howard are getting to be such friends," Edith said brightly. "He needs someone to look after him. But I'm sure you won't mind a word to the wise from an old pal." She dropped her voice the least bit and looked straight at Sybil. "What you and he make of your friendship, my dear, is your own affair. But this much I will say. Don't take him too seriously."

Sybil put her package down on the counter and returned Edith's look.

"Too seriously?" she queried.

"You have that tendency. Do you not?"

"I may have, Edith. But why is Howard not a person to be taken seriously?"

"Because he's a louse," Edith explained quickly. Then she laughed nervously. "Aren't we all?"

Sybil turned away from the counter.

"Well, the first advance won't be made by me," she said. "If that's what you're worried about."

Edith laughed again.

"Oh, I'm not worried about that," she said. "I'm only worried about him. He's really quite wonderful, you know, my terrible cousin. I'm in love with him myself. And *that's* incest."

Chapter
Five

PHILIP WAS NOT enjoying his summer. He had spread his vacation over a series of long weekends rather than taking it all at one time. There had seemed no point in wasting a whole month if he could not go away on a cruise. Of course, he could have done this, but his mother had pointed out the inadvisability of showing such indifference to Timmy before the legal settlements had been made. "Indifference," of course, had been her word. She always put things crudely. He was not indifferent to Timmy at all, but he was accustomed to seeing the boy for short periods in the evening, and it bored him terribly to have to take him to the beach and watch him. It was easier for everybody, including Timmy, if he let him play with Lila's children by the family pool. Lucy made short shrift of his scruples.

"Don't think you can turn yourself into a nursemaid," she warned him. "You haven't the patience. Or the skill. Now get your golf clubs and go off some place where poor Timmy doesn't have to wear himself out being a joy to you."

Philip took her advice, but he found himself resenting what he considered the false position in which Sybil had placed him. A father could not be expected to fuss over a child as a mother did, yet after a separation he had to be demonstrative to prove that he wanted the child at all. Of course, he wanted the child; he would have hated to relinquish custody of Timmy. He knew that the time would come when he would be very proud to go up to Chelton to watch him play football. If Timmy ever did play football. If he did not turn out, that is, to resemble too closely his unpredictable mother. Never had Philip had Sybil so much in mind as during that summer. He could not reconcile himself to the completeness of her independence. He could not conceive that she had really forgotten him.

He had driven over to the beach-club dance at Easton Bay one Saturday night, having heard that she was going to be there. Easton Bay was regarded in Glenville as hopelessly dowdy, but Philip had always liked it. It had some of the charm that Sybil had originally had for him, the charm of the subdued, the good and, above all, the admiring. He had joined an old college classmate and his wife and had ordered a bottle of whiskey when Sybil came in with a large group of people led by a tall, raw woman who was dressed entirely in white and who smoked on the dance floor. Sybil's own appearance took him utterly by surprise. She looked bored and even sophisticated; it was obvious, too, that the man who was with her found her attractive. She did not appear to have looked in Philip's direction or to have seen him, yet when he cut in on her, a few minutes later, she did not seem at all surprised.

"Thank you, Frank," she said casually. "Oh, but look. Here's an old friend."

The man released her and nodded to Philip.

"Well, don't slap him, anyway," he said to Sybil, winking.

"Never fear. He'd slap me right back. He's my husband."

The man called Frank gave Philip a quick, surprised look and disappeared.

"Who's the guy?" Philip demanded, as they started to dance.

"Nobody."

"What did he mean about not slapping me?"

She shrugged her shoulders.

"It was necessary for me, a little while back, to administer a rebuff."

Philip's face darkened.

"What goes on around here, anyway?"

She shook her head several times. Slowly and patiently.

"Nothing, my good Philip," she said. "I can assure you, nothing at all. How is Timmy?"

"Oh, Timmy's fine."

"And Julia?"

"I haven't gone back to Julia," he retorted.

"I thought someone told me you had."

"I don't repeat myself," he snapped.

"I see. Good for you."

There was nothing more satisfactory than this in their conversation, and he returned to his table, greatly irritated. His mood was not improved, either, when he heard from his classmate's wife, a prim, earnest Easton Bay wife and mother, the gossip about Sybil and Howard Plimpton.

"It's the kind of thing you ought to know about, Philip," she said gravely. "They go around together all the time. And you know what *his* reputation is."

Philip didn't know, as a matter of fact, but he was soon brought up to date. He had known Howard at Chelton, and he had liked him in an impersonal way. They had played together on the football team, but he had not kept up with him since, and he knew nothing of his career of emancipation but the few facts, unfavorably presented, now offered for his consideration by his friends. What rankled particularly was that Sybil should have transferred her affections to another graduate of Chelton. He had always assumed that she would never look at another man, but that if she did, it would be a bohemian, an artist, a person, in short, whom someone like himself could not be expected to take seriously. But this was different. This was serious.

The next morning, with a hangover, he felt even worse about the whole thing. After breakfast he went into the living room where he found his mother sitting on the sofa, her shoes off, doing the crossword puzzle in the morning paper. Arlina was sitting at the other end of the sofa stroking a spaniel. She was now an oversized but rather pretty girl of nineteen, with messy bobbed hair and the appearance of one who has just been interrupted roughhousing. She clung to her mother even more than her older sisters did, which Lucy found very trying. Lila was sitting on the floor reading a comic, which, at thirty-two, was still the only part of the Sunday paper that held her interest. It was very hot, and the French windows looking over the lawn to the big meadow with its potato fields and round clumps of trees were opened wide. From time to time a faint breeze percolated the room and stirred the great crowded Gobelin tapestry that hung on the wall behind Lucy's sofa, rippling the faces of Alexander's warriors as they advanced to annihilate their enemy on green and blue Asiatic plains.

"What have any of you heard about Sybil?" he asked, standing before the sofa, his feet apart. "I've been hearing this and that. I suppose the husband is always the last to find out."

His mother looked up at him reflectively. Then she filled in a word in her puzzle.

"You mean about Plimpton, I suppose?"

"Oh, him," Lila said, as if she had been expecting something better. She went back to her comic.

"Well, what about him?" he asked irritably.

"Your dear aunts were the first to tell me about him," Lucy answered. "Trust them. Of course, I was dying to hear all about it, but I couldn't resist the opportunity of telling them that I, at least, took no interest in gossip. After all, one rarely has a chance like that to slap them down."

Arlina laughed and put her spaniel down on the floor.

"Oh, Mummie, superb!" she said. "How they must have glared!"

Philip threw his hands in the air.

"Can't we stay on any point for *any* time?" he protested angrily. "To hell with the aunts. What did you hear?"

Lucy put down her puzzle.

"I didn't hear much, as I say," she said. "Simply that she was seeing a great deal of Howard Plimpton who has deserted a perfectly good wife of his own. Partnership in crime, I suppose."

"Just seeing?" Philip demanded.

"Now don't be fierce, dear," Lucy said soothingly. "Your old ma hasn't let you down. I didn't like to ask people because I didn't think it came well from me. But I've done all right by you. I've hired a detective, and he's taken a room at Easton Bay. Apparently Jo Cummings has a gardener who's touchable —— "

Philip's eyes were wide.

"Mother!" he exclaimed. "You can't mean it!"

Lucy and Lila exchanged glances.

"It's routine, Phil," Lila pointed out. "We did it in my divorce."

"It isn't as if we'd ever *use* this evidence," Lucy explained. "Or even as if Sybil will ever know that we have it. It's a matter of being prepared. Don't forget, my boy, this is war. Separations are always war."

"But we can't spy on Sybil!" he cried. "It's not fair. What has she done, after all?"

"It's abominable!" exclaimed Arlina.

Arlina had never ventured to criticize her mother before, but in the sudden tenseness of the atmosphere her unprecedented outburst went unnoticed. Lucy slapped her hand down on the newspaper in her lap.

"I was afraid you'd be this way, Philip," she said. "That's why I didn't tell you in the first place. We women have to do all the dirty work and then take the blame. You seem to forget, my child, all the questions that have to be decided between you and Sybil. How much she's going to get, for example. Who gets Timmy. If you can put yourself in the driver's seat by spending a few hundred dollars on a detective, it's idiotic not to."

He hung there before her, undecided, swayed by the power of her logic.

"But suppose Sybil has done nothing?" he asked. "And suppose she finds out?"

"Well, since you put it to me, I think she's done plenty," Lucy retorted. "I don't say I can prove it yet, but give me time."

"You've never been consistent about Sybil," he said hotly. "You thought that she was terrible at first. Then you were all for her. Now you're down on her again. How am I to know how you stand or what it's worth?"

Lucy stared at the troubled young man before her. He was, after all, the only person in the world whom she cared for more than herself.

"You can be sure of one thing, my child," she said gravely. "And that is that I'm doing my best for you. That's how I stand and what it's worth."

He turned away from her and left the room. He had a dim, angry sense that these were problems that he should be working out for himself, but there was, as always, a part of him that felt exactly as his mother felt. He did want to know, damn it all, what Sybil was up to, and if she was up to what Lucy thought she was, then he wanted to use proof, however obtained, in the way that would most hurt her. But it was obnoxious, nonetheless, to be in the position of a spy, and it was still in his heart to feel a pang at the thought of Sybil, who had tried so hard to please him, being watched

by a bribed gardener. Yet what else could she expect? Had
he not eaten humble pie and begged her to forgive him?

"To hell with her!" he kept muttering to himself. "She
asked for it, didn't she?"

Later that morning he said this aloud to Lila on the golf
course.

"But why get all stewed up, Phil?" she asked. "It's just a
formality. I'll bet she's having *you* watched."

This was a new and sobering thought, but he was sure,
even as it came to him, that Sybil would never descend to
such a level. There was no point, however, explaining this
to Lila. Like Lucy, she would never understand.

Arlina Hilliard was even more upset than her brother.
Sybil had been the only member of the family who had ever
rivaled her mother in her affections. She went out riding by
herself that morning to consider in all its horror the full
effect of Lucy's revelation. Arlina never quite knew when
her mother was serious and when she was not, but she
hardly thought that even Lucy would joke about a matter
like this. Desperately she took jump after jump, higher than
any that she had ever dared before, as if to lift herself above
the world of hate and suspicion that had so suddenly opened
up to her. Later in the day, lunching at the beach with a girl
friend, she poured out the whole story, telling it as if it had
happened, not to her family but to another. The friend sided
immediately with the wife in the story.

"If I were the husband's sister," she said, "I wouldn't warn
the wife directly. That might be disloyal. But I would certainly see to it that the information got to her."

"You would?"

"Of course, I would. How else could I call myself her
friend?"

Arlina clenched her fists.

"And she *is* my friend!" she cried. "She was the first real friend I ever had! She even came to see me at school recess to tell me when she and Philip were engaged!"

She clapped her hands over her mouth, but the other girl only laughed and told her that she had guessed the secret anyway. Arlina was too miserable really to care. She turned away from her, plunging her fingers into the sand, and contemplated once more the extraordinary inequity of a world where her mother and Sybil could not be friends.

Chapter
Six

SHORTLY AFTER Aunt Jo returned from the Hamptons, Millie came down to Easton Bay with her two children to spend a week and to get away from the cares of housekeeping. She filled the house with an atmosphere of small, neat details and small, exact arrangements and took over, as if by right, the position of senior niece. Aunt Jo, who was capable, in detached moments, of laughing at Millie, was nonetheless flattered and pleased by the constant attention that Millie paid her, an attention, it was true, that seemed premised on the idea that it was only a fraction of the solicitude that would, all naturally, be poured out in return to a young wife and mother, so fragile, so charming and so anxious to do only what was right. Like Sybil earlier in the summer she spent her time entirely with Aunt Jo and with Aunt Jo's friends, but whereas Sybil had been a taciturn and rather sardonic witness of their daily round, Millie, fluttering and pleased and admiring, was immediately taken to their hearts with an enthusiasm that owed at least some of its clamor to the contrast thus afforded to her sister-in-law.

"You're not nice to that girl, Sybil," Aunt Jo warned her one night after she had spent the evening playing solitaire, gloomily aloof from the family group. "You'll regret it one day. You've only got one brother, you know, and you shouldn't antagonize his wife."

Sybil bowed her head.

"I know," she said sullenly. "I'm awful."

"Aren't we feeling just a tiny bit sorry for ourselves?"

They had reached their bedrooms, and Sybil had one hand on her doorknob.

"Oh, Aunt Jo," she said heatedly. "Can't you leave me be?"

And she went into her room and closed the door behind her without even saying good night. It was the first time she had ever been so rude, and she stood for two minutes without moving, trembling at the revelation of what seemed to be happening to her.

Things came to a head towards the end of Millie's visit at a cocktail party which Aunt Jo gave for her. There was no need for Aunt Jo to give cocktail parties when she, unlike the younger generation, was still in a position, with her large house and accommodating servants, to entertain her friends at lunch or dinner, but she liked the idea because she found it modern and a trifle dashing. Her friends felt the same way, although they seemed, unlike Lucy Hilliard's friends, to have little enough use for cocktails; they stood in pairs and trios about the long, stiff, green living room where all could have been seated, in their largest and most shining hats, some with cocktail glasses but more without, talking as earnestly and excitedly as though they had not met, the day before, at a similar party in the house of another friend. Sybil, standing by herself, looked about the room and wondered why she still cared enough to come. She saw Philip's aunts come in, Miss Emily with her quick, jerky stride, waving her arms at Aunt Jo and smiling in anticipation of their imminent embrace, like a great actress in private life who knows, while pretending not to see, that every eye is on her, and Miss Harriet, nodding from side to side, plodding along, picking up the pieces, so to speak, and consoling herself with the thought that if her world was not as romantic as her sister's it was at least more real. Sybil shrank back and let Millie greet them. Millie was good at such things; she went up to the Misses Hilliard as they turned from greeting Aunt Jo and chatted with them in a lively way that seemed designed to meet Miss Emily on her own plane and perhaps a little to distract her attention from Sybil's truculence. Well, it was Millie's world.

Millie, however, could not linger long with the Misses Hilliard. She took her position of guest of honor very seriously and moved from group to group, staying only long enough to hear a single anecdote to which she would listen or give the appearance of listening, with a drawn, rapt expression that broke, as the story reached its climax, into a series of little panting gasps, the components of what she secretly regarded as her enchanting and infectious laugh. Sybil, watching her, wondered if Millie ever really heard what was being said to her. It seemed as though her small quantity of concentration must have been used up in the effort of demonstrating her reaction, in the study of just when and how to throw back her head and shatter the pale generality of her attention with the myriad particulars of that laugh. It may have been that her skepticism was conveyed to Millie across the room through the jangled atmosphere of so many words and laughs, for she glanced at Sybil several times, a bit uneasily, and finally came over to her.

"You know, Sybil," she said, holding her cocktail glass close to her chin as though it were a fan that she was coyly allowing to rest there, "isn't it silly? Here we are, staying under the same roof, and I feel that a crowded party is my only chance to have a word with you."

Sybil looked at her suspiciously.

"A word about what, Millie?"

"Oh, a word about anything!"

"I remember one of our last talks," Sybil said with a touch

of bitterness. "You told me about Philip and Julia. What have you to tell me today?"

Millie looked at her with the wide, half-smiling eyes of the timid who know, half in embarrassment, half in a kind of fascinated pleasure, that they are about to be daring.

"Do you hate me for that, Sybil?" she asked. "Of course, you must. Yet I wonder. After all, you hated me before."

Sybil felt the sudden weariness of having, so unprepared, to take anything like this up.

"I haven't at all, Millie," she said. "You're being absurd."

But Millie only shook her head briskly.

"Oh, no, I'm not," she said in a high, bright voice. "You've never thought that I was the girl for Teddy. I *know*. But then it's possible, isn't it, Sybil, that you don't know your brother as well as you think you do? We all have our childhood dreams, and Teddy, I suppose, was yours. Isn't that true?" She nodded, still smiling, as though to answer herself. "But people do grow up, I'm afraid, in the end. It's one of those things that happens. And if my Teddy hasn't turned into your Teddy, it's quite possible, isn't it, that he may be a better Teddy? Or *must* he be a worse one?"

Sybil knew that one couldn't argue with Millie; she had no sense of the scheme of things, and when her small, metallic mind hit upon a truth, the unexpected illumination served only to emphasize the darkness of the shadows.

"Please, Millie," she begged. "I don't want to talk about it. If I've been a fool about you and Teddy, then I've been a fool. But if it's the past, why must we bother with it?"

Millie stared at her for a moment.

"There's no reason, I suppose," she said in a disappointed tone. "And, of course, Aunt Jo said none of us should plague you. I know you've had a miserable summer."

Sybil almost smiled at the satisfaction in her tone.

"On the contrary," she said. "It's been most enjoyable."

"Oh, Sybil, you *can't* say that!"

"Can't say what?"

"You can't say," Millie explained in her quickest, most nervous tone, "that all this business at Edith Kellogg's has really been enjoyable."

"All *what* business?"

"Sybil, I sometimes wonder if you don't forget who you are," Millie answered, adopting for her own protection a complacent, older sister's tone. "A girl who's married to Philip Hilliard can't be as free as a girl who isn't. Do you think, for example, that he doesn't know everything that's going on here?" She paused for effect. "I can assure you that Arlina Hilliard hinted very broadly to me the other day at the golf club that if you knew what was best for you, you'd watch your step."

Millie had put her glass down on a table as she said this. She was looking at Sybil as severely as she knew how, bracing herself for what she felt sure would be the fury of her rejoinder. Sybil had turned very pale.

"You mean Philip's trying to *get* something on me?" she asked.

"Arlina didn't explain what she meant," Millie answered with dignity.

Sybil turned away from her. The sudden force of the contrast between what Philip had meant to her and what he was now doing made her dizzy. She leaned against the bookcase and shook her head so abruptly when Millie followed her that the latter, hurt, turned back to the party. Left to herself, Sybil breathed deeply and lit a cigarette. It was only another thing to get used to, after all. Another step in the process of her adult education. She looked about at Aunt Jo's friends and thought bitterly how many of their children had been divorced, had had affairs, had done all the things that they went through the form of constantly deploring. But it was different with their children; underneath their defections they maintained a loyalty to the system of marrying and giving in marriage as shown by the very frequency with which they went through its forms. What, in both generations, they could all scent out and resent was a defection that was fundamental, a defection that manifested any loss of faith in the elementary optimism of family chatter, in the idea that everyone was really "all right," that even with ups and downs, given half a chance, they would somehow settle down. There was plenty of room for Philip, even for Julia, in their world. But was there room for anyone who despised the subterfuges and proclaimed openly her own disillusionment? Disillusionment with what? Why, with everything! She rubbed her brow. *Was* she beginning to crack? And was she not even hoping that she would crack? Her mind seemed to be skidding around in smaller and smaller circles. She went over and stood at the sideboard by the shaker and drank her fourth strong Martini in quick nervous sips.

Such a procedure did not pass unnoticed, particularly by the Hilliard aunts. They watched her out of the corners of their eyes until the moment when, nodding to each other, they moved over to stand between her and the room, shielding her from inquiring eyes.

"My dear," Miss Emily began, shaking her head, "I hate to see a young girl taking more than one of those things. I know that everyone seems to do it these days, but doesn't that just make it worse?"

"Are you going to warn me, too, Aunt Emily?" Sybil demanded. "Millie tells me the Hilliards have me under the strictest observation. They want me to slip. Isn't that it?"

The sisters exchanged significant glances.

"If you mean that we're all interested in your welfare, my dear," Miss Emily answered, "then, of course, you're right. I hate to see any member of the family drinking."

Sybil looked defiantly from one to the other. She remembered how much she had wanted to like them and to have them like her in the first years of her marriage. She marveled at the time she had wasted.

"What do you really think of me?" she asked boldly. "Do tell me. Please."

She could see by the glitter in their eyes and their embarrassed smiles that she had shocked them. Being shocked, however, was not for them an unpleasant experience. It amused them to gaze down from the unassailed citadel of their virginity to the flat, dry plane of domestic discord and hear one of the younger generation shouting up at them with a rudeness that was in itself an admission of inferiority.

"I don't think I like your tone, Sybil," Miss Emily reproved her. "One does not ask such questions of one's elders. At least one never did when I was a girl."

Sybil looked at their stiffened jaws, their expanses of flowered print, their big, black shiny hats as if through a haze.

"I wonder if you'd ever have spoken to me if you'd really known what I was like," she said. "Everyone in the Hilliard family makes up to you both because they're after your money. But you *want* that. You knew from the beginning that I wasn't interested in your money, and you thought there was something queer about it." She threw back her head and gave a sudden laugh. "Oh, how I *see* it now!" she exclaimed. "You'd rather be liked for your money than for yourselves! There might be something impertinent in somebody's liking you for yourselves. It might be pity."

For just a moment, as she faced Miss Emily and brought this out, there was a sense of communication between them. Not so with Miss Harriet, the prosaic and resolute, who had already turned away with the air of disgust of the man who cannot stand scenes. But Miss Emily had a certain intelligence and on those rare occasions when she allowed it to peep out from behind the thick curtain of her preconceptions she was capable of a small vision of the world as it was. She could see now, outraged as she had been, that the poor creature who had so outraged her was unhappy and needed help. But it was only for a moment. Then the word "pity" burst in upon Emily Hilliard with its full force.

"If anybody is to like *you*, my child," she said grimly, "it will have to be for something besides yourself."

Once again Sybil was left alone, and she drank another cocktail. She was trembling now from head to foot. It *was* madness; there could be no question about it after what she had said. But she was no longer redeemable, which made it easier than when she had been rude to Aunt Jo. The sky behind her was aglow now with the crackle of burning bridges. If it was strange and terrible, there was also exultation in it. She turned away from the party and went into the front hall.

She was fumbling in her bag for the key to her car when she realized that Nicholas had followed her.

"You're going out for dinner?" he inquired politely.

"I'm going out."

"Can't I take you?" he suggested. "We could dine at a place I know near Glenville. They have excellent oysters."

She found her key and turned back to face him.

"You're being very kind, Nicholas," she said. "But you're afraid I'm drunk and that I'll wreck my car. And I don't care. Can't you see that? I don't *care!*"

He nodded, as in perfect comprehension.

"That is very little consolation, you will admit," he said, "to those of us who do."

She stared into the half-abashed sympathy of his sad eyes and felt, just for a moment, the impulse to surrender to them all. Then she shook her head impatiently.

"Oh, you don't care, Nicholas!" she exclaimed. "None of you care! It's just a tribal fetish. And I'm sick of it. You can't imagine how sick of it!"

She hurried out the door and into her car. How she got down the drive she didn't know; she remembered afterwards the roar of the blue gravel as she sped around the corners at a speed that had never before so insulted its raked orderliness. She went to the roadhouse that she always went to with Howard and drank three cups of black coffee at the counter, looking dolefully at the pale face and messy hair in the mirror opposite her. She decided that she looked picturesquely desperate.

Howard was home and answered the telephone when she called. She was very aggressive.

"Where are you anyway?" she demanded. "Why don't you come down here and buy me a drink?"

"It doesn't sound as if you needed one."

"Well, are you coming?" she asked. "Or aren't you? Do you want me to drive up and get you?"

"God, no!" he said quickly. "I want to live. Stay where you are. I'll get someone at Edith's to run me down."

He came, and they sat at their usual table. while she poured forth, in a rather confused manner, her low opinion of the Hilliard family, her own family and of herself. He had several drinks, but he refused to let her have anything but one glass of beer. By eleven o'clock she was slightly more sober but no calmer.

"Well, if you won't let me drink," she said at last, "there's no point in our staying here."

He paid the check and took her back to her car. He got in himself, however, and took the driver's seat. For a few minutes they drove along in silence.

"But where are we going?" she asked as she suddenly recognized through the rapidly turning headlights the familiar rhododendrons of Aunt Jo's drive. "I don't want to go home. I have no idea of going home!"

"Where do you want to go?"

"I want to go to your place," she said peevishly. "How

dense can a man be? I want to go to your place and have a drink."

He stopped the car and turned it around.

"Very well," he said. "To my place."

"Well, do you *mind?*"

"You're very belligerent tonight, Sybil," he said quietly. "No, I don't mind."

When they drew up before the garage in which he lived he sat for a moment at the wheel.

"Look, Sybil," he said. "I don't want to take advantage of you. You're still plastered."

"Look who's being a gentleman!" she sneered. "Is this your liberation? Is *this* your emancipation?"

"I don't have to be consistent," he retorted. "I live by my own standards."

"I don't give a damn about anybody's standards!" she exclaimed defiantly. "Least of all yours!"

She went up the outside stairway to his rooms, and she heard the click as he turned off the lights in the car and closed the door. Before she reached the landing she heard his step immediately behind her. He turned the key in the lock and opened the door for her, switching the light on as she stepped over the threshold.

.   .   .

She wanted too much and yet nothing. She wanted to be drowned in the eddying green sea of the music of *Tristan* that she had loved as a child in Aunt Jo's box; she wanted to die like Isolde of a love that was identified with the black enveloping honesty of night. There was an element of the indecent, of the suicidal, in her gasping search for an obliteration of her own unfaithfulness to love, and kind as he was, and experienced as he was, he would not allow her to lose herself in him. She could feel that he was holding her back; she felt in his body his own insistence that what they were doing was that and just that, and as she lay back afterwards in the darkness, feeling the throb between her head and the pillow and the thick, slow tears in her eyes, she knew again that she had no one to blame but herself.

When she got up she dressed alone in the dark without speaking to him. She put her clothes on hurriedly in her need to get away as fast as she could. He was lying on the couch, smoking.

"You don't have to hurry off, you know," he said. "It's early still."

"I've got to get home."

"It's never what you think it's going to be, is it, Sybil?" he asked. "Relax. The world isn't going to come to an end."

"I'm not at all sure. Not at *all* sure."

There was a long silence. When he spoke again there was a note of detached sarcasm in his voice.

"You'd rather hold hands, wouldn't you?"

She turned towards him, stung.

"I'm not the only one who misses things," she retorted.

He sat up. She heard his laugh.

"Don't run off, Sybil," he said in a more kindly tone. "Wait a second. I'll drive you home."

"I want to be alone!" she said fiercely. *"Alone!"*

She went out the door and slammed it behind her. She paused at the top of the stairway and looked up into the moonlight, defiant of eyes in the darkness. Then she hurried down the steps and into her car. As she started off, she rolled down the window and let the cool bay breeze ripple her hair. If there was anything wrong, she kept repeating to herself as she drove along, it was the fault of romanticism. A romanticism that she despised for having sunk her in the void where she now found herself. But there it remained, inside her, indestructible. Did she really want anything, she asked herself angrily, fixing her eyes on the fleeting grey of the side of the road, but to be held like a trembling bird in a

large, inert human hand? Or the sense of turning in a ballroom to a waltz or driving along the seashore with the wind
in her hair? Or sitting alone by the radio in Uncle Stafford's
library and listening to Beethoven and thinking of what she
had originally thought of Philip? What a fool she was.
What an absolute fool.

When she had left her car in the middle of Aunt Jo's turn-
around and crossed the gravel to open the front door, she
saw that the lights were on, not only in the hall but in the
living room. She went to the door of the latter and found
Nicholas playing solitaire at the card table in the corner.

"You haven't waited up for me?" she asked.

He mixed the cards on the table before him with a quick
gesture of his long, thin hand.

"I often sit up, Sybil," he said calmly. "You know how
badly I sleep."

She walked into the room and faced him.

"But you did wait up?" she insisted.

He looked at her and smiled his usual smile.

"Surely that's my prerogative, is it not?" he asked. "I'm
not, after all, a child."

She went over to the card table and sat down, leaning her
head on her hands.

"Oh, Nicholas," she groaned. "I'm such a bitch. You have
no idea."

"You always exaggerate, Sybil. You always have."

She looked up at him for a long moment. It was there, in
his eyes, that family faith that dogged her steps, that faith
that she, like all cousins, was surely more sinned against
than sinning.

"If I could only marry you, Nicholas," she said suddenly,
"perhaps I could be saved. Would you, Nicholas?" She got
up and put her hands together beseechingly. "Would you,
please? I'd change my whole life. I'd be good. Good as you
can't believe."

He turned very red. He got up and moved instinctively towards the door.

"Sybil!" he exclaimed. "You don't know what you're saying!"

Too much had happened to her, however, for her to care what she said. Or what she destroyed.

"I've never known better!"

"You must go to bed," he said in a hoarse tone. "You must go upstairs this minute! Or I'll have to call your aunt."

She shrugged her shoulders and walked past him into the hall to the big winding stairway with the white bannister. As she passed each of Aunt Jo's paintings, the cows and the landscapes and the very red cardinals, the shepherds in the fields and the winsome girl on the doorstep with her dog, she reflected, but not very steadily, that all these things had ceased to be referents. But where was she? Alas, and she shook her head bitterly, she was nowhere.

Chapter

Seven

WHILE PHILIP AND ARLINA were having breakfast, two
days later, on the terrace their mother came out and handed
Philip a letter. She sat down opposite him and watched his
face cloud as he read it.

"Well?" she asked.

"Well, what?"

"You said I was prejudiced against her. You said that I
was absurdly suspicious." She shrugged her shoulders. "Now
you can see for yourself."

"I can see that your man has been very thorough," he
said bitterly. "I imagine you have had to pay high."

"But you shouldn't believe people like that!" Arlina cried
unexpectedly. "They get paid more if they turn things up,
don't they? Don't they?" she repeated shrilly.

Lucy and Philip both looked at her in astonishment. The
Hilliards had a way of discussing private matters in family
conclave, but it was not for a junior to interrupt.

"They don't at all, Arlina," Lucy said sharply. "And I
doubt if you know a thing in the world about it."

Arlina blushed and looked down through the glass top of
the table at her feet.

"Anyway, I'm fed up with the whole business," Philip continued angrily to his mother. "It makes me feel like a worm. I'm going over to see Sybil and have this thing out with her. Once and for all."

He got up.

"Don't be a fool!" Lucy exclaimed. "Do you want to ruin everything? How do we know we have enough proof?"

"It's enough for me."

"But, Philip, is it enough legally?" she protested. "Wait a few more days, darling, and I guarantee you'll be in a position to —— "

"I shouldn't have listened to you in the first place," he interrupted. "The whole damn business makes me sick!"

With this he turned and went into the house. A moment later they heard the sound of his car starting. There was an angry spurt of gravel as he drove off.

"He'll ruin everything," Lucy wailed. "The big ox!"

Arlina was sitting quietly in her chair, still staring down at the terrace.

"He's right, Mummie," she said in a low voice. "You should have left Sybil alone."

Lucy looked around again at her youngest child. It was the second time in her life that the girl had dared to talk back to her.

"And just what do you know about it, young lady, I'd like to know?" she demanded.

"I know that if you want Sybil back, you're not going about it the right way."

Lucy stared.

"But I'm not at all sure that I *do* want her back."

Arlina folded her napkin with exaggerated dignity and rose to her feet.

"In that case you've been very clever," she said and left the table.

Lucy looked after her in amazement. A sharp retort died on her lips. Then her anger subsided, and she even managed a laugh.

"Well, I'll be damned!" she exclaimed to herself. "I'll be damned."

When Philip pulled up before the doorway of Aunt Jo's house in Easton Bay he did not even get out of his car. He blew the horn until the old butler, scandalized, appeared.

"Will you tell Mrs. Hilliard that I want to see her right away," Philip called to him.

"I'll see if she's up, sir."

"Well, wake her up if she's not."

The butler disappeared immediately, and a few moments later Sybil came out of the house and walked slowly over to his car.

"Our separation has not improved your manners," she said, putting her hands on the door. "Aunt Jo was wondering if you could possibly be sober."

"I had to talk to you," he said shortly, "and I didn't want to go into the house."

She considered this a moment and nodded.

"I see," she said. "In that case I'd better get into the car."

She came around to the other side, opened the door and got in. She took a cigarette from her pocket and pressed in his automatic lighter.

"Well?"

"I want to know what's between you and Howard Plimpton," he said, leaning his arms against the wheel and looking ahead down the drive. "I want to know what the hell you think you're up to."

She lit her cigarette.

"I thought you had people who told you things like that." He stared.

"People?"

"You know what I mean, Philip."

"How do you know that?" he demanded. "Who told you?"

"I don't see any reason why I should tell you anything," she said coldly. "If you'd come to me in the first place and asked me, it might have been different."

"When I asked you at that party at the beach club what was going on, you said nothing."

"Well, it was true. Then."

"Am I expected to believe that?" he demanded hotly.

"You're expected to believe anything you want to believe."

"Are you being honest, Sybil?"

"I've always been honest," she retorted. "I wouldn't expect you to know what that means."

He gripped the wheel tightly and said nothing for several moments. Then he glanced at the pale face beside him.

"I suppose I don't know what it means to have my wife carry on a perfectly open affair with a guy like Howard Plimpton," he said angrily.

"If it was open, why spy on me?"

"Because I need evidence that I can prove in court!" he exploded.

She nodded grimly.

"I see. I should have done the same thing with Julia. Then the shoe would have been on the other foot."

He had not come prepared to be thoroughly hateful, but then he had not anticipated her attitude.

"That's right," he said nastily. "And you've missed the boat, kid. You've missed it plenty. I had thought we could work things out, but I thought wrong. What I'll have to do now is have the lawyers draw up an agreement and send it to you to sign."

"You mean an 'or else' proposition?"

"Exactly."

"Giving you, I suppose, custody of Timmy?"

"You said it," he snapped.

"You can send me agreements till you're blue in the face, Philip Hilliard," she retorted. "But I shall never sign away custody of my child! Never!"

"Would you rather have a court do it?"

"Much rather!"

He glanced at her to see if she meant it.

"A lot of very nasty things could come out, you know," he warned her. "The papers would make a lot of it."

"That will be your responsibility, Philip. Not mine."

Their eyes met, and her stare was defiant. He looked away and shrugged his shoulders.

"You can let me know," he said, "if you decide to be reasonable."

"You have my answer."

She got out of the car after saying this and went back into the house. Inside the door she waited until she heard him drive away. Then she returned to the breakfast table.

"Was that Philip?" Millie asked.

She nodded.

"Does he always blow his horn instead of ringing the bell?"

"Invariably," she said and turned back to the newspaper.

After breakfast she went to the library and sat there alone for half an hour. She looked up at the bronze stag on the mantel being torn by hounds, at the rows and rows of biographies and court memoirs, at the painting of Uncle Stafford in a leather jacket with his pipe and book; she tried to invoke the spirit of sympathy that must somehow inhabit a room that had been so much a part of herself. Yet it was not there. The things repudiated her.

That morning, in the village, she ran into Howard at the grocer's.

"I apologize for my rotten temper the other night," she said. "It was inexcusable."

"Is this be-nice-to-Howard week?" he asked.

"It's be-nice-to-everyone week."

"You've decided that Aunt Jo's world is your world, after all?"

She looked at him thoughtfully.

"Oh, I don't know about that," she said. "Besides, I may

be thrown out of it. Would you mind if Philip named you as co-respondent in a divorce suit?"

He stiffened.

"Does Philip know?" he demanded.

She nodded.

"How?"

"The usual way."

He swore under his breath.

"I didn't know he'd be such a bastard." Then he shrugged his shoulders. "Well, of course, I don't mind. I have nothing to lose. But what about you?"

As she looked at him she saw that he did mind. He hated to be involved. Oh, he would be good about it, he would do anything that she asked him. He would even go to see Philip, if it came to that. But it was obvious that he hated the idea of having to play a forced rôle in what he regarded as the rigmarole of a pointless legal proceeding. She felt the sterility of his independence. She could look at him steadily now. She could even smile.

"Should I go back to him, Howard?" she asked him for the second time.

"Do you want to?"

They were still standing where they had met, before the counter.

"We always do what we want to, don't we?"

"We always do."

She nodded to him and went out of the store.

Chapter
Eight

PHILIP DECIDED after his interview with Sybil that he was a very wronged man. He was wronged by his wife and wronged by his mother and wronged, as far as he could make out, by all members of both families. No matter what turn events seemed to take, he continued to be blamed for everything. He had tried to be nice to Sybil, and he had been spurned. When he had reproached her, he had been spurned again. Everyone, it seemed, talked at the top of their voices where his marriage was concerned. It was intolerable.

"You'll have to get one thing into your head, Ma," he told Lucy the next morning. "And that is that I refuse to discuss Sybil with you any more. I really mean that."

"Listen to him!" she exclaimed. "I hope you don't think that I *want* to discuss your affairs. I was only trying to keep you from making a mess of them."

"Well, the mess will be my mess," he said sulkily.

"All yours, my boy," she said crisply. "Every bit of it."

He lunched that day in town with Teddy and told him the whole story. Teddy had been forewarned by Millie; he was not taken by surprise.

"The whole thing's out of control," Philip protested, almost childishly, as he finished his tale. "You'd think she *wanted* me to divorce her on those grounds. But I don't, Teddy. You know I don't. All I want is to have her admit that now we're in the same boat. But no. Shouts and screams. All the time. What the hell's eating her?"

"You hurt her, Phil. Remember that."

"*I* hurt her?"

Teddy smiled at the look of surprise on his brother-in-law's face.

"Have you forgotten about Julia?"

"That!" Philip exclaimed. "But, my God, man, that's ancient history. Since then I've eaten crow. What the hell more do you want? Don't you Rodmans have *any* normal impulses?"

Teddy laughed.

"I hope we do," he said. "Or at least I hope I do. But Sib has her pride, Phil. It's a terrific pride. And when she cares about somebody the way she cares about you . . ."

"Cared, you mean."

"No, Phil, cares. Why in God's name do you think she's been acting this way?"

Philip threw his hands in the air.

"She loves me so much that she sleeps with Howard," he said sarcastically. "Is that it?"

"That's it."

Philip looked uncomprehendingly at the assurance on Teddy's face.

"I must be most unsubtle," he said. "I don't get it."

Teddy nodded.

"You are unsubtle, Phil," he said. "You are indeed."

.   .   .

Teddy's theory, however, was far from unpleasant to Philip. It solaced him where he had been most hurt. For if Sybil really still cared, if that was the explanation of her smarting coolness and promiscuous conduct, he would be able to condone with dignity what she had done. For Philip, in spite of everything, still wanted to save his marriage. He detested more than ever the wrangling atmosphere between the families and his dependency on Lucy to provide a home for Timmy. All he wanted was peace. If Sybil, the strange and more interesting Sybil whom he had seen that summer, would only meet him halfway, surely something could be worked out that was better than their present separation.

When he drove up to the house at Glenville that evening, Arlina, who had been waiting in the hall, came out to meet him as he got out of his car.

"Phil!" she said. "Phil, I've got to talk to you."

"What is it, Arlina?"

"It's important," she insisted, holding him back as he started towards the house. "Very important."

"You're in love," he suggested sarcastically. "Is that it?"

"Oh, no, Phil. No!"

He stopped and looked at her. It occurred to him that they all treated Arlina rather shabbily.

"What is it, sweet?"

"It's about you. No. It's really about Sybil."

He frowned.

"Look, Lina, don't you hear enough about love under the Japanese lanterns at your deb parties? Run along, kid, will you?"

She shook her head violently.

"But you don't know!" she cried guiltily. "You don't *know!*"

He stared at her.

"Don't know what?"

"It was I who told Sybil about the detective!" she almost shouted. And with this, she burst into tears, hanging her head down in sudden misery.

Philip watched her in perplexity. Her reaction seemed typical of everyone's reaction to his problems. He sighed and put his arm around her shoulders.

"It doesn't matter, Lina," he said. "I knew she knew. She told me so. Calm down, kid. What did you do? Write her?"

Arlina paused between sobs.

"No. I saw Millie Rodman. I told her to tell her. But that's not the worst of it, Phil." She looked up imploringly and then threw her arms around him. "Oh, darling Phil, can you ever forgive me?"

"Lina, for Christ's sake." He tried to disentangle himself. "Will you calm down, please? What more do you have to tell?"

She took the handkerchief that he offered her and blew her nose.

"Well, you see, I wrote her before it happened," she said finally, looking down at the grass.

"Before what happened?"

"Before the thing happened that the detective wrote Ma about!" she said tensely.

Philip's mouth opened.

"You did?"

"And that's *why* it happened, Phil! Don't you see?" She began to get excited again. "It's all my fault!" She looked up at him with a misty defiance, as sudden and unexpected as her humility.

"What the hell are you driving at, Lina?"

"Oh, Phil, don't you see? She thought you trusted her. She thought she had deserved at least that. And then she hears that you're spying on her. Crash." Arlina drew herself up as though to emulate a stage heroine whose world has collapsed into dust. "She turns to the nearest man. If that's what you're going to think of her, she'll give you something to think about! Why not? She throws herself at Howard's head."

"Lina, for the love of mike —— "

"If you only *knew* Sybil as I knew her," Arlina interrupted him passionately, "if you only knew the nobility of her nature! But what's the use? You won't forgive. You won't see. You won't understand. And who can blame you? You wouldn't really be Phil, I suppose, if it were otherwise."

She turned sadly away from him, overcome with the intransigency of the opposite sex.

"Will you dry up, Arlina?" he called after her. "Will you dry up, please?"

Chapter

Nine

PHILIP MADE UP HIS MIND quickly about things, but, having done so, he left no stone unturned to accomplish his purpose. He knew that he would have to be generous, for the simple reason that Sybil was in the wrong. When he decided to be generous, however, his direct nature enabled him to be very much so. He went into the library after dinner that night and wrote her a letter.

"I want to assure you, in the first place," he said, "that I have no idea of using any evidence that I have against you. That was originally Mother's idea, not mine. I am not, however, trying to shirk responsibility for it. When I found out about it I should have stopped it at once, but at the same time I heard you were seeing Plimpton, and I was so angry that I let Ma have her way. I know it's a hard thing to forgive, but all I can do is hope that you'll forgive it. I'll give you a divorce, Sib, if you still want it, and Timmy can live with you during the school months. Surely that's fair. But what I really want is to have you both back with me and everything the way it used to be. I know you've had a lot to put up with, but if you could see your way to giving me another chance, I really think that we could work things out."

When he reread the letter he was quite moved by it. He

put it in an envelope and drove to the village of Glenville to mail it himself. When he came back he had a pleasant sense of irrevocability, and he sat down again at the library desk to write the other letters which were to buttress his scheme. He wrote to his mother-in-law in Canada, to his father-in-law, to Aunt Jo and to Millie. He even induced himself to write to Nicholas which, all things considered, was handsome of him. He explained to each of them how distressed he was by the continued separation; he described the offer that he had made to Sybil and expressed his hope that they would add their voices to his to persuade her to come back.

"I know that she's the best wife a fellow could have," he wrote. "It's my misfortune that I have discovered it too late."

The reaction to his letters was varied. Aunt Jo was very touched; she handed her letter to Sybil at the breakfast table and simply murmured:

"I hope that you will give this serious consideration, my dear. Very serious. That young man means what he says. I'm convinced of it."

George Rodman was similarly convinced of his son-in-law's sincerity, but then he had been mystified from the beginning by Sybil's attitude. He and Esther discussed the matter one night at their Canadian hotel.

"Where does she think she'll get another husband like Philip?" he demanded. "She's crazy, that girl."

"Maybe she doesn't want one." Esther glanced over the neat lines of her son-in-law's handwriting. "He's awfully prosy, you know. I could never count on a man who was prosy."

George looked at his wife and scratched his head.

"Well, she may snap my head off," he said, "but I'm still going to write her and tell her not to be a fool."

.   .   .

Sybil read her letters with an odd sense of detachment. She was surprised to receive Philip's, and she was impressed with its magnanimity. She saw its prosiness, as did her mother, and she understood perfectly the pleasure it must have given him to write it, but this did not alter the fact that he was throwing away a trump card and doing it in full awareness of the consequences. Philip had his honesty; she knew that. As each additional letter came in and as she traced the careful, almost childish plan that he had conceived to win her back, she could not help smiling.

"Aunt Jo, would you ever go back to a man who described you as a 'model of patience'?" she asked, quoting from Philip's letter to Teddy which the latter had sent on to her. "The whole thing makes me sound like a Griselda. Which, God knows, I haven't been."

"You make fun of everything, Sybil," Aunt Jo reproved her. "And some day you're going to be sorry. A fine literary style may not mean sincerity."

"You know, that's where I think you're wrong, Aunt Jo," she said, smiling. "I think a fine literary style always means sincerity."

But Aunt Jo was not listening. Nobody, as she saw it, would listen to her when Philip took his present tone, not even Teddy. The latter came down to spend a night at Easton Bay to argue it out with her. He had been working on a bond issue, night and day, and he looked tired. The sparkle of his college years had somewhat dimmed, but his smile, if less spontaneous, had much of its old charm.

"I had lunch with Philip the other day," he told her after dinner, when they were alone in the library. "We discussed the whole thing."

"Everybody has," she said coldly. "Except, apparently, Philip and myself."

"I think that his attitude, under the circumstances, is generous. You must concede that, Sybil."

"Oh, I concede nothing," she said impatiently. "To any of you!"

Teddy, however, had come determined to be firm.

"When will you be satisfied, Sib?" he asked. "When Philip has divorced you and taken away Timmy? When you've got everybody in both families against you?"

She shrugged her shoulders.

"You've always been an appeaser, Teddy," she said. "All your life. You've always been for smoothing things out and patching things up. But I'm different. Leave me be."

"I know you think my life is small and dull, Sib," he said calmly. "But then it's impossible for you to understand that I get what I want out of it. And that I gave up smoothing things out. Long ago."

She knew that she had gone too far. She went over and sat beside him on the sofa where they had once looked at Uncle Stafford's illustrated histories.

"Teddy, I don't think your life is small and dull," she protested, putting her hand on his arm. "And you mustn't think I think so. I like everything about your life. And I like Millie, too."

He laughed.

"Come, Sib. You don't have to go that far."

"But I do, Teddy! I *do* now!"

"All right," he said soothingly. "You do."

"And I do believe that what you have means everything to you," she continued feelingly. "And I'm glad it's that way. But you should try to understand me, too. Do you really want to send me back to a man I don't love?"

"But you do!"

She stared at him.

"I do?"

"Of course, you do. That's what I was telling him the other day."

"*You* were telling him the other day?"

He nodded.

"Certainly," he said, as if it were the simplest thing in the world. "I was trying to explain what's been so obvious from the beginning. That Howard was only your way of getting back at him."

She stared at him almost in fear.

"Teddy, are you mad? How could you say such a thing?"

As their eyes met she felt the strange intimacy of their mutual recognition that they did not, after all, really understand each other.

"Because it's true!" he retorted. "You've always been in love with Philip! And you know it too!"

She continued to stare at him as she realized that he believed it. Of course, he believed it! So did they all, her father and Millie and Aunt Jo and Lucy Hilliard and even Philip himself. The crazy picture of her summer fell suddenly into place, and she knew at last what it was really like to be alone.

Chapter

Ten

SHE MADE HER DECISION that night to go back to Philip. She lay awake until three in the morning and then came to her conclusion with a complete calmness of mind. As Teddy had implied, there was really no alternative. It was as simple as that, and simplicity was what, above all, she was most anxious to bring back to the disorganized structure of her life. She had no illusion that her choice was dictated by any sense of morality or duty; if there had been any real alternative, she could have adopted it and flouted the world. But could there ever be such an alternative for one who, like herself, had invested everything in a romantic myth? One could call it neuroticism or even stubbornness, but labels did not help. She had only herself to live with. To Howard she gave hardly a thought. He had given her what anyone might have given her, a sense of his own uneasiness at being taken too seriously. It might be that things would not always be this way, but she was inclined to think they would. It was better to go back and tell Philip everything. Everything, that is, but the change in her feeling for him. To this extent she would lie, and for the first time. She would go along with the generally accepted theory that, however strangely she might have behaved, she still adored him.

She drove over to the Hilliards' in the morning. In the front hall she met Lila who told her that Philip was outside with Timmy. She went out and around the house, to avoid Lucy, and found Philip in his bathing trunks sitting by the pool with his feet in the water, while Timmy and Lila's children played on the grass beside him. Timmy was the first to see her, and he ran over happily. No effort had been made to explain the separation to him, and he had accepted it as a perfectly natural thing. As Lila's children faced the same situation he had no sense of the unusual about it.

"Mummie!" he cried. "Look, Daddy, it's Mummie! Have you brought me a present?"

Philip turned around when he heard Timmy calling and flushed. He got up and ambled over and stood uncomfortably beside her while she talked to the boy, who was telling her in a high, excited voice about a village fair that he had been to. She leaned down while he told her about it and then gave him a kiss.

"Darling, how wonderful. And now will you go and play with the other children? Just for a bit. While I talk to Daddy."

Timmy ran off, and his parents faced each other. Philip looked very tan and well, and his hair was bleached by the sun. He pointed to the white chairs by the pool house, and they went over and sat down. He looked at her a bit sheepishly, but also, she thought, with a certain veiled truculence, as though ready for anything she might have to say.

"Well, Sib? What do you think?"

"I think you've been very big about everything, Philip," she said in a clear voice. "I think you've been fine. I shall be very glad to come back. Truly. And I won't leave you again, no matter what you do. I'm a big girl now."

So there it was. She thought she could read in his embarrassed smile, behind the pleasure that he obviously felt, the faintest hint of disappointment that this was all there was. The tiniest feeling of anticlimax. But she could almost smile now at her own perspicacity and feel the encouragement of knowing that truth would not hurt her and that life *was* complicated. Even with Philip. There were many Philips.

"That's wonderful, Sib. Gee, that really is." He stared down in the grass. "The whole thing's been too damn difficult. It really has."

There was a silence, obviously painful to him.

"You mustn't worry," she said, "if we're constrained at first. It's only natural. It won't last."

He looked at her gratefully, and she smiled. They both turned at the same moment to face the figure of Lucy watching them from across the pool. She was in riding clothes and had just come down from the stable. Philip raised a hand and waved to her.

"Hey, Mom!" he called. "Come on over. Who do you think has just come back to the family?"

Lucy had been astute enough to deduce from their respective expressions what had occurred. Her first impulse had been one of resentment that this girl who had defied them should climb so easily back into her abandoned position. Her second, almost immediately following, had been more charitable. After all, the girl had spunk. They might still do something with her. She might yet do Philip credit. It was like Lucy not to concern herself with what Sybil's attitude in the future might be to herself. She walked around the pool and came over to them.

"Well, Sybil, my dear, we have our faults," she said putting her hand on the back of Philip's neck, "but where would you do so much better than my boy here? I always knew you had sense. Even though you've been awfully good at hiding it recently. You had me guessing there for a bit, I confess. But I'll say this for you. You're the only estranged in-law that we've really wanted back."

The Hilliards passed quickly over embarrassment, and by the time the three of them had walked up to the house the breach had been outwardly healed. And outwardly, Sybil had cause to remind herself in the ensuing year, was all that she had any reason to expect. Philip was glad enough to have her back; he had detested the complications of separation. He took her, as before, very much for granted; she arranged things as he wanted them to be arranged. In due course after their reunion they had another child, a girl, who was christened Emily in deference to the eldest of Philip's aunts. This had almost, if not quite, the effect of making up for the bitter words which Sybil had uttered to her at Aunt Jo's cocktail party.

Everybody was pleased at the reconciliation, and everybody, including Philip's aunts, made Sybil feel that she had not gone too far to be welcomed back. If people flared at the hint of true, as opposed to sham, rebellion, it was nonetheless apparent that they subsided when the anarchist protested his error. Only Esther, the perennial pessimist, seemed to feel, on her return from Canada, that it was not necessarily the perfect solution.

"The same attraction brings her back," she told her sister, Jo, as they drove from the station where the latter had met her, "and I suppose the same repulsion may drive her away again. There's no end to it."

"You assume, Esther," her sister said severely, "that Sybil can't learn anything."

"I don't assume anything," Sybil's mother replied. "You all do the assuming."

Sybil, anyway, showed no signs of being as flighty as her mother so gloomily prognosticated. It was not long after the birth of little Emily that she had reason to suspect that Philip was seeing more of a certain red-haired divorcée whom they had met at a cocktail party at Millie's than he had been absolutely candid about. She had a moment of panic; then she remembered her promise and was even able to smile, albeit dryly, at the ingenuity of some of his reasons for being detained at the office. He would always come back to her; of this she could be sure. Philip was one who, like herself, could not really afford to change his base. As time passed they developed an easy, if mutually critical relationship. It was not unpleasant. She had given Philip too much to have much left for others. If Howard had taught her nothing else he had taught her that. Whenever she thought of the long aimless summer at Easton Bay she shuddered. Life with Philip at least was patterned. It sometimes seemed to her that she was making a life out of the ashes of her love, but there was more left than ashes. There was a grate; there were andirons, indeed there was a whole hearth.

On the eighth wedding anniversary, in the summer of 1949, Aunt Jo gave them a dinner party at Easton Bay. It was a small party, for Uncle Stafford had died the winter before and the family were still in mourning. Nicholas had inherited the whole principal of his father's trust, but with his characteristic generosity and, indeed, out of his own emotional necessity, he had begged his stepmother to let him live with her and maintain her houses on the scale that she had hitherto enjoyed. He sat at one end of the table, as unbending and as kind as ever, with Sybil on his right, and Aunt Jo, who was getting older and beginning to forget things, sat opposite, beside a stouter but still handsome Philip. They were all there, Hilliards and Rodmans, and Lucy made a very funny toast which shocked the Hilliard aunts, and George who drank too many cocktails got up and forgot what he was going to say, and Millie, who blushed furiously and protested when asked to speak, finally rose and made in her small, nervous voice what was generally considered the best speech of the evening.

"I want to propose a toast," she said in conclusion, "to all the Sybils I have known. Even, if not especially, to the silent Sybil of the old days who wouldn't go to parties and read learned books in Aunt Jo's library. Deep down, I confess, I always envied that Sybil. She had something, I guess, that the rest of us didn't have. But I am still glad that she has come out of the library and taken us into her heart."

They all got to their feet to drink her health except Aunt Jo and Miss Harriet, whose arthritis prevented them, and Sybil, looking from one to the other down the long, gleaming table piled with Aunt Jo's heaviest silver, smiled and nodded as if she were thinking of the anniversary and of the dinner and of their kindness and not of how funny it was to find herself, after the years of self-consciousness, without fear, without even embarrassment, in the presence of the assembled tribe.

THE END